Charles Anthony Vince

**John Bright**

Charles Anthony Vince

**John Bright**

ISBN/EAN: 9783337152925

Printed in Europe, USA, Canada, Australia, Japan

Cover: Foto ©Raphael Reischuk / pixelio.de

More available books at **www.hansebooks.com**

# John Bright

# John Bright

By

## C. A. VINCE, M.A.

Formerly Fellow of Christ's College, Cambridge

HERBERT S. STONE & COMPANY

CHICAGO & NEW YORK

M DCCC XCVIII

# Preface

A history of John Bright's career must needs be largely
a record of opinions.  In constructing this record I have
tried, as far as possible, to use his own words, although
the limits of this book do not permit extended quotations from his speeches.  Such a method is facilitated by
the terseness of his style; and inasmuch as his opinions
were always clearly defined, and, being notably independent of circumstances and conditions, were subject to
very little change, I may reasonably hope to have escaped
the error of misrepresenting occasional utterances as
definite judgments.

I have not, however, been content merely to sum-
marize Bright's acts and views, but have throughout
tried to form and to suggest a critical estimate of his
work and its results.  With one exception the controversies in which he was engaged are now sufficiently
remote, and their issues sufficiently developed, to bear
historical treatment.  The exception is the controversy
raised in 1886; upon this subject, therefore, I have
added no comment to the account given of Bright's
opinions.  The space allotted to the different subjects
treated is proportional, not to their importance, but to
the importance of Bright's dealings with them.

For some details of Bright's parentage and early life
I rely on the authority of the biography written by Mr.
W. Robertson of Rochdale.  In studying his parliamentary career I have resorted throughout to *Hansard*
and the newspaper files.  The books of which I have
made most use are Mr. Morley's *Life of Cobden*, Prentice's *History of the League*, the *Histories* of Mr. J. F.

Bright and Mr. W. N. Molesworth, Mr. Kinglake's *Invasion of the Crimea*, Charles Greville's *Journal*, Earl Russell's *Recollections*, Sir G. O. Trevelyan's *Life of Macaulay*, and the collection of Bright's *Public Letters* edited by Mr. H. J. Leech. Wherever I have derived hints from other books I have indicated the source.

I may be permitted to add that I have been from boy-hood a close observer of the political life of Birmingham, and for some years actively engaged in it. This work has made me conscious of the still lasting influence of Bright's doctrine and example on the minds of persons interested in politics in this city. That influence has often been neglected or under-estimated by journalists and speakers who have treated the present state of Liberal opinion in Birmingham as a phenomenon calling for explanation. It has been a task of curious interest to me to amplify and correct, by a complete study of Bright's career, my conception of the character, the methods, the failures and successes, the greatness and the limitations, of a man who did so much to form the political mind with which I am in daily contact.

I have had the advantage of consulting on some points politicians whose knowledge of Bright was intimate and of long duration. In particular, I have to thank Mr. Chamberlain and Mr. J. Thackray Bunce, who most kindly communicated to me some of their personal recollections of Bright. Mr. William Wright of Birmingham has allowed me the use of his large collection of newspaper cuttings, and has given me other assistance, which I here gratefully acknowledge.

C. A. VINCE.

BIRMINGHAM, *Dec.*, 1897.

# Contents

# John Bright.

## Chapter I.

### The Anti-Corn-Law League.

John Bright was born at Green Bank, Rochdale, on
November 16, 1811. He was the second son of Jacob
Bright, a prosperous manufacturer. He came of a
thrifty and pious stock. At the time of the Revolution
his paternal ancestors were farmers at Lyneham in Wiltshire, where there is a field that still bears the name of
Bright's Orchard. Abraham Bright, the great-grand-
father of the statesman, migrated from Wiltshire to
Coventry, and there his grandson, Jacob Bright, was
born. Jacob Bright was apprenticed to William Holme,
a Derbyshire manufacturer; and early in this century
accompanied the two sons of Holme to Rochdale, where
he was employed by them in a cotton mill. Two years
before the birth of his famous son he started a mill on
his own account. He borrowed the capital for this
enterprise, but soon became independent, and in time
wealthy. He was shrewd in business and rigid in principle, but of a just and compassionate disposition, a
generous giver, and, by comparison with other cotton-
spinners of those cruel days, notable for the kindliness
of his dealings with his work-people. He distinguished
himself by the obstinacy of his resistance to church-rates,
consistently refusing to pay until his goods were dis-

trained.  He appears to have been worthy of the veneration with which his son cherished his memory; and all
that is recorded of him is consistent with the belief that
it was from him that John Bright received, whether by
training or by inheritance, his piety of spirit, his un-
bending opinion, and his strong faith in individual
liberty.  Those who attach importance to the remoter
influences of heredity may think it noteworthy that
Bright had a small infusion of Hebrew blood, for his
great-grandmother, the wife of Abraham Bright of
Coventry, was a Jewess.

John Bright received such education as the better sort
of private Nonconformist schools were able to offer at a
time when Dissenters were still excluded from the
universities.  " My limited school-time ", he wrote in
1886, " scarcely allowed me to think of Greek; and I
should now make but slow steps in Latin, even with the
help of a dictionary."  He brought from his school in
Ribbledale a love of angling which furnished him with
a wholesome recreation throughout life, and sufficient
skill at cricket to make him a useful member of the
Rochdale eleven.  He had also acquired a genuine love
of reading, but not any aptitude for systematic study,
and was sufficiently interested in intellectual matters to
join the local Literary and Philosophical Society.  It is,
however, the common experience of provincial societies
bearing this honourable name that they discuss contemporary events and problems with more zest than either
philosophy or literature.  Whatever were the defects of
Bright's education he never affected to deplore them.
His devotion to politics was so complete that he applied
the political standard to everything; and the connection
he discovered between culture and Conservatism led him
rather to respect culture less than Conservatism more.
The observation, which he found frequent occasion to
mention, that the ancient universities returned to Par-

liament the most unreasonable of Tories, made him suspect that the literature studied in those seats of learning was superficial and unsound.

His father, and his ancestors for many generations, were Nonconformists, and members of the Society of Friends. He himself remained faithful to the religious and political ideas and traditions in which he was brought up. A great part of his public conduct cannot be understood by anyone who either forgets that he was a Nonconformist, or is ignorant of the political history of nonconformity. He was proud of his descent from John Gratton of Derbyshire, who was a leader of the Quakers during the life of George Fox, and suffered imprisonment in the persecution of Charles and James. During his boyhood Rochdale was the scene of violent conflicts on the question of church-rates. To this recollection he often recurred; and the sense of injuries to be resented, which Nonconformists of his age had so many reasons to feel, remained in his mind to the last. A certain asperity of temper is commonly imputed by unfriendly critics to political Nonconformists. It is to be explained, if it can no longer be excused, by the bitterness of the prolonged struggle by which they painfully won the elementary rights of citizenship. Throughout his life Bright never spoke with so much vehemence of indignation, and never, it must be added, with so little concern for the susceptibility of his opponents, as when he was pleading for religious equality, and giving voice to his resentment at the privileges of the Established Church.

It is still more important that the student of his career should not for a moment forget that he was a member of the Society of Friends. The discipline of that society has been eminently successful in promoting both private virtue and a generous sense of public duty. Bright's religion was the very foundation of his public as well as of his private character; and the faith he possessed by inheritance and by education was that of a sect whose presentment of Christianity has sedulously given to the consecration of daily life priority over observance and doctrine. There is an air, surely unaffected, as of saintly self-dedication in Bright's own account, quoted below, of his first devotion to political work. It is scarcely too much to say that his political and religious convictions formed in his mind one indistinguishable whole; both were articles of faith, equally unchangeable, equally superior to expediency, and vivified by the same enthusiasm for righteousness. He did not seek for his principles in inductions from the recorded history of nations, nor in any reasoned political philosophy. He was content to deduce his conclusions from comprehensive premises which appeared to him to possess a religious sanction. This is the source of that assertive temper and that disdain of compromise, which both strengthened him as a leader of popular opinion, and disqualified him as a parliamentary tactician. The earnestness by which he kindled the enthusiasm of his friends, and provoked the resentment of his opponents, was akin to the zeal of an evangelist proclaiming the way of salvation. Like Macaulay he was subject to the reproach of being much too certain that he was always in the right. Macaulay's certainty was doubtless based on his consciousness of having grasped all the facts relevant to the issue, and his satisfaction with his own mental processes. The certainty of Bright was the assurance of faith — the confidence which, however exasperating in a debater, has always been recognized as essential to the character of a prophet.

Voltaire had long ago made Quakerism known and respected by French men of letters; and a countryman of Voltaire, M. Challemel-Lacour, has, with eloquence and insight, deduced Bright's public character from his

Quaker training.[1]  "That intrepidity in conflict, that indomitable energy, those speeches with a strain all their own, reveal something deeper than merely political conviction.  Mr. Bright is a Quaker.  He admits that his sect is reputed to be making no progress; but he adds that its principles are gaining more ground than is commonly supposed.  A craving for peace felt more keenly every day, a growing recognition of the incompetence of the state in the region of the religious conscience, a respect for the dignity of manhood even in the most forlorn,—I may add, a sort of utilitarianism exhibited in the increasing regard for useful knowledge, and in the payment of due honour to industry,—here we have traits of society as it is, and these are ideas professed from the first by the sect to which Mr. Bright belongs.  In his speeches, even when he is dealing with the most arid topics, we are always conscious of an undercurrent of religious emotion that rises to the surface only at rare intervals as by an involuntary force."

At the age of fifteen Bright was taken from school and set to learn his father's business.  He was the first son taken into partnership, his elder brother having died in childhood.  The firm became Jacob Bright & Son, and subsequently John Bright & Brothers.  It will be well to say at once what is necessary about Bright's private circumstances.  Though never a wealthy man by comparison with the great magnates of the Lancashire trade, he always enjoyed the means of living in such comfort as satisfied the simplicity of his tastes, and was free from those financial embarrassments into which his friend Cobden was precipitated by his sacrifice of time to the public good.  Those who set any value on Bright's services to the commonwealth must not fail to bestow part of their gratitude on his younger

[1] "Hommes d'Etat de l'Angleterre.   John Bright."—*Revue des Deux Mondes*, Feb. 15, 1870.

brothers, who, with admirable generosity and public spirit, released him from his share in the work of the business as soon as his vocation to public life became apparent to himself and to them.

He interested himself at an early age in the activities of his town, and made several public appearances soon after reaching his majority, which fell in the year of the Reform Bill. His first speech on the Free Trade question was made at Rochdale in 1838. In the autumn of the same year he became a member of the first provisional committee of the Manchester Anti-Corn-Law Association. He was the only member not resident in Manchester. Cobden joined the committee a week later. This association was the nucleus of the famous Anti-Corn-Law League, the date of whose birth is March 20, 1839. Bright took his share in the work of the League from the first; but he dated the beginning of his public services and of his memorable friendship with Cobden from September 13, 1841. What happened on that day, the turning-point of his life, must be recorded in his own language.

" I was at Leamington when Mr. Cobden called upon me. I was then in the depths of grief,—I might almost say of despair,—for the light and sunshine of my house had been extinguished. All that was left on earth of my young wife, except the memory of a sainted life and of a too brief happiness, was lying still and cold in the chamber above us. Mr. Cobden called upon me as his friend, and addressed me, as you may suppose, with words of condolence. After a time he looked up and said, ' There are thousands of homes in England at this moment where wives, mothers, and children are dying of hunger. Now,' he said, ' when the first paroxysm of your grief is passed, I would advise you to come with me, and we will never rest till the Corn Law is repealed.' I accepted his invitation. I knew that the description he had given of the homes of thousands was not an exaggerated description. I felt in my conscience that there was a work which someone must do. From that time we never ceased to labour hard on behalf of the resolution which we had made. We were not the first, though we became, before the public, the foremost. There were others before us; and we were joined, not by scores, but by hundreds, and afterwards by thousands, and afterwards by countless multitudes. At last famine itself, against which we warred, joined us,—necessities became very great,—a great minister was converted,—and finally the barrier was entirely thrown down. Since that time, though there has been much suffering in many homes, yet no wife, and no mother, and no little child is starved to death as the result of a famine made by law."

Such was the inception of a task that occupied more than four years. In a short time Cobden and Bright became famous in every part of England and Scotland as the chief of a great company of apostles of Free Trade in corn. As the anti-corn-law agitation forms the subject of a volume in the series to which this little book belongs, it is unnecessary to attempt here a full account of the work of the League, or of the question at issue between the Protectionists and the Free-traders. But since Bright's future career took its colour from this early work, and since his opinions and methods were largely determined by the experiences of those four years, it will be proper to call attention to those aspects of the controversy which made the most permanent impression on his mind. Of the earlier history of the struggle the briefest summary may suffice.

The Corn Law enacted in 1815, at a time when the close of a long period of warfare threatened a fall in the cruel prices to which food had been forced by the war, prohibited the importation of wheat at any time when the market price of home-grown wheat fell below 80s. a quarter. This limit was lowered to 70s. in 1822. In 1828 the Duke of Wellington's Corn Law established a duty on imported corn varying with the market price. For example, the duty on wheat was 10s. 8d. when the price was 70s., 26s. 8d. when it was 60s., and 36s. 8d. when it was 50s.

From the first there was a body of public opinion adverse to protective duties. "The people", said Bright, "never acquiesced in that Corn Law. You passed it under a protest of the most fearful kind." But for many years there was no attempt to organize a Free-trade party. Mr. Huskisson, until his death in 1830, and, from that time till the advent of Cobden, Mr. Poulett Thomson (Lord Sydenham) were successively regarded by the Free-traders as their political leaders. At the elections which followed the reform of 1832 the question was raised on the hustings of the Lancashire boroughs. In 1833 a resolution condemning the Corn Laws was discussed in the House of Commons, and the next year the policy of a fixed duty, which was afterwards dignified with a place on the official programme of the Whig party, was advocated by Hume, and supported by about one-third of the members voting. In 1837 the anxiety of the Lancashire manufacturers, who had learned to attribute the depression of their industry to a law which prevented the free exchange for foreign corn of the products of their looms, was increased by numerous bankruptcies; and at the elections which followed the Queen's accession many boroughs returned Free-traders. The year 1838, which witnessed the formation of the Manchester Association, was also the first year of Mr. Villiers's annual motion for a committee to consider and repeal the Corn Laws. A Free-trade party was now fairly organized both in the House and in the country.

In 1841 the Whig Ministry of Melbourne was compelled to try to meet a deficiency of revenue by modifying a tariff the severity of which diminished the income of the state by discouraging the importation of duty-paying goods. After a statement on the financial difficulty by Baring, the Chancellor of the Exchequer, Lord John Russell proposed a fixed duty on corn, which was estimated to yield a larger revenue than the variable duty. The "monopoly" of corn, as the Free-traders loved to call it, was part of a system of similar monopolies, of which the most important were those of timber and sugar. The sugar duties were such as practically to exclude from our markets all sugar not grown in a British colony. The new tariff was to be no longer prohibitive, though still offering a large advantage to the colonial sugar-planter.[1] "You monopolists", said Bright later, "all hang together. Neither of these interests really cares one straw for the rest any longer than they all hold together." On the question of the sugar duties, which were taken first, the agriculturists who desired protection for corn, and those who were interested in the maintenance of the sugar or the timber duties, were reinforced by the anti-slavery party; for sugar not grown in our colonies was slave-grown sugar, and the virtual exclusion of foreign sugar was regarded as part of the price to be paid for emancipation. The Government was easily defeated by this combination; Parliament was dissolved; and Sir Robert Peel came in with a majority of about eighty. Mr. Gladstone was Vice-President of the Board of Trade in the new Ministry.

There were now three policies before the country: the Free-trade policy of Mr. Villiers and the League, the

---

[1] Colonial sugar paid 24*s.*, foreign sugar 63*s.*, a hundredweight. It was proposed to reduce the latter duty to 36*s.* The duty on colonial timber was to be raised from 10*s.* to 20*s.* a load; while the duty on Baltic timber was lowered from 55*s.* to 50*s.*

policy of a moderate fixed duty accepted by Lord John
Russell and the Liberal party, and the sliding-scale
policy of Peel and the Conservatives. Though many
causes contributed to the defeat of the Whigs, the incidents that immediately preceded the dissolution gave
to Peel's victory the appearance of a triumph of protection and the agricultural interest. Yet the distress of
the country was so serious that Peel was constrained,
at the risk of dividing his own party, to attempt some
measure of relief.

Parliament met for the session of 1842 on February 3.
The League, exhilarated by the meetings they had held
in the country, and by some electoral successes, includ-
ing the return of Cobden for Stockport, endeavoured to
impress the House of Commons by a demonstration of
their enthusiasm in the metropolis. Delegates from the
provincial associations met on February 8 at the Crown
and Anchor in the Strand, and there Bright made a
speech which was received with great acclamation. The
fame of his eloquence was carried into the country by
the delegates; and from that time he was recognized
as the chief lieutenant of Cobden in the work of propagation.

Peel refused to meet a deputation; but Lord John
Russell, the leader of the Whig opposition in the Commons, had an interview with Bright and five other
Leaguers. He held out no hope of advancing beyond
his timid expedient of an eight-shilling fixed duty.[1] In
spite of this discouragement the Leaguers resolved to
continue their agitation for total and immediate repeal.
This resolution was a final declaration of their indepen-

---

[1] "On the part of the Whigs, I had declared my intention of proposing
a fixed duty on corn. This was likewise an error. Cobden and Bright
proposed the only natural course, that of a total repeal of the duties on
corn. But the Whig country gentlemen were not prepared for so bold a
measure." (*Recollections and Suggestions*, by John, Earl Russell (1874),
p. 236.)

dence of the Liberal party. The cry was: "A fixed duty
is a fixed injustice ".

Peel's new tariff reduced the duties at the prices of
70s., 60s., and 50s. to 5s., 12s., and 20s. respectively.
It was intended that the price should oscillate between
the narrow limits of 58s. and 54s. Cobden denounced
the measure as "a bitter insult to a suffering people";
the price of corn still rose; and by midsummer the distress had again become acute.

The efforts of the Free-traders to enlist the support
of the working-classes brought them into collision with
the Chartists, of whose leaders some, like Feargus
O'Connor, who held that free trade would ruin Ireland,
were Protectionists; others traced the distress to other
causes rather than protection, and all were disposed to
call first for political reforms. The Rochdale Chartists
had carried an amendment against Bright at a meeting
in 1839; and five years later Bright had a public wrangle
with O'Connor himself before the Northampton boot-
makers, resulting in a doubtful vote. It was even
suspected that Chartist agitators were taking the pay
of the Protectionists. In August, 1842, a general strike,
or, as it was then called, a turn-out, was organized in
Lancashire. Bright issued a long address to the work-
ing-men of Rochdale, calling on them to return to their
employment. " Neither act of Parliament nor act of a
multitude can keep up wages. You know that trade
has long been bad, and with a bad trade wages cannot
rise. If you are resolved to compel an advance of wages,
you cannot compel manufacturers to give you employment. Such attempts have always failed in the end;
and yours must fail. To obtain the Charter now is just
as impossible as to raise wages by force. The principles
of the Charter will one day be established; but years
may pass over, months must pass over, before that day
arrives. If every employer and workman in the king-

dom were to swear on bended knees that wages should not fall, they would assuredly fall if the Corn Law continues. No power on earth can maintain your wages at their present rate if the Corn Law be not repealed." The address, which is composed in the plain and nervous style to which Cobbett had habituated the artisans, is a popular exposition of the economic doctrine of the Manchester School, applied to the distresses and discontents of the moment. It is a document of some permanent value, as indicating with precision important and lasting differences between the Radicalism of Bright and that of the trades-unions.

On July 25, 1843, Bright entered Parliament, at the second attempt, as member for Durham city. "The Whigs", said Cobden, "tried to make it a Whig triumph, which Bright spoilt by his declaration at the Crown and Anchor that it was not a party victory." The time had not yet come when Bright could sit in Parliament as a loyal member even of the Liberal party. It was impossible that the leaders of that party should command from him the respect which alone could secure the loyalty of a man of his independent disposition. Lord John Russell, who led the party in the Commons, was regarded by Bright as a timid, time-serving, and unimaginative aristocrat, raised to eminence, despite the mediocrity of his talents, by industry and vigilance, with the prestige of a great historic name. To Lord John's competitor, Palmerston, though he was a man of more popular gifts, Bright had a still more deeply rooted antipathy. It was not until the accession of Mr. Gladstone to the leadership of the party that Bright abated his independence of party obligations.

Bright made his first parliamentary speech on August 7 of this year. He did not fail to speak his mind. "Crime has often veiled itself under the name of virtue; but of all the crimes against the laws of God and the true interests of man, none has ever existed more odious and more destructive than that which has assumed the amiable term of protection." A cabinet minister had argued that the Corn Law was necessary to enable land-owners to discharge the settlements made on the marriage of their daughters. "I have attended", said Bright, "many large meetings of agriculturists, and I have never found a single farmer who seemed to be aware that this House had ever bestowed any attention on the means of providing portions for farmers' daughters." "The increase of our population is every year so great as to require for its support an annual increase of food equal to the whole produce of the county of Warwick. The Government has no power to add a county of Warwick every year to the country."

By this time Bright had addressed meetings on the question in every part of the kingdom. The conversion of the manufacturing towns having been accomplished, he and Cobden began their appeal to the farmers, holding open-air meetings in market towns on market days. Cobden's biographer describes this enterprise as the most striking and original feature in the whole agitation, and gives an animated narrative of some incidents of this campaign.[1] They repeatedly obtained a vote for total repeal from audiences that at the outset were unconvinced or even hostile. In the autumn of 1843 they began a remarkable series of demonstrations in Covent Garden Theatre. Their success at last roused the Protectionists to a sense of peril. "The League is a great fact," exclaimed the *Times*, in a leader that became historic;[2] "a new power has arisen in the state." "If I were the Conservative party of England," wrote Carlyle about this time, "I would not for a hundred thousand pounds an hour allow those corn laws to continue."

---

[1] Morley, *Life of Cobden*, chap. xii.       [2] November 18, 1843.

A list of the labours of a single month may serve as an example of the immense amount of work undertaken by Bright. In January, 1844, he spoke at Bury, Carlisle, Glasgow, Edinburgh, Greenock, Paisley, Ayr, Kilmarnock, Dumfries, Sheffield, York, Hull, Blackburn, and Wakefield. Wherever he went his eloquence, youthful and immature, but always fearless, energetic, and stimulating, never failed of its effect in strengthening the popular resolution.

Notwithstanding the rapid extension of free-trade opinion in the country, the party in Parliament received few accessions, and year by year the divisions showed a strength of only from 120 to 130 votes. But the resistance of the Protectionists was becoming less confident; and the Free-traders often had occasion to welcome grave admissions made in debate by ministers, especially Mr. Gladstone and Sir Robert Peel, who already accepted the theory of free imports, though excepting corn on the ground of the danger of dependence upon a foreign food-supply. These concessions in argument, though barren of practical result, filled the county members with suspicion and dismay, and a band of mutineers, with Disraeli at their head, threatened open revolt. The refusal of Peel to take further measures to satisfy the claims of agriculture, then as now insatiable, elicited, on March 17, 1845, Disraeli's celebrated declaration that a Conservative government was an organized hypocrisy.

During the summer of 1845 the price of corn rose rapidly; and in October it was known that both the wheat harvest in England and the potato crop in Ireland had failed. The scarcity in Ireland was such that the peasantry began to perish of starvation, and urgent demands were made on public and private charity. The practical reduction of the Corn Laws to an absurdity had come at last, if Parliament should be asked at the same time to vote money to feed a starving people, and to maintain the laws that ensured famine prices. "Famine", said Bright afterwards, "was the terrible agent that compelled our boasted constitution to permit the people of this country to purchase their bread freely at the world's market price." Lord Ashley warned the farmers of Dorset that the destiny of the Corn Laws was fixed. The Cabinet met on October 31, and the *Times*, anticipating its inevitable decision, declared that the ports were to be opened. "Henceforth the League may cease to exist. Its spirit has already been transferred to its antagonists." Three weeks later than this revelation, though anticipating by a week the publication of Peel's conversion, Lord John Russell in his Edinburgh letter announced that he abandoned his proposal of a moderate fixed duty. The meaning of this tardy repentance was too obviously this: "I have taken no part in the hunt, but I mean to be in at the death, and to claim the brush".

The victory of the League was won; and the Liberal party and its leaders had no share in it. The League had been constituted and directed by men who had had no previous experience of political life. They had been compelled to renounce allegiance to their party. They had found their speakers in the counting-houses of Manchester and Rochdale and in the pulpits of dissenting chapels. They had organized their agitation, invented their own methods, collected their own funds, without an atom of assistance from the Liberal statesmen. Amateur politicians had accomplished what professed statesmen had not dared, or had not chosen, to attempt. Not a single member of the Liberal Cabinet which shortly afterwards entered into the harvest of their labours had ever stood on the platform of a League meeting. Even Macaulay, who had voted with Mr. Villiers, had curtly refused to welcome the League to Edinburgh.

Russell's letter doubtless served to strengthen Peel's hand in dealing with recalcitrant colleagues; but the divisions in the Cabinet were such as to necessitate his resignation.   Lord John failed to form a ministry; and before the end of the year Peel again accepted office and formed the short-lived " Potato-Peel Ministry ", with the support of all his old colleagues except Lord Stanley. He proposed large immediate reductions of the import duties on all food-stuffs.   The duty on wheat was to be 4*s*., rising a shilling with each shilling of fall in price below 53*s*., till it reached a maximum of 10*s*.   Colonial corn was to be admitted immediately, and foreign corn at the end of three years, at a nominal duty of one shilling.   The Free-traders divided the House for the last time on their motion for total and immediate repeal; but they were well satisfied with Peel's measure, and loud in their gratitude to him.   " When the right hon. baronet resigned ", said Bright, turning to the Protec- tionist benches, " he was no longer your minister.   He came back as the minister of the sovereign, as the minister of the people, and no longer as the minister of a class which made him such for their own selfish objects."   The second reading of the Bill was carried by a majority of 97, 112 Conservatives supporting Peel, and 231, with 11 Liberals, opposing him.   The House of Lords[1] passed the Bill by large majorities.

The success of the Anti-Corn-Law League was the

---

[1] " Preferring their coronets to their convictions," says Froude, ill- naturedly.   But Peel could not rend the coronets from their brows; and many obstinate convictions had been honestly changed.   The obvious fact is, that the argument from the famine was quite irresistible to a House that could not turn ministers out.   Something had to be done without delay to cope with the famine.   It was one thing for the Protectionists in the Com- mons to beat the Ministry, if they could, and then try their own plan what- ever it might be.   It was a different thing for the Lords to reject the method proposed by the responsible Government of dealing with a present calamity. A deadlock at such a time would have been, from every point of view, a frightful disaster.

most remarkable achievement of the art of persuasion in the history of any people. The League were attacking the privileges of a still powerful aristocracy; they were confronted by the active hostility of one, and by the inertia of the other, of the two great parties in the State; they had to persuade the farmers to separate their sympathy from the landlords, and to compete with political reformers for the support of the urban working classes. By common consent the chief credit of this achievement belongs of right to Richard Cobden. The second honours are with almost equal unanimity awarded to Bright.[1] There was a recognized distribution of functions between the two agitators. Cobden's mastery of convincing argument can rarely have been equalled. The part of Bright—though his oratory also was not wanting in lucidity and pertinence of reasoning—was to excite the emotions when Cobden had convinced the understanding. He always spoke after his colleague. Cobden made others think as he thought; Bright made them feel as he felt. Cobden taught the people that they were suffering under a foolish economic error; Bright told them that they were the victims of "a crime of the deepest dye against the rights of industry and against the well-being of the British people". "The freedom for which you struggle", he said, "is the freedom to live; it is the right to eat your bread in the sweat of your brow. It is the freedom that was given to you even in the primeval curse; and shall man make that curse more bitter to his fellow-man?"

Referring to the struggle a few years later, Bright said: "The agitation of the Anti-Corn-Law League was

---

[1] The Leaguers themselves were disposed to give the palm of eloquence to W. J. Fox, an orator who had at his command all the resources of rhetoric, and who abounded in surprising turns and felicitous illustrations, but whose style was awkward and turgid. Bright's eloquence did not reach its maturity till some years later; and from the first it stood the test of the House of Commons better than Fox's.

not an agitation of force, it was an agitation of conviction. It was an agitation which not so much conquered our opponents as converted them." Still less was it an agitation of violence. It is a noteworthy feature of this movement, that, despite the excesses of denunciation which Bright and others permitted themselves to use, the peace of no town was ever imperilled by their operations. At a time when all the conditions that commonly provoke popular violence were present, the League was really a strong force on the side of order. It organized and established the strength of a great body of public opinion outside Parliament, and inadequately represented in Parliament.] Hitherto such a body of opinion had made itself effective only by dangerous methods. Before the Reform Act, for example, there were tumults and the fear of insurrection. "Do they wait", exclaimed Macaulay, "for that last and most dreadful paroxysm of popular rage, for that last and most cruel test of military fidelity?" After the Reform Act the Chartist agitation was dishonoured by destructive riots and a grievous severity of retribution. No man's windows were ever endangered by Bright's philippics. Both then and again and again in his later life he was charged with appealing to popular passion. It must not be forgotten that, at almost any time before he became the idol of mass meetings, that phrase had had a sinister significance in which no one can justly use it of him.

Mr. Kinglake, in a well-known passage, commends the skill, patience, and courage with which Bright and Cobden "carried a great scientific truth through the storms of politics". Undoubtedly at the foundation of their main argument lay the free-trade doctrine of the political economists—the doctrine that a nation must acquire a greater amount of wealth at the expense of the same amount of labour, or as much wealth for less labour, when imports are free than when industries are protected by tariffs. But men who did not comprehend the demonstrations of economic science, and who failed to accept, or accepted only on authority, the fulness of the universal dogma, could yet receive with intelligence as well as enthusiasm the reasoning proper to the special case of imported food-stuff. The appeal was to visible distress and to easily demonstrable causes.

The term protection is an abbreviation of "protection of native industry". In the view of the League, this name was delusive. The whole advantage of the tariff was reaped by the land-owners. Bright often quoted the short speech of a Wiltshire labourer: "I be protected, and I be starving". The wage of this man was 7s. a week. In Dorset the protected labourer starved on a shilling less. "We have always maintained", said Bright, "that the landlord has a right to labour at the market price of labour; but we have denied the right of the landlord to screen himself from competition, while he exposes his labourers to it in the severest form." On another occasion, after depicting the penury of the agricultural labourer, he said: "I tell you what your boasted protection is. It is a protection of native idleness at the expense of the impoverishment of native industry." The farmers were told that whatever benefit they received from protection was less than the advantage they would get from the general revival of commercial prosperity which would follow free trade. The system of duties rising and falling as prices fell and rose was intended to promote stability of prices. It actually increased the frequency and the swing of fluctuations. Importers, by temporarily forcing prices up, could secure, under the sliding-scale, a reduction of duty, which might cover their loss when the ensuing fall brought prices to a level lower than the average on which the farmers' rents were based. Violent oscillations tend in the long run to the advantage neither of the consumer nor the producer, but of the factor, who can more readily forecast and may even manipulate them.   The sliding-scale made many farmers bankrupt.

The battle of the Corn Law was a contention between the middle-class and the landed aristocracy.   It is necessary to dwell upon this aspect of the conflict, in order to understand the reproach of setting class against class, by which Bright was beset throughout his public career.

Bright and Cobden, and with them nearly all the men who made the fortune of the League by munificent subscriptions, belonged to a new order.   The wealthy middle class which both Whigs and Tories had long been habituated to treat with respect, were the great merchants, especially those of the city of London, whose financial assistance had often saved the State from disaster.   But the pride and the power of the manufacturers of Lancashire and the West Riding, luxuriating in wealth newly acquired, and controlling the livelihood of many thousands of working men, were a new portent regarded by the aristocracy with a mixture of apprehension and disdain.   That power had been called into existence by the application of machinery and steam-power to industries before practised by independent handicraftsmen, and by the consequent appearance of the Factory System.   Spinners and weavers had been massed in crowded towns and huge manufactories.   The capitalists who built the mills and provided the machinery claimed a large share of the profits of the industry.   Each workman's labour produced a result enormously larger than when Silas Marner threw his shuttle in his village home, and wove the homespun yarn of the housewives of Raveloe; and multitudes must starve unless new outlets could be found for the cloth of Leeds and the calico of Manchester.   This was doubtless inevitable; but there was honest pity as well as envy in the dislike of aristocratic politicians and Tory essayists to the factory system.

The bitterness of party spirit to-day is not to be compared with the mutual hatred and jealousy of the squires and the cotton-spinners that are revealed in the debates of fifty years ago on the Corn Law and the Factory Bills.   In the mouth of a county member cotton-spinner was a name of contempt, like *épicier*, bagman, or philistine.   These two classes have since been drawn together by the approximation of their social and political aims, and even by those intermarriages which Thackeray thought so ridiculous, but which have helped to conciliate the feuds of classes.   Each class accused the other of grinding the faces of the poor.   The Leaguers told their workmen that the distress could only be remedied by a reform which would at once cheapen their food and provide new markets for their fabrics.   The land-owners retorted by attributing the sufferings of the working cotton-spinner to the cupidity of his employer, and demanding that he should be protected by Factory Acts and Truck Acts.   The League charged the land-owners with enacting the Corn Law to raise their rents. The land-owners in retaliation accused the manufacturers of desiring to repeal the Corn Law in order that they might lower the wages of their workmen and enlarge their own profits.[1]   This suspicion was shared and encouraged by the Chartists.

[1] As a matter of interest to students of mythology, it may be mentioned that this unfulfilled prediction hardened in process of time into the legend that "immediately after the repeal of the Corn Law the firm of John Bright & Brothers reduced the wages of all their hands".

This failure of prophecy may remind the reader of the disappointment of Cobden's confident expectation that the civilized world would soon follow the example of England in the matter of Free-trade.   It would be easy to set against this a hundred examples of his astonishing sagacity in foretelling results.   Those who are interested in falsified predictions will find an inexhaustible mine of such things in the protectionist speeches against Villiers' annual motion.

The view of English politics which Bright held at the time when his indignation drew him from his mill to the platform of the League and to the benches of Parliament, is simple and may be briefly stated. It is a view which never ceased to control his public words and acts. Since the Revolution England had been governed alternately by two aristocratic coteries, each of which had treated the opinions and the interests of the middle-class with a degree of deference and sympathy determined by the vicissitudes of their conflicts with one another. The aristocracy were the land-owners; possession of land rather than noble birth being the test of the caste. The predominance of the land-owners in the House of Lords was in accordance with the intention of the Constitution, and did not form a grievance. But, partly as a natural result of the migration of population from old boroughs to new towns, and partly by an immoral use of the power of landlord over tenant, the land-owners had also acquired an unconstitutional predominance in the Commons, and had so cheated the other classes of their share in the Constitution. The reform of 1832 had failed, and indeed had not been sincerely intended, to destroy the aristocratical control of the Commons. Lord John Russell, a leader of that reform, had acknowledged that the redistribution had been so manipulated as to secure a permanent majority for the agricultural interest; and the agricultural interest was still at the disposal of the land-owners.

The land-owning oligarchy had used this power, acquired in defiance of the spirit of the Constitution, for unpatriotic and selfish ends. The administration of the military and civil services had been conducted by them, not to secure for the tax-payer the best service in return for his expense, but to provide careers at the public cost for their younger sons. But the crowning example and the most cruel result of the selfishness of the ruling class were to be found in the Corn Laws. "This House", said Bright, "is a club of land-owners legislating for land-owners." "The corn law you cherish is a law to make a scarcity of food in the country that your own rents may be increased." "The quarrel is between the bread-eating millions and the few who monopolize the soil." Whether justly or unjustly Bright firmly believed that the land-owners were guilty not of an error but of a sin against the light; and throughout his career he was never able to regard without suspicion and prejudice the acts and the aims of a class against which he had in all sincerity sustained such an indictment.

Bright's disposition was in many respects eminently conservative. He was zealous for the Constitution, an enemy of disorder, and thoroughly disinclined to violent changes. "I like political changes," he said, "when such changes are made as the result not of passion, but of deliberation and reason." He had no theory of the rights of man to vindicate; the most conservative politician in England was not less infected with Jacobinism. He became a leader of democracy, and the protagonist of a democratic reform, because he was first an enemy of oligarchy; and he was an enemy of oligarchy, not so much because the rule of the few appeared to him theoretically vicious, as because the particular aristocracy with which he came into conflict, the aristocracy which made and maintained the Corn Law, had proved itself, in his view, to be selfish, tyrannical, and incompetent. "We are rapidly approaching a time", he said in 1843, "when the middle and working classes will be found in a firm confederacy against the domination of a class."

## Chapter II.

## The Radical Reformers.

Almost simultaneously with the great triumph of the
free-trade doctrine of Bright and his friends another of
their principles sustained a not less remarkable defeat.
In accepting the first and rejecting the second of the
Manchester doctrines, the Parliament of 1846 appears to
be supported by the judgment of posterity, for neither
the victory nor the defeat has since been reversed.

While the Corn-law Bill was passing through the
House of Lords, the House of Commons was considering
a proposal of John Fielden, member for Oldham, the
patron of William Cobbett, to amend the Factory Act.
Lord Ashley's Act of 1833 had restricted the labour of
children under fourteen to eight hours a day, and that
of young persons under eighteen to sixty-nine hours a
week. Fielden's Bill, known as the Ten Hours Bill,
proposed to limit the labour of all women and girls,
and of boys under eighteen, to ten hours a day or
fifty-eight a week. This Bill was opposed by Peel,
Cobden, Bright, and Mr. Villiers, and rejected by a
small majority. In the following session, however, it
passed both Houses, despite a vigorous protest by
Brougham in the Lords.

Bright had already resisted a similar proposal made
by Lord Ashley two years earlier. His speech on that
occasion had been of necessity acrimonious. No one
can now doubt that the motives of Lord Ashley—who is
better known by his later title as the Earl of Shaftesbury,
—were purely philanthropic. But at that time Bright
could not forget that he was a Protectionist, an enemy
of Reform, and a defender of the hated monopolies.
His Bill had been made by Ferrand and other Protec-

tionists the occasion for a furious onslaught on the factory system, and on the inhumanity of manufacturers. The cotton-spinners were put on their defence; and Bright was constrained to reply at length and with much warmth to imputations, grievously exaggerated by the jealousies of the hour, upon himself, his neighbours, and his friends. He was justified in imputing to many of the supporters of the new legislation a desire rather to injure the masters than to benefit the workmen. It was neither his fault nor Ashley's that a measure designed by its author for the protection of the poor had been made a field for ill-tempered recrimination, and for invidious comparisons between the degrees of misery suffered under the protective system by the labourers of Dorset and the weavers of Lancashire. The proposal presented itself to his mind as an attempt to divert the blame of the misery of the operatives from the Corn Law to the factory system. "Let not the House suppose that if they pass the clause now before them they will do more than plaister over the sore which their own unjust legislation has created, instead of endeavouring to renovate the constitution and go to the root of the disease."

This had been said in 1844. On the occasion we are considering Bright reasserted his objection to legislative interference with the working hours of adults, replying to a speech which may be read in the published collection of Macaulay's speeches. The Bill pretended to aim only at a reduction of the working hours of women and young persons; but, so far at least as the textile industries were concerned, its effect would be to reduce also the working hours of men, for the machinery could not run profitably when the women and children were withdrawn. That this was the intention as well as the effect of the Bill was proved by the refusal to accept an amendment of Bright's to allow the women to work in relays. He

declared that, if the Bill passed, the factories then working without profit must close their doors.　The workmen
had always refused a reduction of hours with a corresponding reduction of wages; and they would consider
that Parliament their enemy which should tie their hands
for two hours and take two hours' wages from them.　It
appeared axiomatic to Bright that "ten hours' work can
never yield twelve hours' wages".　"Ten hours' labour
is better than twelve hours; but the ten hours can best
be brought about by voluntary arrangement."　A deceit
had been practised on the working men, who had been
induced to think that legislation could compel an increase
in the wages earned by a given amount of work.　The
Bill was "contrary to all the principles of sound legislation", and "advocated by those who had no knowledge
of the economy of manufacture".

　　Bright's opposition to this and similar bills was in
later years often used against him at elections; but he
never apologized for it, or confessed that he had ceased
to regard the Factory Acts, so far as they limited the
hours of adult labour, as mistaken legislation.　"Most
of our evils", he said, "arise from legislative interference"; and this maxim, eminently characteristic of the
Manchester School, continued to approve itself to him
to the end of his career.　He was, in short, a faithful
adherent of the old radical doctrine of *laisser faire*—a
doctrine held by more modern Radicals, if at all, with so
much laxity in admitting exceptions that it has ceased to
be a guiding principle, and has become merely an occasional weapon of debate.　Many years afterwards, when
he was President of the Board of Trade, his interferences
with the discretion of the permanent officials were rare;
but it was observed that, when he did interpose his
authority, he used it nearly always not to order but to
countermand the exercise of the powers of his Board.

　　The conflict between Bright and his opponents was

one scene of the perennial controversy between those who treat economic laws as immutable by human volition,—insomuch that to legislate in defiance of them is as though we should pass a resolution repealing the law of gravitation in the hope of jumping safely from the top of the Monument,—and those who think more hopefully that, whether by legislation, or combination, or mere clamour, the more painful inferences of economic theory may in practice be somehow circumvented.

Whatever may be thought of Bright's reasoning,—which has at no time commanded the assent of the working-classes, and may therefore be safely neglected by practical politicians,—it is certainly not refuted by the consideration that under the Act hours of work have in fact been reduced, yet wages have in fact risen. The reply is obvious. The repeal of the protective duties, and the free exchange of English fabrics for foreign food-stuffs, increased the demand to such an extent[1] that, by the natural and automatic law to which Bright trusted, the value of a man's labour rose till he earned more in ten hours than he had earned in twelve under protection. Bright could fairly contend that, if the Ten Hours Act had preceded instead of following the repeal of the Corn Law, it would have aggravated the distress of the manufacturing towns.

The same principle led Bright, a few years later, to throw cold water over Sir C. Forster's Bill to strengthen the Truck Act, which was said to be evaded in the Midlands, although in Lancashire, as Bright said, the truck system did not exist. " Under the present conditions of labour in the country, there can be no permanent, continuous, and irritating tyranny such as has been described by the promoters of the Bill, which the working classes are not perfectly well able to correct without

---

[1] The exportation of cotton goods quadrupled itself within thirty years of the Repeal.

coming to the House of Commons for a new measure."
Finally, in 1855, he successfully resisted an attempt of
J. M. Cobbett to improve the Factory Act. "Whenever I
meet my constituents, I have always said that I disapprove
of such legislation as extremely perilous, whatever good
it may do; but that, since the question has been settled
by a judicious compromise, I will not abet in any way
any motion to disturb the settlement of 1850;[1] and I
have always found that answer satisfactory in Lancashire. If I thought the elements of discord were again
to be stirred up, I should myself be glad to leave the
country, and to go somewhere else, where labour and
capital are allowed to fight their own battle on their own
ground without legislative interference."

We now return to the memorable session of 1846. In
destroying the unity of his party for the common good,
Peel had also made sacrifice of his own career. He did
not fail to understand that he could no longer remain,
and could never again become, Prime Minister. He
would not accept Cobden's friendly suggestion that he
should appeal to the country as the leader of a Free-
trade party, conceiving that he could not properly use
the prerogative of dissolution to decide a personal question between himself and the Protectionists. It is possible that the other Radicals, like Cobden, would have
preferred his leadership to that of Russell. But it is
difficult to believe that, if so bold an attempt to ignore
the Whigs and reconstruct parties had been made, it
would not have been easily defeated by Russell and
Palmerston. Anyhow the opportunity, such as it was,
was missed. On the day that the Corn-law Bill passed
the Lords, the Ministry was defeated on an Irish bill.
Peel resigned, and Russell became Prime Minister, with
Palmerston as Foreign Secretary.

---

[1] Ashley's Act of 1850 settled some ambiguities, but made no substantial
addition to Fielden's Act.

The opportunities of private members of the House of Commons were more abundant in those days of scanty legislation than now; and the speeches made by Bright in Parliament in the eight years between the repeal of the Corn Law and the Crimean war cover the whole field of his political aims. He cannot at this time be regarded as the leader, or even as a member, of any organized party or group. Many of the old Free-traders immediately took their place in the Liberal phalanx, and gave no countenance to the Radicalism of Bright and Cobden. Amongst those who commonly voted with them were Joseph Hume, member for Mont-rose, a Radical of long parliamentary experience, the champion of retrenchment and economy, and the most formidable and useful of parliamentary bores; Ricardo, member for Stoke, a nephew of the great economist, and himself known as the reformer who applied free-trade principles to the Navigation Laws; Sir William Moles-worth, member for Southwark, a chief advocate of colo-nial Home Rule; and, after 1852, Edward Miall, member for Rochdale, the general of the militant Nonconfor-mists.

Molesworth may be taken as the connecting link be-tween the Manchester School and the old Philosophical Radicals of the school of Bentham, Grote, and James Mill. There is an obvious gap in the sympathy between Bright—the old-fashioned Puritan, the emotional orator, full of a strong faith in his own intuitions, and appealing to sentiment, compassion, and the New Testament— and the Utilitarians, with their arid philosophy, their odd presumption of a quantitative measure of happiness, their supercilious disdain of national habit, their ungodly hardness, and their dusty logic. But he and they were united in the pursuit of many political ends; and Bright, with his incomparable gift of popular advocacy and his contagious sensibility to injustice, accomplished feats of persuasion to achieve which essays had been written and syllogisms constructed in vain.

Bright derived from the philosophers his belief in the immutability of political economy, and his very wide faith in the doctrine of *laisser faire et laisser passer.* Indeed his devotion to these articles of faith was more rigidly orthodox than that of one who stood nearer than he to the true apostolical succession of the Benthamites, John Stuart Mill. Mill deliberately excepted the regulation of the hours of labour and the provision of education by the State from the general doctrine of *laisser faire.*[1] Bright, as we have seen, set up the principle of non-interference against the Ten Hours Bill; and he was also an enemy of any possible scheme of national education.

In April, 1847, Russell proposed an increase in the grant for elementary education. The prevalent opinion of Nonconformists was then entirely opposed to all grants from the Treasury to the schools, which were mostly under clerical control. It has already been remarked that Bright was above all things an enthusiast of religious equality. " I am a Nonconformist," he said, " being by birth, education, observation, and conviction fully established in the opinion I hold." His hostility to the establishment of religion was associated in his mind with his repugnance to other sorts of privilege. The clergy were in his view a privileged class; and therefore, by reason of the natural tendency of persons so favoured to support not only their own but one another's privileges, the Church, as he thought, had been "uniformly hostile to the progress of public liberty", and "opposed to those opinions and those changes which most men believed to be necessary". To this topic he frequently recurred. He never forgot that when the people were starving, when children were fighting for crusts of bread

[1] *Political Economy*, book v. chap. xi.

picked out of the gutter, when women were pawning their wedding-rings to buy food, and when the dissenting ministers of England turned out wherever the trumpet of the League was blown, the clergy of the privileged church were either indifferent or had joined the defenders of the pitiless monopoly.

Bright admitted that many Nonconformists had been in favour of the interference of the government in 1839. "At that time the Dissenters regarded the institution of a Committee of the Privy Council as a step leading away from that power which the Church of England wished to usurp, of educating the whole people. But from 1839 to this year we have found no step taken by the government which has not had for its tendency the aggrandisement of the Established Church." [1]

Bright's speech, again delivered in reply to Macaulay, defended the old system, described by his antagonist as an experiment tried without success ever since the Heptarchy, by which elementary education had been left to voluntary enterprise and voluntary benevolence, without recourse to the funds or submission to the control of the State. Many years have elapsed since this view became obsolete; but Bright's speeches in its favour are still in a high degree interesting, for his opinion was not isolated or wilful, but intimately connected with the general principles of policy which he never abandoned. The following passage, for example, is of the first importance: "If there is any principle more certain than another, I suppose it is that what a people is able to do for itself the Government should not attempt to do for it. For nothing tends so much to strengthen a people, to make them powerful, great, and good, as the constant exercise

[1] It must be remembered that there was then no Conscience Clause. Bright was one of a very small minority that supported in 1847 an amendment to admit children to all state-aided schools without compelling them to share in the religious instruction.

of all their faculties on public objects, and the carrying out of public works and objects by voluntary contributions among themselves."

We seem to have travelled a vast distance from this position now; and the classes for which Bright won a commanding share in the determination of national policy, have been encouraged to larger and larger expectations of what the State can do and ought to do for them. We may still hear the echoes of Bright's robust individualism in the candour of private conversation, but from political platforms it is banished for ever.

At the general election of 1847 Bright was appropriately rewarded for his services to Free-trade by an unopposed return for Manchester, the headquarters of the League. His colleague, Milner Gibson, was a man of Radical sympathies, though a member of the Government.

Immediately after the election he turned his attention to the second great enterprise of his career, parliamentary reform. That enterprise was destined to occupy twenty years of his life. For ten years he and his friends called for reform in the House of Commons, and from time to time exacted futile promises from Ministers. For ten years more, reviving the methods of the League, he conducted the agitation in the country which at last produced the Reform Act of 1867. Although the Leaguers had resisted the desire of the Chartists to give priority to parliamentary reform over Free-trade, their work and its difficulties had made them sensible of the imperfection of the representative system. They believed that public opinion had always preponderated against the Corn Law, and that it could not have survived the first reformed parliament, if the Reform of 1832 had been sufficient to restore to the people that control over the Lower House of which the aristocracy had deprived them. No one could tell how long the House of Com-

mons might have resisted public opinion if the reasoning
of the platforms had not been reinforced by the irresistible argument of the famine, or if that crisis had not
found at the head of the Conservative party a statesman
who had hereditary sympathies with the manufacturers
as well as the squires.

On April 27, 1848, the movement was inaugurated at
Newall's Buildings, Manchester, the office of the League,
by Bright and Cobden. Two months later Hume moved
a resolution in the House in favour of household suffrage,
the ballot, triennial parliaments, and a more equal
apportionment of voters to seats. This scheme went a
long way in the direction of the People's Charter, and
considerably further than the Reform of 1867. In this
debate Hume once more enunciated the famous Radical
watchword that "taxation and representation should go
together"; and Disraeli declared that "the franchise
was not a right, nor a trust, but a privilege, created by
law, and conferred, not as an odious exception, but as
a general reward". Bright, who had made an earlier
opportunity of declaring his belief that "the constitution would be strengthened by admitting a large number
of people to participate in its privileges", took no part
in this debate, but voted, with Villiers, Molesworth,
Cobden, and Gibson, in the minority of 84. Next year,
in speaking to Hume's motion, he propounded his constitutional theory of reform. "My hon. friend merely
proposes that you should adopt in practice that which
no one will deny is recognized by the theory of the constitution. We have monarchical institutions, in which
we have found no fault. We have a House of Peers,
which is another recognized portion of our constitutional
system. That also has its privileges and prerogatives,
and we find no fault in them. But we maintain that the
constitution recognizes another element,—a popular, or,
if you choose, a democratic element; and we who stand

here, and those we represent, the common people of
England, have as great and undoubted a right to be sole
and absolute in this House as the monarch on the throne,
or the peers in the other chamber of the legislature. But
the system under which we sit in this House is by no
means in accord with the theory of the constitution."
The system, he said, excluded five-sixths of the grown
men of the nation; while the representation of the
middle-classes was a mere pretence so long as so many
boroughs were in the gift of the great land-owners. He
warned the House that the natural result of the disappointment of the working-classes had been "that frightful thing which men call Chartism,—frightful not in its
demand, but because in its discussions passions had been
stirred up, false principles enunciated, and mischievous
animosities engendered". Bright was an enemy of turbulence; but he had learned the first lesson of political
wisdom,—to seek for the remediable causes of popular
discontents, not in the vice of the multitude, but in the
errors of the government.

The demand for parliamentary reform was associated
in the minds of the reformers, and on the banners
exhibited at popular demonstrations, with the cry for
retrenchment. Cobden believed that expense, and in
particular military expense, could be curtailed only by
"giving the people a voice in the government". In
1849 he proposed, with the support of Bright and Hume,
to reduce the national expenditure "to the sum which
within the last fourteen years has been found to be
sufficient", that is to say, from fifty-four to forty-four
and a half millions. The people have since obtained
their voice in the government; and the expenditure has
grown to more than double the maximum proposed by
Cobden.

Bright's speeches on finance are comparatively unimportant. They were indeed merely auxiliary to those of

Cobden and Hume, who could handle statistics and calculations with greater dexterity. He called for an extension of the death duties to real as well as personal property. The Conservative county members retorted by asking that real property should be relieved of its excessive share in local taxation. Bright could not tolerate the clamour of the land-owners for relief to the agricultural interest, and compared them to the strolling players who announced a performance for the benefit of the poor, being themselves, as it afterwards appeared, the poor intended by the advertisement. The Radical plan for the relief of the farmers was to repeal the duty on malt and hops, and to meet the deficiency by a corresponding reduction of expense. The Chancellor of the Exchequer was obliged to refuse all these appeals.

Both at this time and for many years afterwards Bright protested frequently and with insistence against what seemed to him extravagant expenditure on national defence. These protests were inspired partly by his hatred of war, partly by his general belief that the commercial prosperity of the country suffered by excessive taxation, and, not least, by his distrust of an aristocratic service. He was not convinced by the proverb that bids us make ready for war if we desire peace; and indeed those who dispute that time-honoured saw need not be at a loss for apt historical instances. He happily illustrated the fallacy which lurks in the popular belief that large expenditure, on muniments of war for instance, is good for trade, by the parable of the dog fed on its own tail. As for the third reason, he said now, "the cry raised with respect to the defenceless state of the country has its origin entirely in the wishes of a party connected with the military department to increase our expenditure". Ten years later he embodied this suspicion in the most brilliant and memorable of his sayings. "The more you examine the matter, the more you will come to the conclusion that this foreign policy, this regard for the liberties of Europe, this care for the Protestant interest, this excessive love for the balance of power, is neither more nor less than a gigantic system of outdoor relief for the aristocracy of Great Britain."

During the session of 1848 Bright made his first attempt at legislation. The severity of the Game-laws had occupied the attention of eminent Whigs, when that party was in opposition and had a keen eye for grievances. Fox had denounced the Game-law as a law that engendered crime, and Sydney Smith had ridiculed and condemned it in the early numbers of the *Edinburgh Review*. In 1845 Bright had obtained a committee of the House to inquire into the grievance. He had collected information at considerable expense to himself, had called twenty-one tenant farmers to lay their complaints before the committee, and had published the evidence with a preface of his own. The Bill he now introduced, relying rather upon the evidence, and upon his own conclusions therefrom, than upon the cautious and moderate report of the committee, was simple and complete. He called it a Bill for Repealing the Laws with respect to Game, and scheduled all the Acts without exception. The committee had reported that the common law of England had always distinctly recognized a qualified right of property in game; and the effect of Bright's Bill would have been to leave game protected only by the common-law rights of the land-owner in respect of the game on his land.[1]

Bright stated the case against the law under three

[1] The following example of the common-law rights may serve to amuse the non-legal mind :—" If A starts a hare in the ground of B, and hunts it and kills it there, the property continues all the while in B. But if A starts a hare in the ground of B, and hunts it into the ground of C, and kills it there, the property is in A, the hunter; but A is liable to an action of trespass for hunting in the grounds of B and of C."

heads of argument. In the first place, he urged that the preservation of game prevented agricultural improvement and that increase of the production of the land which was required by the increase of the consuming population. Fifty or sixty years earlier the tenant had been contented with the spontaneous produce of the land; now he spent money to increase the produce, and really paid two rents,—one, the rent paid to the landlord, by which he purchased the natural produce; the other, the interest on his capital, in return for which he was entitled to the artificial increase. The land-owner still reserved the right of stocking the land with game, and of thus destroying not only a part of the unassisted produce of the land, but of the increase obtained by the expenditure of the tenant's capital. In the second place, confidence in the law was weakened by the harsh administration of the Game-laws by magistrates personally interested in preservation. The Home Office had found it necessary to order all convictions for poaching to be reported, and had released many persons illegally convicted, and commuted many illegally severe sentences. Thirdly, the law encouraged crime. Graham, the Peelite Home Secretary, had said: " The most frightful source of crime in my neighbourhood is the preservation of game; poaching is the cause rather than the consequence of criminal habits ". All these evils, said Bright, were entailed on the country for the sake of the 35,000 sportsmen who held game licenses.

The Bill was received with derision, and did not reach the second stage. Bright retained his opinion, and nearly twenty years later wrote to a farmer that he saw no good in any changes in the law. " What you want is the repeal of all laws which are made with the object of favouring preservation of game." But he was not satisfied with the support he received from farmers, and he knew by experience that an annual motion in Parliament was useless unless supported by strong pressure from the country. The question slept for many years; and nothing was done by the legislature until Sir William Harcourt's Ground Game Act of 1880. The influence which public opinion has gradually obtained over the conduct of county magistrates has mitigated what Bright treated with reason as a grievance crying for redress.

At this period of his life Bright spoke almost every year in support of an annual motion for the repeal of capital punishment. He said, "I feel more strongly upon this question than upon any other that can come before the House". The sentiment that prompted this avowal was no doubt religious; but he discussed the question, as he afterwards discussed the question of peace and war, without making any assumption repugnant to those who did not share his solemn regard for the inviolable sanctity of human life. This question seems, now that the institution of annual motions has perished, to have passed from the House of Commons into the keeping of debating societies. In regard to another reform, which he advocated from the first, and which was doubtless connected in his mind with this,— the prohibition of flogging in the army,—his views in process of time have prevailed.

The session of 1851 was remarkable for one of the least creditable performances of the House of Commons. The appointment of Roman Catholic bishops with territorial titles had excited the Protestantism of the country, already rendered irritable by the suspicion of romanizing influences in the Oxford Tractarians. Russell, who inherited from his Whig ancestors the strong anti-roman sentiments that originally created the Whig party, and who possibly mistook a passing ebullition of temper for a great national movement likely to bring credit to any man who should put himself at the head of it, thundered against the Pope and the Tractarians in his famous Durham letter, and introduced the futile Ecclesiastical Titles Assumption Bill. Bright was one of the small and enviable minority that opposed the introduction of this "little, paltry, miserable measure", and predicted a rapid subsidence of the indignation that made it for the moment popular. "I shall not be surprised if the noble Lord finds himself devoured by his own hounds." The Bill suggested topics irresistible to a Liberationist. "This is not a subject for a parliament to discuss at all; and we are discussing it in consequence of the errors of our forefathers." No sentence could be quoted more characteristic of Bright,—of his clear vision for what was near, and his inadequate perception of the perspective of history. If Russell, with his historical consciousness of the spirit of the Exclusionists, failed to understand that the time had passed when any effective demonstration of the national Protestantism could be made by Parliament, Bright, with a finer sense of the modern spirit, saw only an error of our forefathers in the parliamentary Protestantism that was once as necessary to the salvation of England as the tolerance and equality of to-day.

It required less than his dexterity in debate to turn Russell's complaint of the "danger within the gates from the unworthy sons of the Church of England" against the Establishment. "The noble Lord has discovered that the great institution that was supposed to be the bulwark of Protestantism turns out to be a huge manufactory of a national and home-made Popery." More worthy of record than this effective taunt is the admirable observation: "It is a common saying that truth is indestructible; but let the House remember that there is another thing that is indestructible, and that is a persecuted error".

Between the first and second reading of the Bill the

Radicals defeated the Government in a small House on a motion to equalize the county with the borough franchise.   Russell, who had other reasons to complain of the listlessness of his supporters, and who was perhaps not sorry to escape from his Bill, made this defeat an excuse for resignation, and was ridiculed in *Punch* as the little boy who chalked up No Popery and ran away. The Conservatives declined to relieve him of his difficulties, and his Ministry returned to office.   But his Cabinet was not very loyal, and his following was still far from enthusiastic.   The life of a Liberal Government without a progressive policy, and supported by little more than the fear of protection, could not be very vigorous.   Within twelve months there was another crisis.

At the end of 1851 Palmerston was summarily dismissed as a punishment for committing the country to approval of Louis Napoleon's execrable *coup d'état* of December 2, without the knowledge of the Queen and the Prime Minister.   In taking, or in assenting to, this course, Russell was aware that "his Government was so much weakened that it was not likely to retain power for any long time".   Palmerston's ostentatious foreign policy, however distasteful to Bright, had been the only part of the conduct of the Government that had touched the popular sympathy.   In a few weeks Palmerston was able to say, "I have had my tit-for-tat with John Russell".   That no circumstance of ignominy should be wanting, the weapon with which he defeated his late friends was an amendment to omit the word Local in the title of the Local Militia Bill.   Lord Derby became Prime Minister, and Disraeli Leader of the House of Commons.

The Free-traders could not see without dismay the statesman who had led the outcry of the exasperated Protectionists against Peel six years before, sitting as the Leader of the House. Preparations were made to revive the activities of the League. Bright joined in the demand for an appeal to the country, at which the question of Protection should be submitted straightforwardly to the electorate. Disraeli's position was indeed awkward, for not only was his party in a minority, but many of the Conservatives who sat for boroughs had by this time declared for free trade in corn. "Your difficulties", said Bright, "are not of our making. They are the difficulties of an impossible policy; and that, I tell you, is a difficulty that we will not allow you to escape from. Either you shall recant your protectionist principles, or you shall go to the constituencies, and let them decide the question once for all and for all of us. You said once you would break up an organized hypocrisy. I say to you, we will try if we cannot break up a confederated imposture."

In the summer of 1852 the appeal was made. Bright stood again for Manchester as a supporter of "commercial freedom, parliamentary reform, and religious liberty", and was re-elected by a satisfactory majority. The response of the country showed that the Conservatives could remain in office, if at all, only by renouncing protection. Accepting the popular verdict, Disraeli finally bade farewell to protectionist principles, which thenceforward were reduced to the rank of a pious opinion tolerated in private members of his party. His palinode did not save him from defeat. In December he was beaten in committee of Ways and Means. The new Ministry was formed by a coalition of the two sections of the Free-trade party. Of the Peelites, Lord Aberdeen became Prime Minister and Mr. Gladstone Chancellor of the Exchequer. Of the old Liberals, Russell became Foreign Secretary and led the House of Commons, and Palmerston was made Home Secretary.

In the early years of this Parliament, Bright had occasion to speak on three questions which to his mind were settled by simple deductions from the general proposition that the State ought to treat all religions alike. The Commons passed a measure, which was more than once rejected by the Lords, to remove the disabilities that prevented Jews from sitting in Parliament. The opposition to this act of toleration, Bright said, had been based on a sentiment which had gradually sunk down to a mere phrase,—that the Bill would " unchristianize the House of Commons ". " What can be more marvellous than that any sane man should propose that doctrinal differences in religion should be made the test of citizenship and political rights?  Doctrinal differences in religion in all human probability will last for many generations to come, and may possibly last so long as man shall inhabit the globe; but if you permit these differences to be the test of citizenship, what is it but to admit to your system the fatal conclusion that social and political differences in all nations can never be eradicated but must be eternal? "

In 1854 the Dissenters were disappointed by the absence of any provision to abolish tests in the Bills for reforming the ancient Universities.  Bright vehemently reproached the Government for their treatment of the just claims of Nonconformists, whose support indeed the Whig party had long been accustomed to purchase or to reward by the stingiest minimum of concessions. " Dissenters are always expected to manifest very much of the qualities which are spoken of in the Epistle to the Corinthians,—' to hope all things, to believe all things, and to endure all things '."  He had before called Palmerston the " political Mrs. Jellaby " by reason of the contrast between his sympathy, often indiscreetly exhibited, with the Liberal movement abroad, and his neglect of Liberal reforms at home.  In the same strain,

he now taunted Russell with leaving the religious in-
equalities of his own country untouched, whilst "undertaking in the most zealous manner possible the establishment of religious equality in Turkey, and asking
the Sultan to do what would be very revolutionary and
horrible if broached in this country".

The third and most important of these questions was
that of the imposition of church-rates on Dissenters.
Bright's speeches on this subject were frequent and
passionate, so passionate indeed that they were perhaps
more likely to provoke obstinacy than to carry conviction. They are full of incidents of oppression, the record
of which it would be cruel to revive. Nor is it necessary
to attempt here any history of that prolonged resistance,
so fruitful in acrimony, which has probably very few
defenders now. The following passage, irresistibly
suggestive of Noodle's Oration, is quoted from Lord
John Russell's speech against the Church Rates Abolition Bill of 1854, as in itself sufficient to explain Bright's
refusal to recognize him as a leader of Liberalism, and
as furnishing a measure of the change that came over the
spirit of the party when the lump was at last leavened
by Bright's inspiriting ideas. "We have a national
church, we have a national aristocracy, we have a
hereditary monarchy, and all these things stand together. My opinion is that they would decay and fall
together. I see no reason why we should prefer to
these institutions those of the United States of America;
and I must therefore oppose this Bill as in my opinion
tending to subvert one of the great institutions of the
State."

Another reform to which the Radicals applied themselves with great energy during the life of the Coalition
Government was the repeal of what they called taxes on
knowledge—the taxes that made newspapers dear. The
cost of the stamp affixed to every copy of a newspaper

had been reduced in 1836 from 4*d.* to 1*d.* There were also a tax on advertisements and an excise duty on paper. The effect of these imposts was, in brief, that while the *New York Herald* was sold for 1*d.*, and the *Melbourne Argus* for 1½*d.*, a paper of the same size in England cost 5*d.*; that even the largest provincial towns had only weekly papers; that in seventy-five parliamentary boroughs no newspaper whatever was published; and that attempts were constantly made to evade the law.

Some of the old Chartists had formed a committee for promoting the repeal of these duties. In the House of Commons Milner Gibson took the lead in pressing for this reform, and Bright gave effective support to his colleague. "Here", he exclaimed, holding up a copy of the *Potteries Free Press*, "is an unfortunate pape which was strangled out of its little innocent life in th most remorseless manner." The expectation already entertained, though destined to a long procrastination, that the working-classes would soon be admitted to the franchise, supplied the strongest argument for cheapening the means of popular information on current events. There were many who feared that cheap papers would pander to this or that evil passion of the multitude. But in Mr. Gladstone, who, though not yet accepting the name of Liberal, was already in many respects more sympathetic with the reformers than the Liberal leaders, Gibson and Bright found a Chancellor of the Exchequer easily convinced of the value of this reform. The revenue stamp disappeared from newspapers in 1855; and many of the great daily newspapers of the provinces date from that era. It was not till six years later, and until after a struggle between the Commons and the Lords, that Mr. Gladstone was able to abolish the paper duty, and so to call into existence a multitude of penny papers. There was none of the many reforms in which he had

had a hand to which Bright referred more frequently and with more satisfaction than to this, in the historical reminiscences which formed the substance of his speeches in his old age.

---

# Chapter III.

## The War with Russia.

We have now reached a period in Bright's career which furnishes the most crucial tests of his public character. A politician acting with a party shares with others, in a degree varying inversely with his eminence, the credit or discredit of his acts and words. When he stands alone, he invites an absolute verdict for or against himself.

Bright's five great speeches on the war with Russia are the summit of his achievements as a parliamentary orator. On the ultimate acceptance of the principles of public action, which he advocated without success at that crisis, he staked and saved his reputation for political sagacity. Long before it was possible to discern the symptoms of that change in the habit of public opinion which he predicted so confidently, as early, indeed, as the first subsidence of the popular passion which had overwhelmed him, he already began to enjoy the reward of his courage and fidelity. He could no longer be classed among the demagogues the breath of whose nostrils is the applause of the populace. Cleon had exhibited the virtues of Cato. From this time forward, though his opinions were often distasteful, and his advocacy of them irritating, to great sections of his countrymen, he was exempt from the reproach of insincerity and time-serving.

With the Russian speeches should be read the lumin-

ous and energetic letter to Absalom Watkin.[1]   The
following outline of the transactions which led to the
war is intended merely to supply what is necessary to
make the letter and the speeches intelligible.

Three men stand at the bar of history charged with
the guilt of this great crime against humanity.   Historians will doubtless never agree upon the distribution
of blame between the fanatical zeal of Nicholas, the
ambition of Louis Napoleon, and the obstinacy of Lord
Stratford de Redcliffe.   Those who acquit the great
ambassador, who is at least entitled to the praise of a
definite purpose and an unbroken consistency, must join
in Bright's condemnation of the " incapable and guilty
administration "—the ministers who weakly surrendered
the reins, at one time to their servant, at another to
their ally.

In the year 1851 the French Government made certain
claims upon the Sublime Porte in respect of the localities
in the Holy Land which have been for many centuries
the resort of Christian pilgrims.   This demand was
based upon a treaty of 1740, in which the Porte had
recognized France as the guardian of the right of the
Western Church to access to the holy places.   The claim
of France was reluctantly conceded by the Sultan, and
in December, 1852, the key of the Church of the Nativity
at Bethlehem was entrusted to Latin monks, and a silver
star bearing the French arms was solemnly installed in
the sanctuary.   The success of this pious enterprise of
the disciples of Voltaire aroused the jealousy of the
Tsar; it was a diplomatic victory of the Latin over the
Greek Church, and of the Greek Church the Tsar was
the acknowledged head and protector.   Russian troops

[1] One of the minor results of the democratic reform of 1867 is that the
art of political pamphleteering has lost much of its importance.  To be successful, political literature must now be brief, and may be shallow.   It is
possible that the letter to Watkin will take rank as the last classical specimen of the lost art of Halifax and Burke.

were ordered to the south-western frontier. The French
retorted by sending a fleet into the Levant. A still more
threatening development of the quarrel now occurred.
The Tsar despatched Prince Menschikoff to Constantinople to require a recognition of the protectorate of the
Tsar over the Greek Christians in Turkey.

The mission of Menschikoff aroused in Britain the
ever-present fear of Russian aggression. In February,
1853, Lord Stratford de Redcliffe, formerly Sir Stratford
Canning, an old antagonist of the Tsar in the diplomacy
of the Eastern Question, was sent as ambassador to
Constantinople, with instructions to watch for any interference with the integrity and independence of the Ottoman empire. The British envoy inspired the Turk to
a strenuous resistance to the Russian claims. After a
struggle of nearly three months between the two diplomatists, Menschikoff finally invited the signature of the
Sultan to an instrument formally acknowledging the
Russian protectorate. This document, which became
famous as Menschikoff's Note, was presented on May 20
as an ultimatum. It was rejected, and Menschikoff
immediately quitted Constantinople. Lord Stratford
had advised the rejection of the note with the full con-
currence of the ambassadors of France, Austria, and
Prussia. The Porte being admittedly unable to resist
Russia unaided, it is certain that by instigating the
refusal of the Russian demand, the British ambassador
committed his country to the duty of supporting the
Turk against Russian coercion.

On May 31 a formal demand for the acceptance of
the note was sent by the Tsar's minister, Count Nessel-
rode, to Constantinople, with a threat that the Russian
troops—which were already massed in great force on the
frontier—would, if the Turk failed to comply, occupy
the Danubian provinces of the Ottoman Empire, that is,
the principalities of Moldavia and Wallachia, which now

form the Kingdom of Roumania.  At the time when this
menace was sent, the Tsar had reason to believe from
the tone of the messages he received from the British
Foreign Office that Lord Aberdeen's ministry was not
minded to support with vigour the firm attitude assumed
by Lord Stratford at Constantinople.  On July 2 the
Russian army crossed the Pruth, and the Tsar issued a
proclamation disclaiming the intention of conquest, and
promising that warlike operations should cease as soon
as the Porte should bring itself to observe the inviola-
bility of the Orthodox Church.

The concert of the four Powers was still unbroken.
On August 12 Lord Aberdeen, the prime minister, and
Lord Clarendon, the foreign minister, assured the House
of Lords that Austria, Britain, Prussia, and France
were "acting cordially together in order to check designs
which they considered inconsistent with the balance of
power".  But at this juncture the British Government entered into what the historian of the war calls "the fatal
transaction which substituted a cruel war for the peaceful but irresistible pressure which was exerted by the
four Powers".  A compact was made with the French
emperor by which, as the event proved, Britain and
France were mutually pledged to execute the common
judgment of the Powers without waiting for the co-opera-
tion of Austria and Prussia, although it was Austria
rather than France or Britain that had occasion to
resent the invasion of the Danubian provinces, and that
was best able to offer protection to the Turk in this
portion of his dominions.  The Queen's Speech at the
close of the session of 1853 contained the significant
announcement that she had united her endeavours in the
cause of peace with those of the Emperor of the French.

Notwithstanding this division of the concert, a conference of representatives of the four Powers had already
assembled at Vienna.  The result of this conference was

the celebrated Vienna Note. This note was in the form of an undertaking to be addressed by the Sultan to the Tsar, and was unanimously recommended to the two disputants by the four Powers. The Tsar at once accepted it as satisfactory. Unhappily it did not recommend itself to Lord Stratford de Redcliffe. He was instructed to urge the Sultan to accept it; but, whilst obeying his instructions, he indicated his disapproval by a demeanour and an expression of countenance that were more eloquent than the language in which he delivered the message of his Queen. The Sultan refused to sign the note without certain specified modifications. These amendments were rejected by the Tsar, who also withdrew a consent that was naturally conditional on the acquiescence of the Sultan. Immediately on this refusal the Sultan declared war, although he was still unfortified by assurances of support from any of the Powers, and even without such reason to expect that support as he would have had if his rejection of Menschikoff's ultimatum had been treated by Russia as a *casus belli*.

The defence offered by the supporters of the policy of war for this fatal obstinacy of the Turk, and for the support given to that obstinacy by Britain and France, is that Russia, when accepting the note, and the Turk, when rejecting it, agreed in putting a construction upon it which had not been in the minds of the representatives of the Powers when they composed it. It was alleged that, according to the interpretation of Russia and the Porte, the Vienna Note, which the Powers invited the Turk to accept, was virtually identical with Menschikoff's Note, which they had advised him to reject, but that the Conference had intended to save the honour of the Sultan by a substantial modification of Menschikoff's terms. The justification of the policy of war rests with its full weight upon this allegation. If it is true, the Ministry finds its excuse at the expense of attributing

to the chosen diplomatists of four great nations incompetence to compose a state paper in unambiguous
language.  But it is not true; and by triumphantly
proving it to be false Bright shattered the formal justification of the war.  The formal justification, however, of
this war, as of others, had but a very remote relation to
the real causes.  These diplomatic inconsistencies enabled Bright to score a point in debate against his enemy
Palmerston, but such a victory provided no remedy for
the suspicious jealousy and fidgety sensitiveness which
Palmerston had educated the nation to regard as elements of patriotism.

On October 22 the British and French fleets entered
the Dardanelles, and a few days later, taking advantage
of the declaration of war, cast anchor in the Bosporus,
from which in time of peace they were excluded by treaty.
The Tsar was not slow to retaliate, and unhappily struck
his blow in such a way as to aggravate the enmity of
Britain.  On November 30 a Turkish flotilla lying in
the harbour of Sinope was annihilated by six Russian
warships.  The news of this disaster raised the war
fever of the British to a degree that called for the effusion
of blood.  The destruction of ships of our ally at a place
barely three hundred miles distant from the anchorage
of the British fleet was regarded as a provocation to
Britain, and an insolent defiance of the naval supremacy
in which every patriotic Briton takes pride.  The
popular indignation expelled whatever disposition to
conciliation still remained in the mind of the Cabinet.
They were, however, at first content with ordering the
fleet to enter the Euxine.  Lord Palmerston thought
that the crisis required more strenuous action, and resigned office.

This was the first of that long series of resigna-
tions which demonstrated so painfully the defects of the
British parliamentary system in the presence of dangers

such as the Roman republic used to meet by the appointment of a dictator. The chosen policy demanded a
statesman who should possess the commanding authority
and the moral intrepidity of Pitt. But instead of Pitt
we had Lord Palmerston and Lord John Russell; instead
of Nelson, Sir Charles Napier; and instead of Wellington,
Lord Raglan; and over all of them the embarrassing
control of the House of Commons.

Once more the Emperor of the French was allowed
to dictate the policy of the British Cabinet. The plan
proposed by him and accepted by Lord Aberdeen was
that the occupation of the Black Sea by the two fleets
should be followed by a message requiring that the
Russian fleet should retire within the harbour of Sevastopol. This spirited action satisfied Palmerston, who
rejoined the Cabinet. The fleets entered the Euxine on
January 4, 1854, and the demand of France and Britain
reached Nicholas on January 12.

Meanwhile the envoys of the four Powers at Constantinople were still pursuing the task of pacification, and
drafting new proposals to be submitted to the belligerents. But the demand of January 12 baffled the efforts
of the peacemakers, broke up the concert of the Powers,
and provoked Russia to defiance. The Russian ambassadors were recalled from Paris and London, and the
French and British ambassadors from St. Petersburg.
A British fleet was ordered to sail into the Baltic under
the command of Sir Charles Napier; but there was still
no formal declaration of war.

Such was the posture of affairs when Parliament
assembled for the session of 1854.

Bright did not take any part in the two nights'
debate on February 19 and 20. The views of the small
remnant that still believed an honourable peace to be
possible were expounded at length by Cobden. He
declared himself opposed to a war " which hangs upon

so fine a thread as whether the Sultan shall sign a note
declaring to the Emperor Nicholas that he will preserve
the rights of the Christian subjects, or whether he shall
give that declaration to all the European Powers. Let
us fall back", he added, "on the Vienna Note." This
suggestion was received with cries of ridicule; but
Cobden protested that, though the terms of the Vienna
Note might be substantially the same as those of
Menschikoff's Note, the honour of the Sultan could not
suffer by accepting terms which came to him as the
proposals of the four Powers, and therefore not as the
proposals of Russia.

Three weeks later, Bright moved the adjournment of
the House in order to call attention to the proceedings
of a banquet by which the Reform Club had celebrated
the appointment of two of its members to the command
of the Baltic and Black Sea expeditions, and at which
Lord Palmerston had presided, and two other ministers
had made speeches. There had been a good deal of
boasting of the sort that does not become him that
putteth on his armour,—boasting to be remembered with
mortification when Napier returned without laurels from
his luckless cruise—and a good deal of what Bright
described as buffoonery and reckless levity. It was
inevitable that two such men as Palmerston and Bright,
the cheery pagan and the grave apostle, the man to
whom politics were a career and the man to whom they
were a mission, should misappreciate one another.
Palmerston's boyish *insouciance* served a useful end by
helping to clear the public mind of cant, but it could
not be anything but disgusting to Bright. To Palmerston the earnestness of Bright ("the honourable and
reverend gentleman" as he called him on this occasion)
savoured of the professional gravity of the pulpit.
Bright spoke with passionate indignation, and was
answered by Palmerston, Graham, and his old ally

Molesworth, with an angry affectation of contempt.
Macaulay, whose sympathy with Palmerston was as
cordial as Bright's antipathy, wrote in his diary: "I
went to the House on Monday; but for any pleasure I
got I might as well have stayed away. I heard Bright
say everything I thought; and I heard Palmerston and
Graham expose themselves lamentably. Palmerston's
want of temper, judgment, and good breeding was
almost incredible." Disraeli contributed some good
jokes to the entertainment; he did not mind the two
fleets being commanded by two sound Reformers, for
"it must be recollected that a sound Reformer is a
gentleman who does not reform". Such was the temper
of our statesmen at the beginning of that period of
confusion, mismanagement, and recrimination. Mr.
Spooner, a county member whose sturdy conservatism
had often been ridiculed by Bright, manfully declared
his sympathy with the protest. But the country eagerly
caught the tone of Palmerston, and thenceforward
Bright's testimony against the war was addressed to
deaf ears.

On March 27 a Queen's message announced to Parliament that the negotiations with the Tsar had ter-
minated, and that she felt bound to offer assistance to
her ally the Sultan against unprovoked aggression, and
to protect the dominions of the Sultan from the en-
croachments of Russia. Four days later the reply of the
Commons was moved by Lord John Russell, and gave
occasion for the first of Bright's speeches on the war.

The tone of this speech is, by comparison with the
emotion and indignation of those which followed, studiously restrained and unimpassioned. Bright declared,
in contradiction to Palmerston, that the Ottoman empire "was gradually falling into decay, and that to
pledge ourselves to effect its recovery and sustentation
was to undertake what no human power would be able

to accomplish. There is no calamity," he declared, appealing to the consular reports, "which can be described as affecting any country, which is not there proved to be present, and actively at work, in almost every province of the Turkish empire." He gave a version of the negotiations, which may now be fully verified by the elaborate narrative of Kinglake. He skilfully directed his attack upon the least defensible point of the case for the war—the rejection of the Vienna Note. "What are we to think of these arbitrators or mediators, the four ambassadors at Vienna and the Governments of France and Britain, who, after discussing the matter in three different cities and at three distinct and different periods, and after agreeing that the proposition was one which Turkey could assent to without detriment to her honour and independence, immediately afterwards turned round, and declared that the note was one which Turkey could not be asked to accede to, and repudiated in the most formal and express manner that which they had themselves drawn up, and which, only a few days before, they had approved of as a combination of wisdom and diplomatic dexterity which had never been excelled?"

Bright attacked the very foundation of the Palmerstonian theory of national obligations by asserting that "the whole notion of the balance of power is a mischievous delusion", and by reiterating his doctrine of "non-intervention in every case where the interests of the country are not directly and obviously assailed". He devoted a few sentences to the injury the war would inflict on the national trade, and turned the favourite phrase of the Palmerstonians against them by asking what would be the effect of an exhausting war upon the balance of power between Britain and the United States, her chief rival in industry and at sea. "Our people, suffering and discontented, as in all former periods of war, will emigrate in increasing numbers to a country whose wise policy is to keep itself free from the entanglement of European politics." Such a contention provoked the retort that Bright cared more to ask whether a policy was cheap than whether it was demanded by honour and justice. But by Bright himself it was never placed in the forefront of his argument.

Another passage has special significance, as uttered by a man in whose mind the ethical aspect of any question of deliberation always held the first place. If we admit the common assumption that the duties of nations are exactly analogous to the duties of persons, the policy of non-intervention must often be comparable with the abnegation of the duty a man owes to an oppressed neighbour. It was characteristic of Bright that he never shrank from any legitimate conclusion of his accepted maxims. "It is not on a question of sympathy that I dare involve this country, or any country, in a war which must cost an incalculable amount of treasure and of blood. It is not my duty to make this country the knight-errant of the human race, and to take upon herself the protection of the thousand millions of human beings who have been permitted by the Creator of all things to people this planet."

No one who reads this memorable speech with a recollection of subsequent history will hesitate to admit that the theory of foreign policy there proclaimed, though condemned at the time by most Englishmen as destructive of the true conception of national honour, has steadily gained ground during the past forty years.[1] No one will deny that in the earlier part of the speech

[1] "They (Cobden and Bright) were routed on the question of the Crimean war, but it was the rapid spread of their principles which within the next twenty years made intervention impossible in the Franco-Austrian war, in the American war, in the Danish war, in the Franco-German war, and above all in the war between Russia and Turkey."—Morley, *Life of Cobden*, ii. 159.

Bright's reasoning was at least so far pertinent as to
deserve a serious and detailed reply from those who
were responsible for the declaration of the war. It is
scarcely too much to say that no reply was attempted.
Lord Palmerston took up Bright's challenge to "explain
what is meant by the balance of power", and supplied
a gloss of that term which may fairly rank with Mr.
Curdle's definition of the Unities of the Drama. Lord
John Russell had nothing to add. They justly relied on
the popular prejudice against Quakerism to annul the
effect of the speech on public opinion.

Bright did not again address the House on the war
until December 22. The intervening period had been
crowded with great events. The hardly won victory of
the Alma had proved that the long peace had not impaired the fighting qualities of the British army; the first
assault upon Sevastopol had been made and repelled;
the British cavalry at Balaklava had performed an
achievement to be commemorated in song or story as
long as courage and discipline hold their place in the
estimation of Englishmen; and at Inkermann the same
obstinate valour that won Waterloo had just prevailed
to avert defeat in spite of the failure of leadership. It
had become apparent that the war into which the nation
had plunged, or drifted, with a light heart, would end, if
in victory, in a victory purchased at an enormous cost
of life and treasure. The spirit of the people had changed
from exultation to anxiety, but it was not less resolute.
Even those who had believed that the war might have
been avoided without detriment to the national honour
could not venture to ask a proud nation to sue for peace
while the fortune of war still hung in the balance.

By this time, too, the grievous Crimean winter had
begun; and already a great cry of indignation against
administrative incompetence had been raised, and was
daily gathering volume and intensity. A people distin-

guished among all the nations of the world by the success
of its middle-class in the organization and direction of
those great undertakings which prosper by patient fore-
sight and the diligent care of details, had entrusted the
business of the State to patrician officials, and now, as
soon as the stress became severe, found that business
hopelessly mismanaged. The Crimean winter was the
crowning opprobrium of Tite Barnacle and the Circumlocution Office. Thousands of men died that winter the
victims of the system of aristocratic patronage, against
which Bright and his friends had testified in vain.

The measure, to pass which Parliament was convened
on the brink of Christmas, was a Bill to authorize the
enlistment of foreigners. This Bill, which involved a
breach of international courtesy for which Palmerston
had to apologize to the United States, was resisted by
the Conservative opposition, and when Bright rose at
midnight on the second evening of the debate on the
third reading, he was secure of an attentive and not
wholly unsympathetic audience. He spoke briefly, but
with an intensity of indignation that carried his invective
to the extreme limits permitted by the courtesy of parliamentary debate. Again and again his mistrust of
Russell and his antipathy to Palmerston were declared
in language bordering on ferocity. Once more he fixed
on the rejection of the Vienna Note as the capital error
of the Government.[1] "You are making war against a
Government which accepted your own terms of peace."
He reinforced his former argument by quoting from a
despatch of which the public had not been in possession
at the time of the first speech. The defence of the rejection of the Vienna Note had been that Russia had, contrary to the intention of the Powers, construed that note

[1] Twenty years later Russell admitted this. "Had I been prime minister
I should have insisted on the acceptance of the Austrian Note."—*Recollections
and Suggestions*, p. 271.

as equivalent to Menschikoff's Note. The despatch quoted by Bright, and suppressed in the blue-books, was one in which the French Government urged Russia to accede to the Vienna Note, for the express reason that "its general sense differed in nothing from the sense of the proposition presented by Prince Menschikoff ".[1]

The peroration of this fine speech was most impassioned. "Let it not be said that I am alone in my condemnation of this war, and of this incapable and guilty Administration. And even if I were alone, if mine were a solitary voice, raised amid the din of arms and the clamours of a venal press, I should have the consolation I have to-night, and which I trust will be mine to the last moment of my existence,—the priceless consolation that no word of mine has tended to promote the squandering of my country's treasure or the spilling of one single drop of my country's blood."

This speech, delivered with unusual vehemence of manner to an audience strongly disaffected towards the Government, penetrated the mind of the House far more deeply than the more elaborate reasoning of the first speech. It was felt that the credit of the Ministry demanded some reply; and, when Bright sat down, there were loud cries for Mr. Gladstone, the only leading minister who had not yet spoken. But neither Mr. Gladstone nor any other minister rose; the division was taken at once; and one of the most spirited and incisive attacks ever made on an English ministry remained for ever unanswered. Charles Greville wrote in his journal: "The third reading of the Enlistment Bill carried by 38, after a very fine speech from Bright, consisting of part

---

[1] The importance of this discovery is curiously indicated by the insertion of the original French in the reports of Bright's speech both in the *Times* and in *Hansard*. Rogers's edition wrongly makes it appear that Bright himself cited the original as well as a translation.

of his letter,[1] with its illustrations. In my opinion this speech was unanswerable, and no attempt was made to answer it. He was very severe on both Lord John and Palmerston. It is impossible that such reasonings as Bright's should not make some impression on the country; but I do not think any reasoning, however powerful, or any display of facts, however striking, can stem the torrent of public opinion, which still clamours for war, and is so burning with hatred against Russia, that no peace could be deemed satisfactory, or even tolerable, that did not humble Russia to the dust, and strip her of some considerable territory."

Bright voted with the Conservatives in this division. Within five weeks the Aberdeen Ministry had fallen. Mr. Roebuck brought forward a resolution for a committee to inquire into the maladministration. Lord John resigned without waiting for the debate. "The hon. member for Sheffield", said Bright, "came forward as a little David with a sling and a stone,—weapons which he did not even use, but at the sight of which the Whig Goliath went howling and vanquished to the back benches." The resolution was carried; but the Conservatives were unable to form a Cabinet, and the Coalition Ministry was reconstructed, Russell, Aberdeen, and the Duke of Newcastle being thrown overboard, and Palmerston becoming Prime Minister. In a few weeks, however, Mr. Gladstone and two other Peelites resigned, disagreeing with their new chief on the appointment of Roebuck's committee; Lord John returned to office, and the Ministry became purely Liberal.

Early in the new year negotiations for peace were opened at Vienna, Russell attending as the representative of the Queen. At this crisis (Feb. 23, 1855)

---

[1] The letter to Watkin had appeared in the *Times* of Nov. 3. "This letter", Greville had written, "as nearly as possible expresses my own opinion on the subject."

Bright delivered a speech, a masterpiece of rhetorical pathos, and notably different in tone from the two that preceded. He did not now deal in invective. The Government had shown a disposition to conclude the war which he strove earnestly to encourage. Not a word suggestive of his animosity to Palmerston was allowed to escape his lips. Even when repeating a description given just twelve months before of Russia as "impregnable within her own boundaries, but nearly powerless for any purposes of offence", he forebore to remind the House that it was Palmerston who had said this,[1] — Palmerston, who was now invading that impregnable empire in order to prevent those impossible aggressions. He did not even plead for any modification of the terms offered to Russia. "You have offered terms of peace, which, as I understand them, I do not say are not moderate." But he still feared the influence of the extreme war party in the House and the country. He besought the Government to neglect those who "have entertained dreams, — impracticable theories, — expectations of vast European and Asiatic changes, of revived nationalities, and of a new map of Europe, if not of the world, as a result of the war", and to hold in good faith to the terms they had proposed.

Bright's reputation as the greatest English master of the oratory of sentiment may confidently be staked upon the last few sentences of this speech, — sentences pure and unlaboured in diction, majestic in rhythm, and reflecting even in the irregularity of their construction the tumult of noble emotion.

"I cannot but notice that an uneasy feeling exists as to the news which may arrive by the very next mail from the East. I do not suppose that your troops are to be beaten in actual conflict with the foe, or that they will be driven into the sea; but I am certain that many

---

[1] Feb. 20, 1854. Bright slightly exaggerates Palmerston's words.

homes in England in which there now exists a fond hope
that the distant one may return—many such homes may
be rendered desolate when the next mail shall arrive.
The angel of death has been abroad throughout the
land; you may almost hear the beating of his wings.
There is no one, as when the first-born were slain of old,
to sprinkle with blood the lintel and the two side-posts
of our doors, that he may spare and pass on; he takes
his victims from the castle of the noble, the mansion of
the wealthy, and the cottage of the poor and the lowly,
and it is on behalf of all these classes that I make this
solemn appeal. I tell the noble lord that, if he be ready
honestly and frankly to endeavour, by the negotiations
about to be opened at Vienna, to put an end to this war,
no word of mine, no vote of mine, will be given to shake
his power for one single moment, or to change his position in this House. I am sure that the noble lord is not
inaccessible to appeals made to him from honest motives
and with no unfriendly feeling. The noble lord has
been for more than forty years a member of this House.
Before I was born he sat upon the Treasury bench, and
he has spent his life in the service of his country. He is
no longer young, and his life has extended almost to the
term allotted to man. I would ask, I would entreat the
noble lord to take a course which, when he looks back
upon his whole political career, whatever he may therein
find to be pleased with, whatever to regret, cannot but
be a source of gratification to him. By adopting that
course he would have the satisfaction of reflecting that,
having obtained the object of his laudable ambition,
having become the foremost subject of the Crown, the
director of, it may be, the destinies of his country, and
the presiding genius in her councils, he had achieved a
still higher and nobler ambition,—that he had returned
the sword to the scabbard—that at his word torrents of
blood had ceased to flow—that he had restored tran-

quillity to Europe, and saved this country from the inde-
scribable calamities of war."

At Vienna the Allies claimed four main concessions
from Russia, of which three were not resisted.  These
were the withdrawal of Russian troops and influence
from the Danubian provinces, and the relinquishment of
the claims of Russia to the exclusive protectorate of the
Christian subjects of the Porte, and to the control of the
mouths of the Danube.  The Allies also stipulated that
the predominance hitherto secured by treaty to Russia
in the Black Sea should cease.  Upon this demand, the
third of the famous four points, the negotiations broke
down.  This failure compelled Bright, in June, to resume
his former attitude of bitter hostility to the Government.
His expectation that they would conduct the negotiations
in a pacific spirit had been disappointed.  The solution
proposed of the Black Sea difficulty had been that Russia
and Turkey should be allowed eight ships each, and
France and Britain four ships each, on the Sea.  An
alternative to this proposal was that the Sea should be
declared inaccessible to war-ships of all nations.  Russia
had refused to "give herself up disarmed at the good
pleasure of the Napoleons and the Palmerstons, who
would themselves be able to have armed forces in the
Mediterranean".  "If any diplomatist from this country,"
said Bright, " under the same circumstances that Russia
is placed in, had consented to terms such as the noble
lord has endeavoured to force upon Russia, when he
entered this House, he would be met by one universal
shout of execration, and, as a public man, would be
ruined for ever."  Bright's salutary practice of trying to
see the enemy's side also of such a question has since
been improved by some of his followers, who too often
refuse to see any other.

Bright's invective was now more than ever personal
to the two "authors of the war", Russell and Palmer-

ston. He taunted them with failure: "they have not yet crippled Russia, although it is admitted that they have almost destroyed Turkey". The country had been "the sport of their ancient rivalry", and was in peril of becoming "the victim of their policy". He told Russell, who three years before had rudely dismissed Palmerston from his Cabinet for insubordination, that he was now "going to sea with no chart on a most dangerous and interminable voyage with the very reckless captain whom he would not trust as mate". He accused him of "that description of moral cowardice which in every man is the death of all true statesmanship". He spoke of Palmerston as "a man who had experience, but with experience had not gained wisdom; who had age, but who with age had not the gravity of age". "You, who now fancy that you are fulfilling the behests of the national will, will find yourselves pointed to as the men who ought to have taught the nation better."

He assailed Palmerston still more injuriously six weeks later, when Russell, who had admitted at Vienna that he himself approved terms of peace which his instructions obliged him to reject, had been compelled to expiate this indiscretion by yet another resignation. Bright suspected that the Cabinet had had no intention of making peace, and had sent Russell, whose aim was really pacific, to Vienna on a fool's errand; and saw in his resignation the triumph of "a disreputable and contemptible cabal". He charged the younger members of the Cabinet with ingratitude to their old chief, and Palmerston with the motive of a jealous desire to get rid of his competitor, and with indifference to the desolation and sorrow caused by his policy. "The Queen", he said, "may make a minister or a prime minister, but it is not in royalty to make a statesman."

The war lasted a few months longer. In September Sevastopol fell, and the negotiations were resumed. In the end Russia accepted terms which opened the Black Sea to commerce, and closed it to the navies of all nations alike. This stipulation Russell calls "very harsh and unusual". In his first speech on the war Bright had said: "What do you propose to do? How is Turkey to be secured? Will you make a treaty with Russia, and force conditions upon her? What security have you that one treaty will be more binding than another? It is easy to find or make a reason for breaking a treaty, when it is the interest of a country to break it." This prediction has been exactly fulfilled. In 1870 the Tsar declared the Black Sea clauses of the Treaty of Paris null and void, and no attempt was made to enforce them.

There are three great epochs in Bright's career, each marked by an act of revolt from the Liberal party. In 1843 he took the lead of the Free-traders who rejected Russell's compromise on the question of the Corn Law, and pursued an agitation in defiance of party discipline. In 1854 he refused to accept the guidance of Russell and Palmerston on a memorable question of foreign policy. In 1886 he rebelled against the only leader whom he had ever followed with the loyalty of respect.

No political orator appealed more frequently or with so much confidence to the verdict of history. Upon the secessions of 1843 and 1854 that verdict may be said to be already recorded and to be recorded in favour of the appellant. The first revolt was justified by immediate success; the second has been justified by the gradual acceptance by statesmen of all parties of principles of action approximating to those which Bright stood almost alone in defending. The time has not yet come when any writer can affect impartiality in giving his judgment on the third.

# Chapter IV.

## India.

In January, 1856, at a time when the prospect of peace had become certain, Bright's health began to break down, and for more than two years he was unable to take any active part in public affairs. " From apparent health", he said after his recovery, " I was brought down to a condition of weakness exceeding the weakness of a little child, in which I could neither read nor write, nor converse for more than a few minutes without distress and without peril." His physicians feared serious injury to his mental powers,[1] and before the end of the year, which was spent by him in travel, the reports of his condition filled his friends with grave anxiety. Cobden wrote in November: "Bright's loss, if permanent, is a public calamity. If you could take the opinion of the whole House, he would be pronounced by a large majority to combine more earnestness, courage, honesty, and eloquence than any other man. But we will not speak of him as of the past. God grant that he may recover!"

Early in the following year his offer to resign his seat for Manchester was rejected with a unanimity and generosity which would seem scarcely consistent with the catastrophe of a few months later, did we not remember that elections are determined by the votes of persons the great majority of whom pay little attention to public affairs between one election and the next.

---

[1] Some of his opponents saw in the disease of the brain a proof that his illness was a Divine judgment on his unchristian love of peace. "One Scotch lord told a great audience that I was afflicted by a visitation of Providence, and that I was suffering from a disease of the brain. His friends can tell whether that is a complaint with which he is ever likely to be afflicted."

During his absence from Parliament Palmerston pursued the now popular policy of quarrelling and warfare. In 1857 we were at war with Persia and with China. The dispute with China turned on the question whether the coasting schooner *Arrow*, on board of which the Chinese police had arrested certain Chinamen suspected of piracy, was or was not a vessel entitled to the protection of the British flag. The evidence showed clearly that she was not so entitled, and that the violent measures of the Government had no justification. A vote of censure moved by Cobden was supported not only by the small party that still habitually voted with him, but by the Peelites who had helped to make the Crimean war, and by the Conservatives who had at least condoned it, Disraeli, Cobden, and Mr. Gladstone voting in the same lobby. By this "fortuitous concourse of atoms", as Palmerston called it, the Government was defeated. Bright wrote to his friend from Rome: "I need not tell you how greatly pleased I was with the news, and especially that the blow was given by your hand".

Palmerston took a course then more unusual than it has since become. Instead of resigning he appealed from the Commons to the country, with a confidence, fully justified by the result, that the popularity he enjoyed as a strong minister, and that distrust of a coalition of factions which is characteristic of the British electorate, would carry him triumphantly through a general election. He had recently visited Manchester, where he was received by Bright's constituents with ominous enthusiasm. It was not to be expected that his friends in that borough would spare the man who had assailed their leader with a vehemence exceeding the customary bounds of political enmity. Two local Liberals of Palmerston's school, whose undistinguished names may be found in the poll-books, were nominated against Bright and Milner Gib-

son. Nothing could be more complete than the victory.
In 1852 Bright and his colleague had had a majority in
every ward except one; in 1857 they were in a minority
in every ward. Bright was at the bottom of the poll,
nearly 3000 votes below his leading antagonist. Manchester appeared to have renounced the Manchester
School. Doubtless many causes contributed to this
disaster; but the testimony of the time agrees in attributing it mainly to the unpopularity of Bright's opposition to the war. The inexpiable offence had been the
letter to Watkin, which, unhappily for its author, had
been translated and circulated in Russia by order of the
Tsar. At the same time Cobden suffered defeat at
Huddersfield.

It would be idle to repeat here the charge of ingratitude with which the Manchester Liberals were assailed.
By revolting from the party to which his constituents
were attached, Bright had accepted the risk of losing
their support. His claims on their gratitude were no
doubt exceptional, for they were the master cotton-
spinners, who had most eagerly desired the repeal of
the Corn Law, and who owed to the victory won by the
extraordinary exertions of Bright and Cobden the aug-
mentation both of their wealth and their political and
social dignity. But it was not unreasonable to argue
that the intention of representative institutions would
be frustrated if men were deterred by gratitude for past
services, however eminent, from casting a sincere vote
on a question of present importance submitted to the
suffrages of the country. The outstanding question at
that crisis was, not whether Bright had served the
country and his order well fifteen years before, but
whether his enemy Palmerston was still to be prime
minister of England. Palmerston was the only possible
prime minister of the Liberal party—indeed, he was the
only possible prime minister of any party, if the proba-

bility that the supporters of Disraeli would outnumber any combination of Liberals, Radicals, and Peelites was small enough to be neglected; for no stable Government could possibly be formed by the temporary coalition that had driven him to appeal to the country.

Bright took leave of Manchester in an admirable letter, in which his characteristic self-confidence is expressed with singular dignity. Neither then nor afterwards did he condescend to complaint or reproach, unless in a single sentence of his first speech at Birmingham. "If there be those in the defence of whose interests the prime years of my life have been spent, who, when I was stricken down and enduring a tedious exile, subjected me to passionate and ungenerous treatment, I have the consolation of knowing that their act was not approved by the country."

This boast was fully justified. If the burgesses of Manchester expected the applause of the nation for postponing gratitude to patriotism, they were entirely disappointed. The *Times*, which had strongly resented Bright's protest against the war, and which was at that time supporting Palmerston's claims, had before the election supported Bright's candidature with a generosity rarely permitted by the exigence of party warfare. After the defeat, Conservative journals joined with the independent Liberal press of the provinces in such expressions of regret at his disappearance from Parliament, as prove that Cobden had scarcely exaggerated the general esteem in which his friend was held.[1]

On the 10th of August, 1857, whilst still abroad and ill, Bright was returned without opposition by Birmingham, a constituency which he continued to represent

[1] The *Saturday Review*, for example, said: "Rarely have politicians retired from the parliamentary stage attended by so general an expression of respect and esteem as that which Mr. Cobden and Mr. Bright have received from those who were most opposed to the ideas and principles by which their careers were guided".

without interruption until his death thirty-two years later. Manchester had enjoyed the distinction of giving its name to the advanced school of Liberal politicians. Almost simultaneously with Bright's change of constituency, Birmingham became, and for many years remained, the recognized head-quarters of Radicalism. The share taken by this town in the anti-corn-law agitation had been comparatively insignificant; but it had played a more conspicuous part in the movement that preceded the Reform Bill of 1832, and at Bright's first visit to his new constituents he invited them to take the lead with him in a new agitation for parliamentary reform. The history of this enterprise will form the subject of the next chapter. Another subject, in which Bright interested himself with scarcely less ardour, claims attention first.

The first question of importance with which Parliament had to deal after Bright's return was that of the government of India. The Mutiny, which befell at the time of the general election, had forced upon all parties the necessity for such constitutional reforms in the administration of that part of our Empire as Bright had already advocated. For fifteen years he had been the foremost assailant of the East India Company, and of the system, established in 1784, and from time to time renewed with modifications, by which India was governed by the Directors of the Company, checked by a Board of Control responsible through its president to the sovereign and to Parliament. In 1858 that system was suddenly abandoned and the Company abolished. "That was exactly what we had asked them to do in 1853," said Bright later; "but nothing is done until there comes an overwhelming calamity, when the most obtuse and perverse is driven from his position." It has appeared convenient to defer to this point the history of Bright's earlier dealings with the Indian question.

Before his opinions are recorded we have to confront
the view that he was disqualified by ignorance and prejudice from holding any respectable opinions on India at
all.  He had, we are often told, no trustworthy knowledge of India, and his religious antipathy to war and
conquest predisposed him to disparage the conduct
of an authority acquired and held by force of arms.
This view is presented with some severity in Mr. Leslie
Stephen's account of an attack made on Bright by Sir
James Fitzjames Stephen in 1877.  The immediate question at issue was whether the British Government had
done what it was reasonable to expect for the improvement of Indian irrigation.  Stephen accused Bright of
gross ignorance of the facts.  Thirty years before Bright
had been chairman of a committee of the House of
Commons appointed to consider this very subject; and
it may be remarked that the imputations of ignorance,
so easily made by persons who have served in India
whenever a member of Parliament offers an opinion on
Indian affairs, bring us perilously near the conclusion,—
surely anti-imperialistic,—that Parliament, that is, that
Britain, is not well qualified to govern India at all.
"His wrath, however," says the biographer of Stephen,
"was really aroused by the moral assumptions involved.
Bright, he thought, represented the view of the commonplace shopkeeper, intensified by the prejudices of the
Quaker.  To him ambition and conquest naturally
represented simple crimes.  Ambition, retorts Fitzjames,
is the incentive to all manly virtues; and conquest is an
essential factor in the building up of all nations.  We
should be proud, not ashamed, to be the successors of
Clive and Warren Hastings and their like", and so
forth.

In point of fact, it would be difficult to collect from
Bright's speeches any certain evidence that he was
proud, or that he was ashamed, of the performances of

Clive and Hastings. Probably he was indifferent. He was little interested in historical problems, even in those that raise ethical discussion, such as the still vexed question of the morality of the conquest of India. "I accept", he said, "our possession of India as a fact. There we are; we do not know how to leave it; and therefore let us see if we know how to govern it." But it is not to be denied that he was insensible of the glory of conquest, that he had no share whatever in the pride that rejoices in the mere vastness of the Empire, and that, in estimating its value, he was contented with the standards of measurement that are supplied by the returns of the Board of Trade. Further, it is certain that the wars by which, even during his own lifetime, the Indian Empire was extended and consolidated filled him with mere horror; for the enthusiasts of peace at any price are not easily persuaded that peace must sometimes be purchased at the price of war. "It may be our unhappy fate", he said, "to demonstrate the truth of the saying, 'There is no sure foundation set in blood'."

Bright was, in short, an early and not a highly-developed example of the order of politicians who are called, in the most recent political slang, Little-Englanders. This admission, which will be made with equal readiness by those of his admirers who share, and by those who dispute, the preconceptions with which he approached all questions of imperial policy, must of necessity modify, in the minds of those who are not ashamed of the pride which Bright renounced, the respect to be paid to his deliverances on such matters as the government of India. On the other hand, the questions at issue in the deliberations in which he took part were largely practical questions of administrative aims and methods, which it was, perhaps, an actual advantage to regard with eyes undazzled by the glamour of imperial vainglory. After all, the insensibility which allowed Bright to mention India without feeling his bosom swell at the remembrance of Plassey, did not altogether disqualify him from sound views on the condition of the ryots and the economic demerits of the Indian land system; and his dissatisfaction with the Jos Sedleys of his own time was not in itself inconsistent with the most favourable opinion of the virtues of Hastings.

Like other British statesmen, Bright could not help occasionally falling into errors such as could be avoided only by actual experience of Indian affairs. It is quite possible that he sometimes fathered the complaints of the native population without due allowance for oriental duplicity and hyperbole. It is possible that, being versed in the politics of a country where the first condition of good order is that the government should be popular, and the second that it should be strong, he did not adequately recognize in his criticisms that in India it is more important that the government should be strong than that it should be popular. Accustomed as he was to declaim against the failings of a decadent aristocracy, and habitually incurious of the lessons of past history, he may not have acknowledged to himself that nearly every nation that has become great has owed its greatness in the first instance to the great qualities of its aristocracy, and that it is in India, if anywhere, that what remains of the ancient virtues of the English oligarchy may still be rendering service to humanity. His hatred of oligarchy predisposed him to criticise with severity the conduct of a government which was not only oligarchical, but foreign. But, if he was eager to discern the faults of a system of arbitrary rule, he, at least, did not proceed to the absurdity of applying to India without discrimination the commonplaces of British democratic sentiment. Nor is there anything in his speeches which would justify us in imputing to him the extreme opinion which, as Mr. Morley tells us, was held by his friend Cobden; who, it is said, "had always taken his place among those who cannot see any advantage either to the natives or their foreign masters in this vast possession".

Whatever weight may be assigned to these admissions, the service that Bright rendered to good government in India cannot fairly be denied; and nothing could be more unjust than to dismiss him as a visionary or as a mere grumbler. In the first place, although hostile criticism must often be unjust criticism, it is infinitely more wholesome than mere acquiescence. Bright set his face against that indolent or insincere optimism of officials, which easily becomes inveterate if nobody takes the trouble to disturb it. In the second place, he asserted the right and the duty of the Imperial Parliament to make independent investigations; and he prepared himself for discussion by a study, laborious if incomplete, of all accessible facts. Herein he set a useful example to his colleagues, upon whose shoulders the burden of imperial responsibility sat too lightly. "No one out of office", he declared in 1853, "has paid so much attention to this question as I have done." In the third place, he insisted with salutary iteration that in India, as elsewhere, "the test that indicates the true character of the Government is to be found in the condition of the people that are governed".

Bright's attention had been first directed to India by the requirements of his own occupation. In 1847 he had asked for a committee of the House to inquire into the culture of cotton in India. The Company had spent £100,000 in experiments, without improving either the quality or the quantity of the cotton received by Lancashire from India. Bright already foresaw the cotton famine that nearly ruined his county and his industry in 1862. "We ought not to forget that the whole of the cotton grown in America is produced by slave labour; and, no matter how long slavery may have existed, abolished it will ultimately be, either by peaceable or violent means." The committee he asked was granted the following year, and, under his own chairmanship, collected such evidence as was accessible to a committee sitting in Westminster. It reported that the natural conditions of soil and climate were favourable to the cultivation of cotton, and the people accustomed to the work. But there were four conditions unfavourable to the success of the industry, which, in Bright's opinion, could at least be mitigated by good government. These were, bad roads; insufficient irrigation; the condition of the industrial population, who were so poor that they resorted to the money-lender to buy seed, and mort-gaged growing crops; and bad fiscal arrangements, especially the land assessment, which was regarded as rent paid to the State, but differed from rent in not being determined by the free competition of landlords for tenants and of tenants for land. He attributed the first two conditions to the niggardliness of the Company, whose expenditure on roads, bridges, canals, and tanks was only one-half per cent of their revenue. The condition of the people, he declared, could not be amended without the interference of Parliament. For these reasons Bright proceeded, in 1850, to ask for a Royal Commission. This request, though supported both by Peel and by Lord George Bentinck, the pro-tectionist leader, was refused by the President of the Board of Control, Sir J. C. Hobhouse (Lord Broughton), "one of the most contented and somnolent of statesmen that ever filled that or any other office". Twelve years later, when the disaster against which he had tried to provide had befallen, Bright reproached Broughton bitterly as "having neglected in regard to India every great duty that appertained to his high office".

In the session of 1853, Bright laid his views on Indian government at length before the House in three speeches before and during the debates on Sir C. Wood's India Bill. This Bill made no substantial change in the relations of the Board of Control and the Directors; and the reforms proposed, though elaborate, and intended to increase the power of the Imperial Government and to diminish the privileges of the Company, were, with one exception, unimportant in comparison with the heroic measures for which Bright had called. This exception was the partial abolition of patronage and favour in the civil service of the Company, and the institution of open competition by examination for admission to Haileybury, the training school of Indian civil officers. "Some of Bright's objections", wrote Macaulay, after the first reading, "are groundless, and others exaggerated; but the vigour of his speech will do harm. I will try whether I cannot deal with the Manchester champion." Macaulay's speech was chiefly occupied with an animated defence of the proposed system of competitive examination; and it is certain that Bright strangely under-estimated the value of this reform, which struck, not ineffectively, at the root of many of the evils he had denounced.

His indictment was certainly sweeping. He protested that the Indian Government as represented in the House was fluctuating, uncertain, and incompetent; that the presidents of the Board of Control were so frequently changed (four persons had filled this office within ten months) that there was no continuity of policy and no disposition to grapple with difficulties; that responsibility was divided and concealed; that the division of authority was fruitful in procrastination; that there was a constant underground wrangling between the two authorities; that Indian opinion was unanimous in calling for a constitutional change, and in

complaining of the delay and expense of the law-courts,
the inefficiency and low character of the police, and the
neglect of road-making and irrigation; that the destitu-
tion of the people was such as to demonstrate of itself
a fundamental error in the system of government; that
the well-meant statute authorizing the employment of
natives in offices of trust was a dead letter; that taxation was clumsy and unscientific, and its burden intolerable to a people destitute of mechanical appliances;
that the salt-tax was cruel, and the revenue from opium
precarious; that the revenue was squandered on unnecessary wars, while the Company had spent less on
public works in the whole dominion than the city of
Manchester had spent on its water-supply; that the
civil service was overpaid; that there was no security
for the competence and character of the collectors,
whose power was such that each man could make or
mar a whole district; that the best men were kept out
of the Directorate by ignominious canvassing;[1] that
Parliament was unable to grapple fairly with any question of India, or to deal with any grievance there as
they could deal with grievances at home or in the
colonies; finally, that India was ruled by a government
in a mask, and that the people and Parliament of Britain
were shut out from all consideration in regard to it.

Such was Bright's indictment against British rule in
India. Even after the reconstruction of the Government, he reasserted many of its counts from time to
time on such occasions as the annual debates on the
Indian Budget. There is always something ungracious
in the criticism of the doer by the talker—in the task of
one who points out faults to be amended, if at all, by
the wisdom and the skill of others. But it is a task

---

[1] Bright succeeded in carrying a clause prohibiting canvassing. He failed
in another amendment designed to bring the offices of the two authorities
under the same roof.

rendered necessary by the natural indolence of humanity
and the natural conservatism of office; it is a task imposed by the spirit of our constitution upon the Opposition, and, in a sense, Bright was always, until he
became a minister himself, in opposition.

When he took his new seat in Parliament early in
1858, he found his colleagues engaged on the first of the
three India Bills of the session, that of the Liberal Government. But on February 19 Palmerston's Ministry
fell, the Manchester School again striking the fatal blow.
The attempted assassination of the Emperor of the French
by conspirators who had concocted their plot in England,
produced one of those crises at which the admirable
patriotism of the French nation commonly breaks out in
the silly fashion which recalls Chauvin and Barère.
Before the gasconading had subsided, the British Government hastily brought in the Conspiracy to Murder
Bill. The Opposition thought, or affected to think, that
it was undignified to legislate in a hurry to oblige the
Frenchman. Whether this view was right or wrong,
poetical justice was satisfied when Palmerston became
the victim of that touchy national dignity which he had
loved to encourage. He was roasted in his own brazen
bull. A resolution condemning hasty legislation on the
criminal law, and reprimanding the Government for
leaving the French remonstrance unanswered, was moved
by Bright's old colleague, Milner Gibson, who now sat
for Ashton, and seconded by Bright himself. Palmerston
did not fail to congratulate them on appearing for the
first time as the champions of the honour of their country.
But they were supported not only by the Conservatives
but by the Peelites and by Russell. The Government
was defeated, and Lord Derby became Prime Minister
and Disraeli leader of the Commons. The Peelites declined, and the Radicals were not asked, to join the new
Ministry.

The task of reforming the constitution of India therefore passed unexpectedly to Disraeli.   His first attempt
failed; and before introducing the third India Bill, he
took the sense of the House on a series of resolutions
laying down principles on which legislation was to proceed.   The first of these resolutions transferred the government from the Company to the Crown.   The feeling
against the Company was so strong that Mangles, its
mouthpiece in the House, did not venture to call for a
division.   The subsequent resolutions directed the appointment of a Secretary of State, or other responsible
minister, through whom the Queen should exercise her
authority; an Indian Council, over which he should
preside, and which would take the place of the old Board
of Control; and the transference of the proprietary rights
of the Company to the Crown.   The Bill as passed also
established a Viceroy to exercise in India the imperial
authority over all the provinces alike.

    The debate on the resolutions was interrupted by an
incident which curiously illustrated the demoralization of
the Liberal party.   Lord Canning, the Governor whose
intrepidity and prudence had saved the Indian Empire at
the terrible crisis of the Mutiny, had proceeded to measures of retribution, which, although they so far disappointed the natural vindictiveness of the British in India
that he was nicknamed Clemency Canning, exceeded
the limits which appeared just and prudent to the Home
Government.   He issued a proclamation confiscating the
lands of the Kingdom of Oude, with the exception of
the estates of nobles whose loyalty to the British rule
was inviolate.   Lord Ellenborough, the new President
of the Board of Control, at once sent a despatch ordering
the withdrawal of the proclamation, and was so anxious
to dissociate himself from a vindictive policy that he
communicated his despatch to Bright, who was in a
manner recognized as the champion of the native Indians

in Parliament. When an outcry at the premature publication of the despatch was raised, Ellenborough tried
to save his colleagues by resigning office. But an
attempt was made, with great confidence of success, to
reunite the Liberal majority on a resolution which, without approving Canning's proclamation, condemned the
peremptory tone of the despatch. The disunion of the
Opposition had been such that the appearance of Russell's
and Palmerston's names together on the list of guests
at a dinner-party was hailed as a momentous political
event. Bright on this occasion performed the function,
not unfamiliar to him, of the candid friend of his party.
He not only told his friends that they would be disin-
genuous if they blamed the Government for condemning
a measure which they themselves disapproved,[1] but
declared that he was better satisfied with the Conservative Government than with the administration it had
superseded, or than he was likely to be with any that
the Liberals could form until the affairs of the party
were in better trim. After this speech the Opposition
collapsed with a suddenness which Disraeli, who was
provokingly cheerful for a minister with a minority,
compared to the instantaneous ruin of an earthquake.
The resolution was withdrawn; and for the rest of the
session the Government was as secure as if supported
by a loyal majority.

The Bill, under which India has since been governed
without any necessity for further constitutional change,
did not entirely satisfy Bright's zeal for reform. He ob-
jected to the Council, which, he predicted, would within
five years be abolished as either obstructive or as having
fallen into contempt. The constitution of the Home
Government should be simple, to correspond with the

---

[1] Bright, however, paid a tribute to the humanity and justice of Canning.
The intention and effect of the proclamation seem to have been misunder-
stood by all parties.

simplicity of its function of control rather than legislation. He was not satisfied that the new constitution, which still involved perpetual reference from Calcutta to Westminster, would be free from the "circumlocution, delay, and neglect" which had distinguished the old dual system. Procrastination, he said a few years later, was the very nature of the Calcutta Government. But his most serious objection was taken to the office of Viceroy, and to the expectation which such an institution implied, that the provinces of India could be "bound up and consolidated into one compact and enduring empire". "You lay duties on the Governor-general which are utterly beyond the mental and bodily strength of any man who ever existed." How could one man grasp the government of "a country of twenty nations speaking twenty languages"? We could not expect a succession of Alexanders. "No doubt there have been men strong in arm and in head and of stern resolution who have kept great empires together during their lives; but as soon as they went the way of all flesh, and descended like the meanest of their subjects to the tomb, the provinces they had ruled were divided into several states, and their great empires vanished." Bright was in favour of further decentralization. His own plan was that "the country should be divided into five or six separate, and, as regards each other, independent, presidencies of equal rank, with a governor and council in each, and each government corresponding with, and dependent upon, and responsible to, a secretary of state in this country".

Ten years later Bright declined Mr. Gladstone's offer to him of the Indian Secretaryship of State. Probably he refused this opportunity, not so much because he had lost his sense of the deficiencies of Indian administration or his faith in his methods of reform,—for he very rarely admitted any change of opinion,—as because he had not enough confidence in his own ability to execute his designs.　He was at that time fifty-seven years of age, and wearied by the long struggle for Reform; his second illness was imminent; and in him the energy of youth was abated somewhat early in life.　During his last twenty years he was perforce a comparatively idle man.

It is probable that Bright's vigorous and prolonged animadversions on Indian government helped to inspire the internal reforms by which the viceroyalty of Lord Ripon (1880–1884) was distinguished.　Bright at any rate regarded those reforms with satisfaction.　He wrote to an Indian correspondent: '' The principles which have distinguished the administration of Lord Ripon seem to me to be those which promise to be beneficial to you and creditable to us".　Intelligent and liberal opinion is still far from unanimous in approval of the policy of popular concession initiated by Lord Ripon.　If it should be finally condemned, much of Bright's fault-finding, and some of his suggestions, will share the condemnation. But he will always deserve applause as the first private member of Parliament since the days of Burke who set himself with diligence and ardour to investigate and redress the wrongs of the voiceless millions of India.

## Chapter V.

### Parliamentary Reform.

In October, 1858, at the first meeting at which he addressed his Birmingham constituents, Bright set afoot the popular movement for Reform.　Ten years had elapsed since he and Hume first propounded their scheme to the House of Commons; and he was now able to say that already four ministries—those of Rus-sell, Aberdeen, Palmerston, and Derby—had pledged themselves to Reform.　The first steps taken by the

Radicals in the House of Commons have already been recounted. It is now necessary to resume the history of the movement from that point to the autumn of 1858.

The scheme of the Chartists had included five heads of Parliamentary Reform—universal suffrage, the ballot, annual parliaments, the abolition of the property qualification for membership, and the payment of members. In 1848 most Radicals had declared for four of these five points, though they substituted household for manhood suffrage, and triennial for annual parliaments. The payment of members was at no time admitted by Bright into his scheme. He rarely or never alluded to that proposal in his Reform speeches. His judgment upon it is given in the following passage of a much later speech. "I am satisfied that the results of payment of members, in some countries at least, are highly unsatisfactory. The condition of things in the United States is deplorable. I think that in any country it introduces into the list of candidates men who are willing to make the occupation of party life a trade from which they may get a comfortable income."

Bright had advocated triennial parliaments for two reasons. He thought it desirable to counterbalance by a more immediate fear of the constituencies the influence which the Treasury could exercise over members of Parliament by means of its patronage. In the second place, it appeared to him mischievous that legislators should be fettered in judgment by those specific pledges which constituencies were tempted to exact from representatives elected for so long a period as seven years. But on this point his opinion suffered some change; and by 1858 it had disappeared from his scheme of Reform.

Faith in the Ballot was part of Bright's inheritance from the older school of Radicals. Long before he entered political life Grote and others had called for this method of protecting the independence of voters, and had convinced even so sound a partisan of Whig finality as Macaulay. It may appear surprising that a man so eminently outspoken and veracious as Bright should have been enamoured of a device which must either be inefficient or succeed only by the aid of habitual falsehood. The example of America as well as the precepts of the philosophical Radicals may have weighed with him. For whatever reason, he was uniformly and undoubtingly persistent in asking that the voter should "give his vote by a machinery which should protect him against the influence of his landlord, his creditor, and his customers". He declared that, if the workmen of the towns were admitted to the franchise, they too must be protected against the influence of their employers. His reply to Palmerston, who had argued that a man's morality would be injured if he were taught to violate an open promise by a secret vote, gives his judgment on the ethical question. "The noble Lord appears not to be aware of the fact that if a man is made to promise contrary to his conscience he by that promise is equally guilty of immorality; and if he votes in accordance with his promise he doubly violates the rule which the noble Lord professes to support."

Bright was also at all times consistent in declaring that he was not afraid of the widest possible extension of the suffrage, though it is certain that he would have been content, and probable that he would have been better pleased, to give first a fair trial to a suffrage less wide than household suffrage. But his speeches show that in 1858 he assigned the greater importance to redistribution; and that his main purpose was to secure for the large manufacturing and commercial towns, in which the principles of public action to which he was devoted had found widest acceptance, a preponderant influence in the control of the national policy. It must be added that at this period he never spoke on Reform without indicating his confidence that that influence when acquired would be used in favour of a peaceful and unenterprising foreign policy, and of a great reduction in the national expenditure. No self-governed people, he declared, had ever wasted, or would ever waste, so much of the national wealth as had been squandered by the class that since the Revolution had governed England, and had made unnecessary wars, created unnecessary offices, and contracted the national debt.

As early as 1848 Russell had cautiously admitted that "it would soon be advisable to consider the extension of the franchise". In 1849 he raised the question of introducing a new Reform Bill in the Cabinets. In 1851 he promised a Bill. "But," said Bright, "looking at the speeches of the noble Lord on this question, and leaving out of view his antecedents twenty years ago, there is no reason for believing that he is about to submit such a Reform Bill as would excite the enthusiasm of the country."

In the session of 1852 the first of many abortive Reform Bills was introduced by Russell. The Act of 1832, while preserving some of the ancient franchises conferred on different boroughs according to varying qualifications, established in general a £10 occupation franchise in boroughs, and in counties a £50 occupation, and a forty-shilling freehold, franchise. Russell's Bill proposed to reduce the rated value qualifying an occupier for a vote from £50 to £20 in counties, and from £10 to £5 in boroughs. The new qualification in the boroughs would have admitted working men paying as low a rent as half a crown a week, and was therefore by no means an illiberal concession. The Bill also offered the franchise to all persons both in boroughs and counties paying forty shillings in direct taxation. This qualification would have admitted a large number of persons resident in counties, who were neglected in the Act of 1867, and waited for their citizenship until 1884. Russell also proposed to extend the boundaries of sixty-seven small boroughs for the purpose of parliamentary elections. Before this Bill came up for a second reading the Ministry had fallen. Bright had given it the coldest of welcomes. He thought that the county franchise should be further reduced, and that, without some further measure of redistribution, the House would still continue to misrepresent the balance of opinion in the country.

In the session of 1854 Russell brought in the Reform Bill of the Coalition Ministry. This Bill proposed an occupation franchise of £10 in counties and boroughs alike, with a £6 qualification for dwelling-houses in boroughs only. It repeated the taxation franchise of the former Bill, and further proposed to give votes to graduates, to every man who had an income of £100 not paid weekly, or who enjoyed an income of £10 from Bank Stock or East India Stock, or possessed £50 deposited for three years in a savings-bank. The redistribution clauses took sixty-two seats away from fifty-two small boroughs; and bestowed some of these upon the large boroughs, but most of them upon the more populous county divisions. The Bill was also remarkable for the first appearance of the minority vote. In the constituencies which received three members each under the redistribution each elector was to vote for two candidates only.

The Bill was not popular; and little regret was exhibited when it was withdrawn in consequence of the Crimean war. Bright explained why it had been received without enthusiasm. "The noble Lord seems to have forgotten how he carried his Reform Bill in 1832. That measure was carried by the heartfelt response from all the towns of the United Kingdom. But in the present Bill I am unable to discover what should induce the towns of England to support it. The great towns are not likely to be enthusiastic in favour of a measure which gives members to counties already over-represented, and overlooks the claims of the borough constituencies."

During the recess between the sessions of 1858 and 1859, Bright addressed great popular meetings at Manchester, Edinburgh, Glasgow, Bradford, and other towns, as well as at Birmingham. These meetings constituted an event the importance of which could not be gainsaid. It was impossible that they should not recall to the minds of men the old days of the League, the appeal of the Leaguers from the politicians to the population, and their triumph over the moderation of the compromising Whigs. Bright himself informed the House of Commons next session that the meetings had "exceeded in numbers and in influence almost every meeting that was held by the Anti-Corn-Law League". The statesmen of the Liberal party were still scarcely less disinclined to reform than their Conservative competitors. Both parties regarded reform as an inevitable event of the future; both were anxious not to anticipate the necessity, and angry with Bright for opening the throttle-valve while they were trying to screw down the break; yet both were eager to intercept the credit of being the first to yield to the popular will as soon as it should become obviously irresistible. The Bills of 1859 and 1860, which will shortly be considered, are to be regarded merely as finessing moves in the party game, or, at the best, as mere *ballons d'essai*. But the Liberals of the great towns, tired of the tame domestic policy of the past ten years, as well as the unenfranchised working men, eagerly responded to Bright's spirited appeals. Among those who joined him at this time were J. A.

Roebuck of Sheffield, Duncan Maclaren of Edinburgh, Samuel Morley of Nottingham, W. E. Forster of Bradford, and many other leaders of the Liberal opinion of the great provincial cities. " Bright's agitation will bear fruit", wrote Clough, in January, 1859. " He is scoffed at in the metropolitan papers and at all clubs; but his hold on the country is such as no M.P. whatever, except himself, possesses."

Bright's popular oratory still retained all the fire and indignation of his speeches against the Corn Law, while it had improved vastly in the higher qualities of eloquence. He was now the greatest living master of demagogic rhetoric, if not indeed the greatest that England had ever known. If the end of such oratory is popular enthusiasm and determination, what could be more effective than the closing sentences of his Birmingham speech? " Shall we then, I ask you, even for a moment, be hopeless of our great cause? I feel almost ashamed even to argue it to such a meeting as this. I call to mind where I am, and who are those I see before me. Am I not in the town of Birmingham, England's central capital, and do not these eyes look upon the sons of those who not thirty years ago shook the fabric of privilege to its base? Not a few of the strong men of that time are now white with age. They approach the confines of their mortal day. Its evening is cheered with the remembrance of that great contest, and they rejoice in the freedom they have won. Shall their sons be less noble than they? Shall the fire which they kindled be extinguished with you? I see your answer in every face. You are resolved that the legacy which they bequeathed to you you will hand down in an accumulated wealth of freedom to your children. As for me, my voice is feeble. I feel now sensibly and painfully that I am not what I was. I speak with diminished fire, I act with a lessened force; but as I am, my countrymen and my constituents, I will, if you will let me, be found in your ranks in the impending struggle."

During the first three or four years of the agitation Bright's chief topic was the conservatism and wastefulness of the class which controlled through the unreformed House of Commons the policy of the country. "A House of Commons so formed becomes for the most part an organ of the great territorial interests of the country. It hates changes with an animosity that nothing can assuage. It hates economy. It hates equality of taxation." "All we have done of late years has been to vote with a listless apathy millions of money for which you have toiled." "The House of Commons presents itself to us as a body caring, I fear, very little for the great internal interests of the country, and reckless—I will not hesitate to say profligate—in the expenditure of public money." Against the fears of those who dreaded the evil possibilities of democracy he constantly appealed to the example of the United States. "In America there is a franchise as wide as that I have proposed. Yet in America we find law, order, and property secure. Are we less educated, are we less industrious, are we less moral, are we less subject to the law, are we less disposed to submit to all the just requirements of the Government?"

At a conference of reformers held in the Guildhall in November, 1858, Bright was entrusted with a commission to prepare a Bill. His scheme was a £4 rental or £3 rating qualification in the boroughs, a £10 franchise in the counties, the ballot, and a redistribution by which 130 seats were to be taken from the small towns. Of these seats eighteen only were given to counties, and the rest to the large towns, forty of which were to return three, four, or six members each.

Early in the session of 1859 Disraeli introduced the

promised Reform Bill of the Conservative Government. He clearly distinguished his purpose from that of Bright. He declared himself one of those reformers whose aim was to "adapt the settlement of 1832 to the England of 1859"; and repudiated sympathy with the new school, which thought that "the chief, if not the sole object of representation was to realize the opinion of the numerical majority of the country". Bright had anticipated that the Bill would be like a Spanish feast—"a very little meat and a great deal of tablecloth"; and, whatever its merits, it proposed no satisfaction to the hope of enfranchisement with which Bright had inspired the working classes. The county franchise was to be assimilated to that of the boroughs, but no reduction of the qualifying value in boroughs was offered. The people, said Bright, who were most eager for enfranchisement were to be disappointed. "Every one of these men, working, toiling, serving, paying taxes, and fulfilling all the duties of citizenship, will see that, as he was left an outcast by the Bill of 1832, he must remain an outcast by the Bill of 1859."

In place of a general enfranchisement of the workmen, Disraeli proposed to bestow the vote as a special reward for thrift or education. He offered it to clergymen and ministers of religion, to certificated schoolmasters, to solicitors, barristers, and proctors, to qualified medical men, to pensioners, to persons possessed of £10 a year from funded property, and to every man who had £60 in the savings-bank. Some of these qualifications were borrowed from Russell's Bill. But, so far as the Reform party in the country was concerned, Bright damned them for ever by a single contemptuous epithet. He called them the fancy franchises. No nickname was ever more successful. Disraeli, who was himself our greatest artist of such phrases, was naturally irritated by its success. "Alliteration", he said, "tickles the ear, and is a very popular form of language among savages. It is, I believe, the characteristic of rude and barbarous poetry. But it is not an argument in legislation." Whatever the value of the argument, it sufficed to convince the savages.

Disraeli's plan of redistribution was equally cautious. He condemned "those rattling schemes of disenfranchisement with which we have been favoured during the autumn". He took one seat from each of fifteen towns returning two members, and allotted eight of these seats to counties and seven to new boroughs.

The part of Disraeli's scheme selected for the first combat by the Opposition was rather oddly chosen. During the free-trade agitation many Free-traders had, on Cobden's advice, obtained county votes by the purchase of small freeholds in towns. Disraeli now proposed that a man who held a freehold in the town in which he lived should vote in respect of that property for the borough instead of the county. The irony of destiny has since decreed that the Liberal party should have the greater cause to complain of that swamping of rural opinion by urban freeholders which Cobden encouraged, and for which Disraeli tried to find a remedy. But at the moment the proposal meant a transference of Liberal votes from the counties, where they might turn the scale, to the towns, where they were not needed. Russell protested successfully against the change. The Government was defeated on this issue, and appealed to the country. The dissolution deprived Bright of the opportunity of bringing in his own Bill.

As soon as Parliament reassembled Lord Hartington moved a resolution of no confidence in the Conservative Government. Bright spoke and voted for this resolution; but he was careful to withhold any unqualified promise of support to the coming Liberal Ministry. " I wish to pursue the same course that I have pursued in the past—a course of vigilance in regard to the Government." He gave two reasons for his desire to see a change of Government. The war between France and Austria had led the Government to strengthen the national defences; and Bright, always jealous of such expenditure, interpreted it now as conveying a menace to France. His second reason was that he had more confidence in the reforming intentions of Russell than in those of Disraeli. Disraeli had "pretended to pay a portion of the debt that had been long due to the people, but he had offered them notes of the Bank of Elegance". Russell had during the election given assurances which, though they proved to be worthless, were for the moment accepted as honest and satisfactory by the Radicals. "It will be the duty of the new Government", said Bright, "to bring in at an early period a measure of reform very different from the measure of the Chancellor of the Exchequer."

The Derby Government being defeated by a narrow majority, Palmerston became Prime Minister and Russell Foreign Secretary. Mr. Gladstone, although he had voted with the Conservative Ministry in both the fatal divisions, took office as Chancellor of the Exchequer, and from this date may be regarded as a member of the Liberal party. The Peelite group had disappeared by absorption. Palmerston was known to be disinclined to reform, but Russell's pledges had been so precise that the reformers looked forward with a good hope to the coming session.

During the recess, and in the temporary suspense of the agitation for reform, Bright turned his attention to finance. The brilliant series of budgets by which Mr. Gladstone carried to its conclusion the work begun by Peel, and satisfied the free-trade theory of the Manchester School, was still incomplete; and Financial Reform Associations were calling for the removal of the duties on between three and four hundred articles of import. Bright's zeal was not satisfied even by this hope. He secured the approval of the financial reformers of Liverpool for a remarkable scheme, the audacious simplicity of which is so characteristic of his mind that, though it might claim no place in the history of the financial policy of the country, it cannot be omitted from any record of the opinions of its author. He proposed in brief to dispense altogether with indirect taxation.[1] He asserted the "simple principle of justice that taxes should be levied from the people in proportion to the property which every man possessed by reason of the security which Government gave him". The established methods of taxation he regarded as "essentially mean and singularly cruel". All taxation ought to be direct. He proposed also to abolish the existing income-tax. The deficiency of twenty-seven millions incurred by these remissions he proposed to meet partly by retrenchment, but chiefly by a tax of eight shillings per cent on all property, except that of persons whose possessions were worth less than £100. This was equivalent, if the annual yield of the property taxed were taken as five per cent, to a tax of eight per cent on all incomes derived from property, the earnings of work of any sort being left untaxed.

The poor man's luxuries still continue to yield revenue to the State; but within a few months of this speech, after the great budget of 1860, Bright was able to say with exultation that "four hundred obstacles to the free development of our industry have been struck out of the pages of our statute-book". Some years later his own suggestion made a partial reappearance in the form of a proposal for "a free breakfast-table", which supplied an attractive motto for the decoration of political assembly rooms.

[1] This proposal had already been made by the Chartists notably by Lovett in 1848.

The Reform Bill which Russell introduced in 1860 in fulfilment of his election pledges proposed a £10 qualification for the counties, a £6 qualification for the boroughs, and a meagre scheme of redistribution, by which twenty-five seats taken from the smaller boroughs were allotted, fifteen to counties, nine to boroughs, and one to the University of London. Four boroughs were to have three members each, but one of the three was to represent the minority.

Bright was willing to accept the compromise so far as the voting qualification was concerned; but, " with the candid audacity", said Disraeli, " which in his case greatly neutralizes the pernicious opinions he expresses, and the dangerous courses he pursues ", he announced that he would continue the agitation for the ballot, and for a more generous measure of redistribution. Disraeli did not divide the House on the second reading, but he probably did no violence to the prevalent opinion when he described the measure as "unnecessary, uncalled-for, and mischievous". Greville, who knew all the Whigs, wrote: " It is impossible to meet with any man who approves of this Bill, and who does not abhor the idea of any reform ". Such, no doubt, was the view of the clubs.

The first important division showed so small a majority for the Bill that Russell withdrew it before the first clause had passed committee. To ask the House of Commons to reform its own constitution is at any time to invite some of its members to commit political suicide; and, notwithstanding the success of Bright's agitation in the great provincial towns, there was as yet no such popular outcry as had forced the reform of 1832 upon Parliament. Yet Bright was justified in warning his colleagues that they were misreading the signs of the times. " There is no turbulence ", he said. " The passion of 1832 is past. There is no howling wind and no imminent convulsion, but there is the steady, the ever-growing, the irresistible tide of public opinion. There is the consciousness among millions of your countrymen that Parliament does not adequately represent them and is not just to them." Six years later he elaborated this simile with singularly fine effect. "You have stood on the sea-shore in an hour of quiet and of calm, when no tempest drives the waves, and the wind passes as it were but with a whisper; and yet you see the tide coming on, urged as it were by some latent and mysterious power. You see the loiterers on the beach driven from point to point by the advancing waves, and by and by and finally the whole vast basin of the ocean seems filled to the very brim. There is no violence; there is not even menace of force; but we all feel that opinion is growing and that the tide is coming on. We feel that those who oppose—ignorant some of them may be, insolent others may be—are being gradually driven back, and by and by barriers will be thrown down, and privilege and monopoly will be swept away. The people will be enfranchised, and the measure of their freedom will be full."

For the moment, however, public attention was occupied by other matters. The Free-traders were watching with interest Cobden's great enterprise of the French Commercial Treaty. The credit of this achievement is to be divided between Cobden and Mr. Gladstone. But the germ of the project was a suggestion derived by Michel Chevalier from a speech of Bright's. Politicians were also interested less in reform than in the great Free-trade Budget of the year, and in those ambitious projects of Louis Napoleon which caused the deplorable Invasion Panic.

This disquietude gave occasion for another assertion by Bright of his principle of non-intervention. On March 4, 1860, Lord Malmesbury wrote in his diary that he had heard Bright deliver " the most un-English speech he had ever heard in his life ". It is well known that Bright's sentiments were very often reproached as un-English. The reader may perhaps be assisted in assigning a meaning to this indeterminate epithet as applied to Bright, by a citation of those passages of this speech which gave gravest offence. The speech provoked an immediate and vivacious rebuke from the present Duke of Rutland. Sir Robert Peel, the son of the statesman, had interrogated ministers on the annexation of Savoy by the Frenchman, and, according to a custom then permitted, had introduced his question with remarks of his own intended for the guidance of the Government. Before the question was answered Bright interposed a protest against discussing such a question in Parliament at all. " What does the hon. baronet propose to do? We are not the Parliament of France—we are not the Parliament of Savoy—we are not the Parliament of Europe—but we are the Parliament of England. Unless it can be shown that there is any direct and obvious interest which this country has in any of the foreign questions which are constantly brought before us, what an absurd spectacle do we offer to Europe with all these repeated discussions!" He believed that France would not gain, nor Savoy suffer, by the annexation; but he added: " Perish Savoy, rather than that we the representatives of the people of England should involve the Government of the country with the people and Government of France in a matter in which we have really no interest whatever. Have we not for generations past endeavoured to settle the map of Europe? Have we not, as if it were not worth a thought, spent blood and treasure for the purpose of fixing certain boundaries, and declaring that certain provinces and kingdoms should belong to certain families; and have we not utterly and ignominiously

failed in every attempt that we have made?" There
were many hectoring protests against the annexation as
a flagrant breach of European law, but nothing particular was done. The "English" policy to which
Bright took exception proved to be a policy of loud
barking, and no biting at all.

Bright had accepted the great Budget as a reasonable
excuse for the withdrawal of the Reform Bill of 1860.
"I know you cannot get twenty wagons at once
through Temple Bar", he said; and the phrase passed
into a proverb. But his indignation broke out when
early in the session of 1861 Russell announced, "with
a jocularity that was absolutely contemptuous to those
who placed him on that very seat that he might advocate that very measure", that the Ministry did not
intend to waste time by introducing another Reform
Bill. The country, he said, did not seem to care about
the question. "What do you want?" cried Bright.
"You want six-sevenths of the people to make a demonstration which you have put it out of their power to
make in a peaceable fashion." Five years later he had
to make a similar reply to a similar argument. "There
is nothing more marvellously obtuse than the expression
of these men at head-quarters, that we need not give the
extension of the suffrage because the working people
are quiet." "The foundation of revolution", he said in
1866, "has in every country been laid by those who
pretended to be especially conservative."

To wait for the perilous argument from disaffection
has always, as Macaulay so often remarked, been a
common error of English statesmanship. Bright's indignation was not without reason; but Russell and the
Government had good grounds for apprehending that no
Reform Bill could pass the Parliament with which they
had to deal. A struggle for parliamentary reform is
inevitably of the nature of a struggle not only between

parties in Parliament, but between Parliament itself and the country; and further demonstrations, whether peaceful or turbulent, were necessary before Parliament would yield. Further, as matters then stood, the death or incapacitation of Palmerston was a necessary condition preliminary to such a reform as would satisfy Bright. Even after the death of their chief the Palmerstonians succeeded once in scuttling the ship.

It is possible that a renewal of the popular agitation would have proved without delay the accuracy of Bright's estimate of public opinion, but for the momentous event abroad which diverted attention from reform, and imposed upon Bright a new duty. The march to reform had been arrested by the Crimean war; it was now delayed by the civil war in America. No foreign event since the French Revolution has produced in this country so much animosity of divergent opinion. It made a schism among the reformers. Roebuck, for example, and Scholefield, Bright's colleague in the representation of Birmingham, were strong partisans of the South.

The secession of the Southern States, and the appeal to arms made by Lincoln, brought into conflict two of Bright's strongest antipathies—his hatred of war, and his hatred of slavery. Yet he had less hesitation in declaring his adherence to the cause of the Federals than his friend Cobden, who was at first disposed to sympathize with the seceders, as free-traders throwing off the yoke of a protectionist government. Bright perceived at once through the cloud of pretexts that the one issue at stake was that of slavery or emancipation. That this was so is now a matter of history. At the time it was a matter of opinion; and it is certain that many Englishmen, like Dickens, who had been most vehement in using the slavery of the South as a reproach against the whole American nation, sympathized with the South, and even regarded the proclamation of liberty made by the Federals as disingenuously intended to enlist philanthropy on their side, and to distract attention from an oppressive attempt to subvert the independence of the disaffected states.  Bright found plenty of evidence that English sympathy with the secession was due in part to jealousy of the growing strength of the Republic, and that opinion was perverted by the apprehension, so distasteful to him, of a disturbance of the Balance of Power.

"The object of the South", he said, "is this—to escape from the majority who wish to limit the area of slavery; to found a slave state free from the influence and opinions of freedom, a state whose corner-stone is the perpetual bondage of millions of men; to maintain in bondage four millions of human beings; to perpetuate for ever the bondage of all the posterity of those four millions of slaves."  "If the American Republic should be overthrown, there will be a wild shriek of freedom to startle all mankind."

Bright at all times cherished for the institutions of the United States a singular admiration, which inspired some of the most ambitious flights of his eloquence.  He was ready to believe everything that was good of a country where the will of the majority was law, and where there was no territorial aristocracy, no remnants of feudalism, no establishment of religion, and no class, except the slaves of the South, condemned to such hopeless penury and dependence as the agricultural labourers of England.  He was silently tolerant of American protection, and of what Mr. Morley calls "the political corruption which for the moment obscures the great democratic experiment" he showed no consciousness during his period of activity.

There were always persons to whom Bright's constant admeasurement of Britain with America appeared to be un-English and unpatriotic; and his use of this topic supplied his opponents with the rather nauseous retort that he was trying to Americanize our institutions. But it is apparent that his affection for America was based on consciousness of the ties of a common blood and a common language; and that he felt the same sort of satisfaction in contemplating the growth and forecasting the greatness of the great English-speaking nation of the new world that other Englishmen feel in watching the expansion of our own empire.   When Mr. Gladstone had declared his belief that the cause of the North could not succeed, Bright replied in words that will never be forgotten in America.   "I cannot believe that such a fate will befall that fair land, stricken though it now is with the ravages of war.   I cannot believe that civilization in its journey with the sun will sink into endless night in order to gratify the ambition of these men, who seek to 'wade through slaughter to a throne, and shut the gates of mercy on mankind'.   I have another and a far brighter vision before my eyes. It may be but a vision, but I will cherish it.   I see one vast confederation, stretching from the frozen north to the glowing south, and from the wild billows of the Atlantic westward to the calmer waters of the Pacific main; and I see one people, and one language, and one law, and one faith, and over all that wide continent the home of freedom and a refuge for the oppressed of every race and of every clime."

There is surely nothing unpatriotic, nothing that is not entirely admirable, in these great hopes for humanity. Yet it is one who reveres Bright's memory who comments thus on this famous peroration.   "Would that it were possible to set beside this noble vision some passage, conceived in the same strain, but inspired by an equal faith in the high destiny of his own country! If only I could read that majestic sentence without thinking of the scorn and derision with which Bright would have visited any man who had used the same magniloquence in predicting the future of the empire of Britain!"

It was necessary from Bright's point of view to make a demonstration of sympathy with the North, in order to prevent the Confederate party in Britain from actually involving us in hostility with the American Unionists, especially after the arrest of two Southern emissaries when sailing under the protection of the British flag, and when the North resented the piracies of the *Alabama*.  He made the advocacy of the Northern cause his mission; and despite his love of peace did not allow his zeal to be dismayed even by the horrors of Sherman's march.  For a short time he seemed to be in almost as small a minority as at the time of the Crimean war.  But he had now the British hatred of slavery to appeal to, and he carried with him, not indeed all England or all Liberals, but the two sections of the community that accepted his oracles—the Nonconformists and the working men.  It cannot be doubted that he did good service to his country by speaking, as he said, "for that policy which gives hope to the bondsmen of the South, and which tends to generous thoughts, and generous words, and generous deeds, between the two great nations which speak the English language and from their origin are alike entitled to the English name".  The sympathy of England could not avert the defeat of the Confederates; and that sympathy, if it had been unbroken, might have engendered a dangerous international animosity.

The war brought some misfortune to Bright himself.  The blockade of the Southern ports cut off the supply of cotton, and paralysed the industry of Lancashire.  Bright's private fortune was impaired by the generosity of his firm to their workmen for whom they could not find employment.

The American war, the Schleswig-Holstein question, and the cotton famine had combined to prevent the agitation for reform from proceeding with the vigour with which it had been begun in 1858. In 1865 the general election gave the Reformers another opportunity. The Liberal leaders had promised reform six years before, and, with whatever excuse, had failed to redeem that promise. Except for the Gladstone Budgets they had done little to encourage the loyalty of the Radicals; and the sluggishness of the Government and the House gave Bright a new reason for pressing for a change without which he could not pursue hopefully his crusade against privilege.

The feeling of the outgoing Parliament towards reform had been tested by a Bill introduced in the last session by Edward Baines, member for Leeds, to reduce the voting qualification in the boroughs. In the debate the coming schism had been foreshadowed by a remarkable speech made by Robert Lowe, a Liberal placeman, in which the case against the enfranchisement of the masses was presented with admirable skill and force. He warned his party that by espousing reform they would ruin the party, if they failed, and the country, if they succeeded. Lowe's Australian experiences had led him to take an unfavourable view—or, as Bright said, a "Botany Bay view"—of the competence of the working-classes for politics. But the speech was portentous, because Lowe had sat for thirteen years as a member of what was ostensibly a Reform party, had held office in two ministries pledged to reform, and had voted for the earlier Reform Bills. "The Reform question", cried Bernal Osborne, the chief jester of the Liberals, "has fallen from its high estate. It is 'deserted in its utmost need by those its former bounty fed'. It is reserved for an independent member at a morning sitting to present a fragmentary stump of the Bill, the whole Bill, and nothing but the Bill, to contemplative Reformers on the eve of an expiring Parliament." The division gave point to this irony. Fifteen years after the leader of the Liberal party had declared for an extension of the suffrage, in the seventh year of a ministry that had come into power on the cry of reform, and in a House in which the Liberals commanded a substantial majority, the Bill was defeated by a majority of seventy-four.

Before Bright entered on a campaign which was to end in his greatest victory, he had sustained the heaviest blow that fortune could deal at his happiness. In March, 1865, three months before the election, Cobden died. The memorable friendship between Bright and Cobden was based on an identity almost absolute of political aims,—for, except on the Maynooth grant, they never differed on any public question,—and on the recognition by each in the other of powers of mind denied to himself. The inner history of that friendship has not yet been written, and perhaps will never be written, for Bright refused to Cobden's biographer the use of the correspondence in which he and Cobden had interchanged their most intimate thoughts. For many years after the death of his friend Bright scarcely ever dared to mention his name in public, lest he should be overpowered by a rush of emotion. In his old age he once told a friend that nearly every night he was visited and consoled in his dreams by the spirits, or by the memory, of two of the departed. One was his father, the other Richard Cobden.

Bright was returned without opposition. But for the Reformers the most auspicious event of the election was the rejection of Mr. Gladstone by Oxford University, and his return for an industrial constituency.

A comparison of Bright's reform speeches in 1858 and 1859 with those delivered in 1865 and the two years fol-

lowing reveals two striking differences of topic. In the
former period he devoted the greater part of his addresses
to the necessity of checking by popular representation
the extravagant expenditure of the governing classes.
In the latter, the topic of retrenchment is almost forgotten. He now spoke as one desiring democracy for its
own sake. He had said, for instance, at Glasgow in
1858: "I hope that an improved representation will
change all this; that that great portion of our expenditure which is incurred in carrying out the secret and
irresponsible doings of the Foreign Office will be placed
directly under the free control of a Parliament elected by
the great body of the United Kingdom. Then, and not
till then, will your industry be secured from that gigantic
taxation to which it has been subjected during the last
hundred and fifty years." When he spoke in the same
city in 1866 he said: "The class which has hitherto
ruled in this country has failed miserably. It revels in
power and wealth, whilst at its feet, a terrible peril for
the future, lies the multitude that it has neglected. If a
class has failed, let us try the nation! That is our faith,
that is our purpose, that is our cry: Let us try the
nation!"

The second difference is this. In the earlier agitation
he had laid most stress on his proposal of a redistribution
of seats in favour of the large towns. In the speeches
of the second period he made the extension of the suffrage
to the working-classes the first and indispensable element
of reform. He still spoke of the county representation
as "a dead body tied to the living body of the borough
representation". But he was chiefly indignant at the
attempt to "erect the middle-class into a sort of oligarchy" by treating the settlement of 1832 as final. An
extended suffrage must come first; for the ballot and
redistribution he was content, if necessary, to wait, provided the artisan got his vote. Both in the towns and

in the House he gave three reasons for advising the Reformers to be content for the moment with this instalment of reform. In the first place, the small boroughs constituted a general grievance, not a class grievance; the grievance that cried aloud for redress was that of the excluded class. Secondly, he believed that opinion was more ripe upon the question of the suffrage; and thirdly, he saw that it would be more difficult to carry a scheme of disfranchisement through the House in face of the natural hostility of the representatives of the threatened boroughs. Any possible scheme of disfranchisement, he said, must needs be trifling and unsatisfactory.

These speeches are also distinguished from the former by the ferocity of his attack on the Conservative party and its leaders. He accused the Tories of permanent and virulent hostility to commerce, and of a sustained and persistent hatred of popular institutions. The course of the Tories was factious to the very last degree; they were a decaying faction, a supercilious and insolent party, and so forth. Conservatism was the great enemy of order; its principles would have led to anarchy. At the general election many Conservatives declared for a well-considered measure of reform. Bright interpreted this provoking qualification in the light of the fancy franchises of 1859, and of a phrase newly invented by Disraeli,—who was, said Bright, the "mystery-man" of the party, and "did the conjuring business for them",— the phrase of "the lateral extension of the franchise". He meant, said Bright, " It is true you are shut out; the Reform Bill was not satisfactory; the representation must be amended; and therefore we will admit somebody else".

Hitherto Bright's invective had hardly discriminated between the two great parties. He had castigated Palmerston more frequently and with greater gust than Disraeli. His speeches were now strongly impregnated with the party spirit which he had formerly disowned. The fact is that he had now good reason to be hopeful of the Liberal party of the future. Russell had by private overtures convinced Bright of his sincere desire of reform; Palmerston died shortly after the election; and Mr. Gladstone was already secure of the reversion of the leadership. It was already apparent that under Mr. Gladstone's leadership the policy of the Liberals would be more democratic. As early as 1860 his colleague, Lord Clarendon, had remarked to Greville that Bright and Mr. Gladstone were converging from different points to the same end; and again, that Mr. Gladstone was moving towards a democratic union with Bright. Palmerston, too, had uttered the famous prediction: "Gladstone will soon have it all his own way; whenever he gets my place, we shall have strange doings". The more Mr. Gladstone came to the front the better disposed Bright became to act loyally with the party. He had at last found his leader. He was more versed in reprehension than in encomium; but by his animated and unstinted eulogy at this time he associated Mr. Gladstone with himself in the popularity he had won, and contributed not a little to the establishment of his ascendency in the hearts of the common people. Even so self-reliant a man as Bright is happier if he can lean on another; and it is noteworthy that his devotion to Mr. Gladstone ripened rapidly from the date of the loss of Cobden.

On March 13 the Reform Bill of 1866, the fourth and last of Russell's failures, was introduced by Mr. Gladstone. The Bill was a moderate one as compared with the measure which Bright had for so many years advocated, or even with Russell's earlier efforts. It reduced the county qualification from £50 to £14, provided the occupation included a dwelling-house of £7 value, and the borough qualification from £10 to £7. The fancy franchises made no reappearance, except that £50 in a bank was to qualify for a vote. Bright recognized at once the essential virtue of this Bill,—that, though studiously moderate and redolent of compromise, it was at least a Bill intended to pass and not merely for show. "It is not a Bill", he said, "which if I had been consulted by its framers I should have recommended." He calculated that out of five or six millions of men in the United Kingdom who were not yet enfranchised, the whole number of the working-classes to be admitted in the boroughs of England and Wales was only two hundred thousand. " I found, when Mr. Gladstone brought forward the Bill, that it differed in almost every particular from the Bill I had urged him and his colleagues to prepare." But he welcomed it as an honest Bill, and as offering "a very sensible advance toward fair representation"; and he persuaded the Reformers in the country to adopt this opinion.

It was soon discovered that the enemy the Reformers had to fear was the Palmerstonian section of the independent Liberals. Lowe, who sat for one of the rotten boroughs threatened by the Radicals, took from the first the lead of the opposition to the Bill, and was joined by Horsman, member for Stroud. Bright, who always picked out for attack the strongest man in the adverse host, fell upon Lowe with all his energy both in the House and in the country. The real fighting in the debates, says Lowe's biographer, was between Lowe and Bright. "The right hon. gentleman", said Bright in his speech on the first reading, referring to Horsman, "is the first of the new party who has retired into what may be called his political Cave of Adullam; and he has called about him every one that was in distress and every one that was discontented. He has long been anxious to form a party in the House. At last he has succeeded in hooking the right hon. gentleman the member for

Calne. There was an opinion expressed many years ago by a member of the Cabinet that two men would make a party. When a party is formed of two men so amiable and so discreet as the two right hon. gentlemen, we may hope to see for the first time in Parliament a party perfectly harmonious, and distinguished by mutual and unbroken trust. But there is one difficulty that it is impossible to remove. This party of two reminds me of the Scotch terrier which was so covered with hair that you could not tell which was the head and which was the tail of it."

The simile of the Cave of Adullam has become a permanent addition to our political slang; and that of the Scotch terrier was enjoyed at the time with a relish which posterity can never taste in a personal joke. But the Cave contained before long many more than two malcontents.

At the outset Lowe gave a terrible advantage to his antagonist. With that engaging aptitude for saying and doing unpopular things, which will long keep his memory green, and which perhaps was itself a cause of his distrust of a populace which he could never hope to please, Lowe remarked: " Let any gentleman consider the constituencies he has had the honour to be concerned with. If you want venality, if you want ignorance, if you want drunkenness and facility for being intimidated, or if, on the other hand, you want impulsive, unreflecting, and violent people, where do you look for them in the constituencies? Do you go to the top, or to the bottom? "

This passage (which is here given as cited in Lowe's biography from a revised issue of the speech, rather than according to the report quoted by Bright) was construed by the Reformers as a general description of the working-classes of England. If this was a mistaken interpretation, it was an inevitable one, inasmuch as the sentence formed part of an argument against the enfranchisement of a select few of the most skilful and thrifty of the industrial class.   Nothing could illustrate better the difference between different conceptions of patriotism than the applause with which this imputation upon a class that formed the majority of Englishmen was greeted by the very men to whom Bright's sentiments so often appeared un-English and unpatriotic.  No one ever says this sort of thing without meaning it; and Lowe therefore deserves the praise which should always be given to a politician when he is sincere.  But no statesman ever said a thing less likely to serve his own purpose. Bright took full advantage of his adversary's indiscretion.   "I would recommend", he said, "that these passages from that celebrated and unhappy speech should be printed on cards, and should be hung up in every room in every factory, workshop, and clubhouse, and in every place where working men are accustomed to assemble."   He repeated the quotation at every meeting.  Lowe had raised himself, with some assistance from Bright, to the eminence of the most unpopular man in the country.   At the reform meetings pictures of the Scotch Terrier were exhibited amidst shouts of ridicule and execration which recalled the time a century before when the Jack Boot was the symbol of the object of popular hatred.   Those who regard the reform of 1867 as excessively democratic must lay the blame upon the indiscretion of Lowe as well as on the zeal of Bright. "It is Mr. Lowe's speeches", said Forster, "that have aroused the working-classes from their apathy, and enlisted them one and all in the cause of reform."

The danger from the Adullamites was pressing; and Bright, instead of waiting till the autumn, roused the country in the short Easter recess.  It was not till the end of April that the long debate on the second reading ended in a victory for the Bill by a majority of five only.

A separate Bill for redistribution was then brought in, and the two Bills were committed together. This Bill again fell far short of Bright's Bill of 1858; it dealt with forty-nine seats only instead of the 130 scheduled by Bright. The defeat of the Government was now certain; and on June 18 they were beaten by the Cave and the regular Opposition on a vital clause by a majority of eleven. The second Derby-Disraeli Cabinet succeeded. The Adullamites refused to join the Ministry, and by this refusal, as it turned out, sacrificed whatever the cause of oligarchy had gained by their disloyalty.

The anger of the provincial towns blazed fiercely throughout the autumn. The working men were now thoroughly aroused, and flocked to the banner of Bright and his lieutenants with a unanimous enthusiasm that at last startled Pall Mall and Downing Street. Bright was able to tell the House next session that a thousand meetings had been held, that at every one the doors were open for any man to enter, and that at every one an all but unanimous vote for reform had been taken. No public hall was large enough for the demonstrations of the great towns. At Birmingham, Glasgow, Leeds, and Edinburgh the local Reformers, recruited from the surrounding country, marched in procession to large open spaces, and there assembled in numbers which in each case exceeded the adult male population of the town itself. Bright's command of the popular mind had now reached its zenith; he was the Mirabeau of the moment; and it is hardly too much to say that had he chosen he could have ordered and guided a revolution. He spoke at Birmingham, Manchester, Leeds, and Glasgow; then he crossed the channel and inflamed the zeal of the men of Dublin; and finally addressed a great meeting of the trades-unions in London.

"The accession to office of Lord Derby", he said, "is a declaration of war against the working-classes."

"Justice is impossible from a class; it is certain and easy from a nation." "If the Clerk of the House of Commons were placed at Temple Bar, and if he had orders to tap upon the shoulder every well-dressed and apparently cleanly-washed man who passed through that ancient bar until he had numbered six hundred and fifty-eight, and if the Crown summoned those 658 to be the Parliament of the United Kingdom, my honest conviction is that you would have a better Parliament than now exists. It would be a Parliament that would act as a jury that would take some heed of the facts and arguments laid before it. It would be free at any rate from the class prejudices which weigh upon the present House of Commons. It would be free from the overshadowing presence of what are called noble families. It would owe no allegiance to the great land-owners."

The statistical case for reform was put by Bright thus: out of every hundred grown men in the United Kingdom, eighty-four had no votes; and the votes of the enfranchised sixteen were so distributed that half of the House of Commons represented one-seventh of the electors, so that less than three per cent of the population could command a majority of votes in the House.

One incident of these meetings deserves special notice. Bright was by nature a constitutionalist and therefore a loyalist; and his loyalty to the Throne, like that of all Englishmen of his time, was associated with a great veneration for the character of the Queen. In the early years of her reign, when she was for a short time unpopular with the Tory party, he had taken occasion in one of his first recorded speeches to rebuke one of his opponents in the church-rate dispute at Rochdale for some act of disrespect to the sovereign. There was now in London a certain amount of dissatisfaction because the Queen, after the death of the Prince Consort, had declined those public appearances which appear to metropolitan loyalty to form a large part of the duty of a limited monarch. At the reform meeting in St. James's Hall, a Liberal statesman, whether speaking seriously or essaying a tasteless jest at the expense of the audience, tried to involve the meeting in the absurdity of complaining because the Queen had not shown herself to a procession of Reformers which had passed her windows on its way to the Park. Bright treated as an insult to the Queen what was perhaps intended only as an insult to the audience. He rose in great indignation. "I could not sit here", he said, "and hear that observation without a sensation of wonder and of pain. I think there has been by many persons a great injustice done to the Queen in reference to her desolate and widowed position. And I venture to say this, that a woman, be she the queen of a great realm or the wife of one of your labouring men, who can keep alive in her heart a great sorrow for the lost object of her life and her affections, is not likely to be wanting in a great and generous sympathy with you." By making this use of an unexpected opportunity Bright had the satisfaction of doing real service to the Queen. The working men who filled the hall—the same men of whom Carlyle spoke as "Beales and his roughs"—responded with the utmost warmth; and the classes that were really responsible for the grumbling were shamed into silence.

When Parliament met for the ever-memorable session of 1867, the recalcitrant Liberals and probably the greater part of the Conservatives still meditated resistance to the popular clamour. But the great statesman who led the House of Commons knew that the hour of democracy had struck, and was resolved to turn the inevitable concession into a personal triumph for himself, and if possible to the advantage of his party. To suppose that Disraeli did not foresee the end of the session from the beginning, that he was unaware whither the

course he had marked out would lead him, that he had
not designed the policy of yielding bit by bit after flattering his followers with a show of conservative caution,
is to refuse justice to his extraordinary shrewdness.
Probably he never shared the distrust of democracy
prevalent in his party. Mr. C. A. Cooper reports Bright
as saying of him: "He is what you will hear more of
in the future—a Tory democrat. He has no love for
those who now lean upon him. He has ability above
most men of the time; and he will use his ability to lead
his friends into ways they have abhorred." The history
of the century must be misread by a man who cherishes
the preconception that the Liberal was essentially a
democratic, and the Conservative essentially an aristocratic, party. The Liberal party, as we have seen,
threw off their aristocratic fetters with not a little reluctance; and Disraeli's feat of democratizing the Conservative party was scarcely more arduous than Bright's
feat of democratizing the Liberal party. But it was
more astonishing because it had the appearance at least
of being the unaided achievement of one man, and of
being performed with the rapidity of a stroke of leger-
demain.

There must always be room for divergent conjecture
as to Disraeli's motives, for no one will reproach him
with that indiscreet candour on which he ironically feli-
citated Bright. But the real and permanent difference
between his political theory and Bright's related, not to
the democratic, but rather to the imperial, idea. If we
may credit him with the expectation that the new democracy might be educated into his conception of political
or imperial purposes as readily as into that of Bright,
such a hope finds some justification in subsequent history.

The Queen's speech promised a measure which should
freely extend the elective franchise without unduly dis-

turbing the balance of political power. On February 11 Disraeli declared that parliamentary reform should no longer be a question to decide the fate of ministries. Judging by the repeated failures of the past, it was evident that reform might be indefinitely postponed if each successive ministry staked its existence on the details of its own measure. In 1859, he said, the Liberals had turned him out on a captious point of detail, and then, having incurred the responsibility, had shrunk from fulfilling their duty by passing their own measure. This was fair enough. Disraeli seemed to be inviting the House of Commons to reform itself; he was really inviting it to help himself in forcing upon his party a gradual but swift reversal of its traditional policy. If any trick was intended, it was a trick in favour of reform; but the Reformers not unnaturally misconstrued the intention.

Disraeli next laid on the table thirteen resolutions, by accepting or modifying which the House was to instruct the Government what sort of Bill to bring in. The resolutions vaguely prefigured a measure whose salient feature should be an apparatus of checks to prevent the predominance in the electorate of the working-classes. But in moving the House into committee on the resolutions he gave the details of the Bill which was in the mind of the Government. It was to include a revival of the fancy franchises of 1859, a general qualification of £20 rating in counties and £6 in boroughs, an enlargement of the areas of boroughs, and a redistribution of thirty seats. Lowe and Bright agreed in suggesting that the resolutions should be omitted and the Bill at once printed. This course was adopted; but there was a short delay due to the withdrawal of Lord Cranborne (now Marquis of Salisbury) and two other members of the Cabinet, who had agreed to the resolutions, but who refused to support the measure sketched by Disraeli.

On March 13 the actual Bill was at last introduced.
Already a startling concession had been made.  What
was now proposed was a £15 rating qualification in
counties, and a household qualification irrespective of
value in towns.  There were four collateral franchises—
an educational franchise, admitting members of certain
professions and men who had passed certain examina-
tions, a savings-bank franchise, a property franchise,
and a direct-taxation franchise.  As for redistribution,
seven seats were at the disposal of the Government
owing to the disfranchisement of four corrupt boroughs;
twenty-three boroughs of less than 7000 inhabitants,
and returning two members, were to spare one member
each; and of these thirty seats, fourteen were allotted
to new boroughs, fifteen to counties, and one to the
University of London.  A new proposal was that electors
were to be permitted to vote by paper without personal
attendance at the poll.

If the Conservatives were taken aback at finding
household suffrage, the dream of the impracticable
Radicals, thrust into the Bill of a Conservative Government, the attention of the Reformers was fixed on the
checks by which the Bill proposed to preserve the predominance of the educated classes.  The first was a
provision requiring two years' residence, instead of the
twelve months fixed by the Act of 1832, as a condition
of registration, and so excluding the migratory class
of which the lowest stratum of the population is largely
composed.  The second was the dual vote.  A man who
was qualified as a ratepaying householder and also as
paying twenty shillings in direct taxation was to exercise
his suffrage under both qualifications.  The third and
most important was the requirement of personal payment
of rates as a condition of the franchise.  This provision
excluded not only householders exempted from poor-
rates on the plea of poverty—a class which Bright called

the residuum, and which he also was willing to exclude—
but the compound householders, whose rates, according
to a method established by local habits and local Acts
of Parliament, were paid by the landlord and counted
in the rent. The effect of this restriction would have
varied in different towns. In Sheffield, for example,
the clause would have admitted 16,000 householders;
in Birmingham, according to Bright, it would have
admitted 2400 and excluded 36,000.

Mr. Gladstone formulated ten objections to the Bill
as it stood; and Bright declared it very unsatisfactory
and very bad. "I think", he said, "it has marks of
being a production not of the friends but of the enemies
of reform." Nevertheless the Reformers of the Liberal
party, confident in their majority, addressed themselves
to accept Disraeli's invitation and amend the Bill, Bright's
desire that they should rather upset the Government by
rejecting the Bill and produce a measure of their own
being overborne by the general sense of the party. But
once more their counsels were divided by a new schism.
A group, known from the place in which they laid their
conspiracy as the tea-room party, revolted from Mr.
Gladstone's lead, and defeated his amendment to admit
the compound householder. Immediately after this
division the House adjourned for the Easter holidays.

Then came, with dramatic suddenness and completeness, the catastrophe of the play. The indignation of
the towns broke out again, and the demonstrations of
the previous autumn were repeated. Bright went to
his constituency, and told them the Conservatives were
bewildered. "The whole Tory party has been dragged
from its anchorage. They find no longer any holding-
ground, and in their confusion they offer they know not
what." But he directed all the force of his invective
against the tea-room party—the forty Reformers, who,
in the phrase he borrowed from Bernal Osborne, "had

had salt put on their tails". For the first time he appeared as an enthusiast of party loyalty. "What can a party do in Parliament if every man is to play his own little game? Why, a costermonger's donkey-cart, that would not travel from here to London in a week, yet, by running athwart the North-Western Line, might stop and bring to destruction a great express train. And so twenty very small men, who during their whole political lives have not advanced the question of reform by one hair's-breadth or by one moment of time, can at a critical moment like this throw themselves athwart the objects of a great party, and mar a great measure that ought to affect the interests of the country beneficially for all time." The cry of the mass meetings was that Disraeli should be turned out, and the cause of reform entrusted to Mr. Gladstone.

The donkey-cart proved as successful an argument as the Scotch terrier. The revolting Liberals, astonished at the storm they had raised, were persuaded or intimidated into loyalty. Disraeli made at first a mere show, and then not even a show, of resistance. Within three weeks of the day when Parliament reassembled all the three safeguards had disappeared. The dual vote was abandoned; the two years' residence was reduced to one; and finally Disraeli completed the consternation of the Cave by promising to devise a plan for the admission of the compound householder. Lowe uttered his solemn protest against "a clause which comprises in itself a whole revolution". "Your repentance," he said, "bitter as I know it will be, will come too late." But on this occasion he went beyond the safe generalities of a cautious prophet, and injured the effect of his prognostications by condescending upon particulars. The new electorate would repudiate the National Debt and institute an inconvertible paper currency.

Further concessions to the Reformers followed. The

vote was granted to lodgers in towns; the collateral or fancy franchises were abandoned; the qualifying value in the counties was reduced to £12. The redistribution of seats was also extended, the limit of population under which a town should not return two members being raised to 10,000. Finally, the Government at first refused, and then consented, to allot a third seat to the four largest provincial towns; and the proposed system of voting-papers was abandoned.

Lord Cranborne gave voice to the grief of the unconvinced Conservatives, and Lowe to that of the disaffected Whigs; but Disraeli's triumph was complete; and the Bill was read a third time without a division. It was left for the melancholy Jaques of Chelsea to shake his head over the triumph of "John of Bromwicham" and of "the superlative Hebrew conjuror, spell-binding all the great lords, great parties, great interests of England to his hand, and leading them by the nose like helpless, mesmerized, somnambulant cattle to such issue". But the general feeling in the country was one of satisfaction that, for good or for evil, the long-vexed question was settled; that the settlement was broad enough to last a generation; and that the occupation of the agitator was gone.

Bright had been one of a small minority that voted for John Stuart Mill's amendment admitting women to the franchise. In regard to this vote he afterwards made an admission very uncommon with him—that he had voted with hesitation and misgiving, and in deference to Mill, whose services to the cause of reform had latterly been very valuable. On this question his opinion always wavered. Peradventure his reason was convinced, but the old Adam of sentiment resisted.

In the form in which it ultimately passed into law, the Bill entirely satisfied the conditions which Bright had for so many years laid down, except in three particulars, in regard to all of which he lived to see his

views adopted.   The readjustment of seats fell short of
his scheme of 1858; the ballot was not conceded; and
the Lords had been allowed to enact a provision taken
from Russell's old Bills, by which the minority were
to have a chance of returning one member in each of
the three-member constituencies.   This device, carried
against a strong protest by Bright, disappeared without
a word of regret in 1885.

The passing of the second Reform Bill was the crowning triumph of Bright's career.   " It is discovered in the
year 1867 ", he said with pardonable exultation, "that
my principles all along have been entirely constitutional,
and my course perfectly patriotic.   The invective and
vituperation that have been poured upon me have now
been proved to be entirely a mistake."   He had been
for many years the unquestioned leader of the Reformers;
he had borne the brunt of many battles, and had outlived many defeats.   It was he who had forced the
question upon Parliament, as Cobden had forced free-
trade, in despite of the indisposition of Whigs and
statesmen.   There are elements in the eulogy of his
first enterprise that must of necessity be omitted from
any commendation of the second.   Free trade in corn,
if a good thing, was a good thing in itself; its benefits
were immediate and direct; the hungry were fed, the
idle found employment, and wealth flowed into the
country through the open ports.   Parliamentary reform
is to be judged by remoter results; its benefits are indirect and relative, and will always be diversely estimated.
The people who were starved by protection knew that
they were hungry, and only needed to be told why.
The discontent of the unenfranchised working man was
created in part by Bright and his helpers.   In the
motives of the Reformers there was necessarily a partisan
as well as a patriotic element; the new votes were
wanted for party purposes.   But we may confidently

claim that Bright's zeal for democracy was as little tainted as any man's could be with the spirit of faction or ambition; and those who hold his purpose to have been mistaken may be safely challenged to admit that his intention was patriotic.

It is impossible to suppose, in the light of his earlier speeches, that Bright can ever have been entirely satis- fied with the results of his success. The speeches of the enthusiastic leaders of any victorious movement will always provide congenial food for the cynic. It would be easy to treat ironically the contrast between the bygone ardour of the unenfranchised shouting for votes and the present apathy that requires the mechanism of associations and the importunity of canvassers to push and pull the voter to the poll. The reflection that is borne in upon the reader of *Hansard* is that, if no reform has ever done a tithe of the harm apprehended by its adversaries, neither has it accomplished a quarter of the good predicted by its advocates. This is perhaps part of a still more general truth—that politics do not count for so much as politicians suppose. But there remains one consideration more, that we must reckon not only the good that such a measure has done, but also the evil it may have averted. The apathetic policy of Palmer- ston, scornful of the multitude, looking for public opinion very little further than the lobby and the metropolitan clubs and newspapers, and setting more store by the chatter of a Whig lady's salon than by the clamour of a mass meeting in Manchester or Glasgow, might, if it had long survived his death, have been disagreeably interrupted by disorder or by something like revolution. One may reject one-half of what Bright said of the delinquencies of the unreformed Parliament, and yet recognize that there was no guarantee in its constitution that it would not sooner or later commit some disastrous error of the sort that breeds anarchy.

Bright always maintained that he was a sounder Constitutionalist than the oligarchs; and the ground of this
claim at least deserves examination.   He did not, according to the common idea of demagogy, call upon his
clients, whom his eloquence could have moved as easily
one way as another, to overthrow or destroy anything
whatever; he showed them that there was a place for
them in the Constitution, and made them content to ask
for admission, not as men storming a hostile citadel, but
as entering into an inheritance.   If he helped to create
the excitement, his authority made for restraint and
order when it was at its height.   He called out an army
of a million indignant men; and when the storm had
passed, a few overthrown palings in Hyde Park represented all the material damage of the turmoil.   It is
admitted that democracy was inevitable, and could not
without peril have been long delayed; and even those
who regret it ought to be grateful that at the critical
time the leader of the victorious masses was a man so
singularly free from the common vices and common
ambitions of the demagogue.

## Chapter VI.

### Ireland.

The Reform Bill of 1867 had dealt only with England.
The session of 1868 was partly occupied with the passage
of similar Bills for Ireland and Scotland, Disraeli, who
early in this year succeeded Lord Derby as Prime Minister, refusing, in spite of several defeats, to resign or
dissolve until he had completed his task of reconstructing
the representative system.   An appeal to the new constituencies was imminent; and it was proper that the

Liberal leaders should propound some legislative enterprise that should attract the support of the new and
untried electors.  It was not yet thought necessary to
ask the working-classes, who now formed a majority in
nearly every urban constituency, to use their votes to
get something for themselves; and a generous tribute
was offered to their disinterestedness when Mr. Gladstone proposed that the new power should be used first
of all to redress an Irish grievance.

The perennial problems of Irish discontent had recently
been forced on the attention of politicians by a series of
unhappy events.  In 1865 had occurred the disclosure
of the plots of the Irish Republican Brotherhood of
Fenians; in 1866 the Fenian invasion of Canada; in
1867 Davitt's attack on Chester Castle, the rescue of
Fenian prisoners in Manchester, and the Irish demonstration of sympathy with three of the rescuing party
who were hanged for the murder of a policeman; finally,
in December of the same year came the attempt of Irish
conspirators to blow up Clerkenwell Prison.

In January, 1868, Bright wrote to an Irish correspondent: "For twenty years I have always said that the
only way to remedy the evils of Ireland is by legislation
on the Church and Land".  But he added: "To strike
down an established church and to abandon the theory
of our territorial system by one Act of Parliament would
be too much for Parliament, and would destroy any
Government that suggested it.  Our rulers, though un-
comfortable, are not sufficiently alarmed to yield.  The
Whigs are almost as much afraid as the Tories are of
questions affecting the Church and the Land, and they
seem to have almost no courage.  The English people
are in complete ignorance of Irish wrongs, and know
little or nothing of the real condition of your country."
"Mr. Gladstone", he said in the same letter, "hesitates,
and hardly knows how far to go.  He does not feel

himself very secure as leader of a powerful and compact party."

This letter proves that, despite the warmth with which Bright had welcomed Mr. Gladstone's leadership, he had not yet adequately recognized his capacity for command or his zeal for reform.   It also suggests that Bright did not at first realize how much nearer he himself stood to the centre of gravity of the party since the extension of th electorate.   But he was not deterred by these forebodings from the experiment of engaging the interest of the new voters in the Irish question.   A few days later he devoted a long speech at Birmingham to the exposition of his views on the Irish Church and the Irish Land Law.   This speech differed from his earlier exhortations to his constituents in exhibiting more of the thoroughness of the practical statesman, and less of the vehemence of the agitator; the shadow of coming official responsibility seemed already to have fallen on the orator.   But it fully achieved its purpose; and we may fairly suppose —unless indeed Bright had been entirely mistaken in his opinion of the hesitation of his leader—that the success of this speech was a determining cause of the bold and well-omened stroke by which Mr. Gladstone, three months later, committed his party to a strenuous Irish policy.

Hitherto we have omitted any account of Bright's earlier dealings with the Irish question.   It will be convenient at this point to justify the assertion quoted above, of his twenty years' advocacy of the policy that was embodied in the legislation of 1869 and 1870.

Bright had always shown a facility of sympathy with the Irish people such as, at least in the earlier half of his career, was not common among English politicians. He was curiously successful in forging graphic phrases that were eagerly accepted by Irish patriots as reflecting the national sentiments of the dolorous island.   "I

believe that, if the majority of the people of Ireland
counted fairly out had their will, and if they had the
power, they would unmoor the island from its fastenings
in the deep, and move it at least 2000 miles to the west."
"When the ancient Hebrew prophet prayed in his
captivity, he prayed with his window open towards
Jerusalem.    The followers of Mahomet when they pray
turn their faces towards Mecca.  When the Irish peasant
asks for food and freedom and blessing, his eye follows
the setting sun, the aspirations of his heart reach beyond
the wide Atlantic, and in spirit he grasps hands with
the great Republic of the West."   Nothing could suggest more felicitously than these images the incongruity
that is, it may be, destined still to baffle the wisdom of
many generations of statesmen,—the incongruity between the political union inexorably ordained by the
disposition of territory and the irrevocable course of
history, and the disunion of sentiment that has been
engendered by racial antipathies and by ancient crimes.

Bright had from the first associated himself with that
section of the Liberals that was disposed to trace Irish
disaffection to the establishment of a Protestant Church
in the midst of a Catholic population.   Two methods of
redress were already under discussion when he entered
public life—the disestablishment of the Protestant
Church, and the concurrent establishment and endowment of the Catholic Church.   A small beginning of the
second scheme had actually been made by a vote of
public money to support the Catholic College at Maynooth.   This grant was regarded as an equivalent to
the *regium donum*, the grant made to the Irish Presbyterian ministry by William III. as a reward for the
support he had received from the Irish dissenting Pro-
testants in the civil war that followed the Revolution.
To the Maynooth Grant, which enabled peasants destined
to the priesthood to learn their Latin in Ireland without

going abroad, many observers have attributed the trans-
formation of the kindly and genial priest who laughs
and prays in the pages of Lever into the sullen and
underbred tyrant of the Meath Elections.

Bright always declared for disestablishment and disendowment, and missed no opportunity of enforcing his
opinion. His first speech on any Irish question was
made when Peel proposed a large increase of the Maynooth Grant. Bright joined Disraeli in opposing this
increase. By his speech and vote on this occasion he
separated himself, for the only time in his parliamentary
life, from Cobden, who was a Churchman, and regarded
the question from another point of view. The surprise
that has been expressed at this vote is surely unnecessary. Bright was a Nonconformist; the English Nonconformists, who also possessed colleges, had never
asked for a subsidy, and, if they had done so, would
certainly have been rebuked both by those who supported and those who opposed the grant to Maynooth.
The reasons he gave are quite intelligible. He disapproved of any expenditure of public money on any
ecclesiastical institution. He saw in the grant the
beginning of a policy of endowing the priesthood; and
that policy was certainly in the mind of some statesmen.
He believed that the endowment of the Catholic priests
in Ireland would have the same effect which he attributed to the endowment of the clergy of the English
Church; that it would make them allies of privilege, and
indifferent to the wrongs of the people among whom
they lived. He was also of opinion that the grant
diverted attention from the real causes of disaffection.
Peel's policy in short missed the mark at which it aimed;
and the grant would provide a new and shabby excuse
for the continuance of the Protestant establishment,
which was the real root of the evil, so far as that evil
grew out of ecclesiastical jealousy.

In 1852 Bright put before the public a scheme of dis-establishment in an elaborate letter addressed to Dr. Gray of Dublin. He proposed a Church Property Commission, which should gradually, as benefices became vacant, possess itself of the whole property of the Irish Church. The Commissioners were to be directed to appropriate certain portions of the fund as a free gift to the Protestant Episcopal Church, to the Presbyterian Church, and to the Roman Catholic Church. These gifts were to be absolute and irrevocable. The gift to the Catholic Church was to consist of a house and a plot of land for the priest in every parish; the cost to be, at a rough estimate, a thousand pounds for each of a thousand parishes, or £1,000,000 in all. The gifts to the other two churches were to be of about the same value. In consideration of these endowments the Maynooth Grant of £26,000 and the *regium donum* of £40,000 were to be withdrawn. Three millions being thus spent in endowing the churches, the remainder was to be a fund for education and for providing free libraries.

This scheme was sharply criticised by the Liberation Society; it was indeed hardly consistent with those rigid principles of political nonconformity of which Bright was in general an adherent, or with his own argument against the Maynooth Grant. Despite this opposition he repeated his proposals sixteen years later at the Birmingham meeting already mentioned. He expected and deprecated Nonconformist opposition. "I hope", he said, "that some of my Nonconformist friends who have a very strong opinion on this question, and perhaps have not looked at it in the same light as I have, will have a little charity for me when I say that it would not be just to take the £13,000,000 into the hands of the Government and throw the whole of the present Church bare and naked upon the country." In the same temperate spirit he said in the House of Commons a few weeks later: "When you are about to make a change which is inevitable, and which shocks some, disturbs more, and makes hesitating people hesitate still more, it is a great thing if you can make the past slide into the future without any great jar, and without any great shock to the feelings of the people. In doing these things the Government can always afford to be gracious to those whom they are obliged to disturb."

Bright's proposals were so often in advance of public opinion that they could not but appear to his critics violent and revolutionary. But the sentences just quoted, with their strong tincture of that reasonableness in which Matthew Arnold found Nonconformists so lamentably deficient, illustrate a quality of his mind less frequently displayed than the thoroughness which was so exasperating to less resolute politicians. The rigidity of his principles of action seriously narrowed the field of compromise for him; but within that field he was not always disposed to obstinacy.

In his speeches on the disestablishment of the Irish Church Bright could do little more than repeat reasons that had been perceived and enforced before his time, though he is entitled to a share of his own in whatever credit any man may be disposed to give to the feat of 1869, inasmuch as it was he who enlisted the sympathy of the new voters in the project at a time when he spoke to them with an authority possessed by no other politician. But his share in the deliberations that led directly to the Irish Land Act of 1870, and indirectly to many later enactments, was of far greater importance; here, at any rate, he is entitled to the credit of initiative. "From first to last", said his colleague, Mr. Chamberlain, many years later, "Mr. Bright laid it down that there could be no satisfactory solution of the Irish Land difficulty which did not give facility to the tenant to become the absolute owner of the land he cultivates.

Every provision of legislation which has been based on this principle of Mr. Bright's has been a success." This is the claim we have now to substantiate.

It had been Bright's practice to turn to account the opportunities afforded by the Bills suspending Habeas Corpus in Ireland, or permitting extraordinary methods of enforcing the law, by descanting upon the causes, as he understood them, of the disaffection which made such disagreeable precautions necessary. It was never his custom to vote against measures of coercion when required by the responsible Government. When therefore he uttered, after long experience, his famous dictum, "Force is no remedy", he had already defined, by the action he had consistently taken, the exact meaning of that excellent maxim. Lawlessness was as abhorrent to him as to any man; he was willing to use any necessary force rather than that the law should be broken with impunity; but he always held that it was the second duty of legislators confronted by an outbreak of lawlessness to look elsewhere than to coercion for the remedy of disloyalty, as he looked elsewhere than to the native wickedness of the law-breaker for its remediable causes.

Bright's sympathy with the people of Ireland was at one period of his career warmly reciprocated, and he received at Dublin a welcome rarely accorded there to an English statesman. But with the Irish members his relations were often by no means cordial. Both they and he represented sections of the community that considered themselves unjustly treated by the legislature. Bright and the English Radicals were always ready to define their complaints by bills or resolutions. The Irish members appeared to him to be active in complaint but indolent in devising measures of relief. "The Irish members", he said in 1847, "complain very justly of the past legislation of this House. But when we call to mind that there are 105 of them here, of whom 60 or

70 are of Liberal opinions, and that above 30 of them
are repealers and hold very strong views in regard to
the mismanagement of Irish affairs by the Imperial Parliament, I think we have a right to complain that they
have not laid on the table of the House any one measure
which they believe to be necessary to the prosperity of
their country." Two years later he spoke of the inca-
pacity and disagreement of the Irish members as one of
the greatest misfortunes under which Ireland laboured;
and was angrily rebuked by Barron, member for Water-
ford, who declared that Ireland had been brought to
ruin and misery by the policy of the Manchester School.

In the failure of helpful advice from his Irish colleagues, Bright, as one of those English politicians that
thought some other remedy than force to be wanted,
was obliged to seek a remedy himself. The peculiar
service that Bright rendered to Ireland was that, if he
was not the first to look for the remedy of discontent in
a modification of the Land Law, he was most persistent
in thrusting upon the view of the country and of Parliament that part of the Irish difficulty which has now for
many years been recognized by common consent as the
most important, and as affording the largest hope that
it will not be found insoluble. Further, he was for
years foremost, if not alone, in putting forward that
solution of the agrarian problem which for thirty years
after the Reform Act has been actually adopted in a
series of legislative experiments by both the great parties in the State.

" The great cause of Ireland's calamities is that Ireland is idle. Ireland is idle and therefore she starves;
Ireland starves and therefore she rebels. We must
choose between industry and anarchy. I defy the
House to give peace and prosperity to that country
until they set agoing her industry, create and diffuse
capital, and thus establish those gradations of rank and

condition by which alone the whole social fabric can be held together." The last sentence of this extract from a speech delivered in 1847 deserves remark. The object of Bright's Irish policy was to bring the land into the possession of the occupier, and so to promote the wealth of a country dependent on agriculture by attracting capital and increasing the agricultural production. But he foresaw social as well as economical advantage in the creation of a middle-class of independent farmers corresponding to the manufacturing middle-class to which he himself belonged. He wished to see intermediate between the idle aristocracy and the labouring classes a body of yeomen, industrious, well-to-do, giving employment to labour, with a stake of their own in the prosperity of the country, and with a strong motive for the encouragement of order. "What you want", he said in Dublin in 1866, "is to restore to Ireland a middle-class proprietary of the soil." "I believe", he told the House of Commons in 1867, "that you can establish a class of moderate proprietors who will form a body intermediate between the great owners of land and those who are absolutely landless, which will be of immense service in giving steadiness, loyalty, and peace to the whole population of the island." A great gulf had been created by the circumstances of the conquest between the owner and the occupier; the problem was to build a bridge over that gulf. The solution of the social and of the economical problem seemed to him to be the same; but it is noteworthy that the social problem was always present to his mind even when the attention of England had been directed to Ireland by economic disasters.

When Bright first interested himself in the Irish question, Ireland was still labouring under the evils which the Encumbered Estates Act of 1848 was intended to alleviate. "There were", as he said, "vast

tracts of land which, if left in the hands of nominal or
bankrupt owners, would never to the end of time support
the population which ought to live on them." "It is
the absence of all demand for labour that constitutes the
real evil of Ireland. The land there enjoys a perpetual
Sabbath. There is the land; and there is labour enough
to bring it into cultivation. But such is the state in
which the land is placed that capital cannot be employed
upon it. You have created such a monopoly of land by
your laws and your mode of dealing with it as to render
it alike a curse to the people and to the owners of it.
Why should land be tied up any more than any other
raw material?" All these things were said by Bright
twelve years or more before the first serious attempt to
grapple with the problem.

In 1847 and for some years after, Bright was content
to ask that every obstacle that legislation could remove
from the distribution of land should be removed. He
desired a simplification of conveyance and titles, a
parliamentary title for the purchaser, a restriction of the
power to make settlements in favour of unborn heirs,
a remission of all stamp duties on transfer of land, the
abolition of entails, and a repeal of the rights of primo-
geniture in the administration of intestate estates.

In 1850 he prepared a draft of a short Bill, after an
independent study of the evidence and report of the
Devon Commission, which had sat from 1843 to 1845.
This Bill was shown to the Irish members, and was
regarded favourably by a few of them on either side of
the House; but the majority refused any support.
Russell also saw the draft, and submitted it to Irish
officials with a Bill of his own. Russell's Bill was
regarded as establishing a machinery too complex to
work smoothly; and that suggested by Bright also failed
to get any official favour. Politicians in general were
indisposed to touch the question at all. Bright attri-

buted the reluctance of the governing classes to grasp the nettle firmly to the presence in every Government of persons who were themselves land-owners in Ireland. Although the measures proposed would do no injury to the fortunes of Irish land-owners, they might diminish the political power which landed property conferred even upon those who were being dragged by their unlucky inheritance to financial disaster. "The question is," he said in 1852, "can the cats wisely and judiciously legislate for the mice?"

The Bill which Bright had in mind was never submitted to the judgment of Parliament. He thought it better, he said, when challenged to take it out of his pocket, that a man who was not connected with Ireland should not bring forward a measure which did not meet with the approval of the Irish members. But when in 1852 W. S. Crawford, member for Rochdale, introduced a Bill which, anticipating an important provision of Mr. Gladstone's Bill of 1870, proposed to give legal sanction to the Ulster Custom, Bright put in an urgent plea for doing something in the face of the agrarian crimes. "It is in the eternal decrees of Providence that so long as the population of a country is prevented from the possibility of possessing any portion of their native soil by legal enactments and legal chicanery, these outrages should be committed, were it but as beacons and warnings to call the legislature to a sense of the duty it owes to the country which it governs." Such a reading of the moral of agrarian outrage, if not of its final cause, is now the merest commonplace; but forty-five years ago it required all the courage of a man hardened against vituperation to utter such a sentiment.

The lasting feud between Bright and the landed aristocracy of England made it natural that he should look to the landlords and the land system for the causes of Irish discontent, and natural also that his testimony

should be treated as prejudiced, and his motives suspected. It is curious to observe that he had to defend
himself against the charge of designing confiscation,
robbery, and what not, when he was only propounding
schemes which have since been not only accepted but
developed by the emulation of statesmen of all parties.
In point of fact he was conservative of the rights of
property, and in his land-purchase scheme always postu-
lated the consent of the land-owner. " If it is intended
by a Bill with this title ", he said of a Bill promised by
an Irish member, " to vest the ownership of land in the
present occupier, I believe that this House will never
pass it; and if it did, it would prove most fatal to the
best interests of the country."

His own scheme of land-purchase was explained in
detail to the people of Dublin in 1866, and to the House
of Commons in a speech delivered early in 1868, on the
occasion of a motion for a committee of the whole House
to consider the state of Ireland. He proposed to entrust
five millions of public money to Commissioners, who
should purchase by agreement the Irish estates of English or absentee landlords. The sale was not to be
forced, except in the case of lands belonging to the City
Companies; and he did not propose any purchase of the
land of owners who resided on their estates. He assumed
that the land could be bought at twenty-five years' purchase; that the tenants could pay five per cent annually
on the purchase-money; and that the Government might
without loss be content with three and a half per cent
interest. The accumulation of the balance of one and
a half per cent would make the tenant the absolute
owner in thirty-five years. These were exactly the terms
adopted in the land-purchase clauses of the Act of 1870.
He believed that there was in Ireland a great amount
of saved money, which the tenants, for lack of security,
would not invest in their farms. This saved money

would at once be used as capital for the improvement of the land. "I would negotiate with land-owners who are willing to sell, and with tenants who are willing to buy. I would make the land the great savings-bank for the future tenantry of Ireland."

Such was the germ of the legislation for the creation of a class of small proprietors in Ireland which has since been developed in a long succession of enactments with results the value of which must still be left to the judgment of posterity.

The speech that has just been quoted included a renewal of the plea for disestablishment. It contained also another of those happy comparisons which have passed into political proverbs. Lord Stanley had suggested, as a sort of alternative for disestablishment, the endowment of a Roman Catholic University in Ireland. Bright thought this proposal "grotesque and imbecile", and added that Stanley reminded him of the man mentioned by Addison "who was not a Cabinet Minister, but only a mountebank", and who "set up a stall, and sold pills that were very good against the earthquake". It was a rather dangerous jest in the mouth of a man who had a prescription of his own for Irish discontent. The pill of disestablishment was administered; but the Irish earthquakes have continued.

A fortnight after this debate Mr. Gladstone moved three resolutions committing the House to the disestablishment and disendowment of the Irish Church. The debate and division proved that the fear Bright had expressed a few weeks before, that there was no man strong enough to unite the party on so great a question, had been too timid. The Cave was deserted, and the Adullamites joined the hosts of Israel against the Philistines. "The people of three kingdoms", said Bright, "are waiting with anxious suspense for the solution of this question. Ireland waits and longs for a great act

of reconciliation.  England and Scotland are eager to
make atonement for past crimes or past errors." He
made effective use of a species of argument very familiar
to readers of his later speeches.  He set up against the
predictions of evil which the opponents of disestablishment had uttered, the failure of former vaticinations of
the same oracles.  "You have always lions in the path.
But when you have seen and handled them, these things
are found after all to be only hobgoblins.  You have
learned that they are perfectly harmless; and when you
thought we were doing you harm and upsetting the
Constitution, you have found that after all we were doing
you good, and that the Constitution was rather stronger
than it was before."  The colonies were more easily
governed and more loyal since the changes in the colonial system brought about by Molesworth and Hume.
The revenue was larger since the tariff was simplified.
Free-trade had been a frightful monster; but the land,
which, it was predicted, would become valueless and go
out of cultivation, was selling at a higher rate in the
market than it had ever touched before.  The Balance
of Power, once the beginning and end of our foreign
policy, was forgotten; yet England was as much respected as when she was ready to meddle with every
stupid quarrel on the Continent.  Only the year before,
the Conservatives had boldly faced another hobgoblin;
and Disraeli would agree that there was nothing to be
afraid of, and that Parliament would henceforth be more
strong and more venerated by the people than it had
ever been before.  The argument is, of course, merely
rhetorical; it dissolves at the first touch of the com-
monest logical tests, and it is evident that it is equally
available in the defence of any proposal whatsoever.
But it was always effective; and Bright, as a successful
slayer of hobgoblins, had a better right than most men
to use such a plea.

The division on the first of Mr. Gladstone's resolutions gave a majority of sixty-five in his favour and against the Government. The conduct of the Government after this defeat raised a grave constitutional question, which was discussed with much heat. Disraeli had, when defeated in committee on the Reform Bill, escaped the usual consequences of defeat by accepting the amendments; but when the Irish Church resolution was carried against him, he was put in a position in which the unwritten law gave him only the alternative of resigning in favour of the victor, or of submitting the question at issue to the country by a dissolution. But to dissolve Parliament at once would have been to appeal to the unreformed constituencies to the exclusion of the new voters; and Disraeli did not conceive that, when precluded by so rare an accident from dissolution, he was restricted to the alternative of resignation. He therefore resolved to postpone the dissolution till the Reform Bills of the year were carried, and the new electorate properly constituted. His refusal to resign was sharply criticised by the Opposition. The constitutional mode of government, said Bouverie, member for Kilmarnock, a Liberal authority on such points, was that "the House of Commons gave its support to the Government, and the Government represented the Crown"; but if Disraeli's views were carried out there would be "a renewal of those differences between the Crown and the House of Commons which all who take an interest in good government must have hoped had ceased for ever".

In these difficult circumstances Disraeli thought proper to give an unusually detailed account of his discussion with the Queen, using language in which Bright discovered "a mixture of pompousness and servility". His narrative appeared to the Opposition to imply that he had left it to the Queen's personal discretion to decide whether he should resign, and so to throw upon her the responsibility which the Constitution imposed on himself, and to put her in the position of seeming to keep in office by her own will a Government opposed to the policy which the Commons had decreed. If this interpretation, which was disputed by the supporters of the Government, was correct, a grave error had been committed. Bright, who seems to have suspected that some manœuvre was contemplated by which Disraeli would take the settlement of the Irish Church question, as he had taken Reform, out of the hands of the Liberal party, gave voice to the indignation of the Liberals at the use Disraeli had made of the name of the Queen. He "feared that Disraeli had not stated all that it was his duty to state in the interview he had had with his sovereign". "The minister who deceives his sovereign is as guilty as the conspirator who would dethrone her." He added, amidst a hurricane of cheers from the Opposition: "Let me tell hon. gentlemen opposite, and the right hon. gentleman in particular, that any man in this country who puts his sovereign in the front of a great struggle like this, who points to the Irish people and says from the floor of this House, 'Your Queen holds the flag under which we, the enemies of religious equality and justice to Ireland, are marshalled', is guilty of a high crime and misdemeanour against the sovereign and against his country; and there is no honour, there is no reputation, there is no glory, there is no future name that any minister can gain by conduct like this which will acquit him to posterity of one of the most grievous offences against the country that a prime minister can possibly commit". Whether or not the occasion justified language of this degree of vehemence, a strong protest was necessary, lest a highly dangerous precedent should be set up.

Parliament was dissolved in November, and Bright

went to Birmingham to fight for his seat under conditions of some doubt. Birmingham was one of the few
constituencies the solidity of whose representation was
endangered by the minority clause in the new Act.
That clause had been accepted by the Commons against
his protest, and it may be suspected that it was passed
partly for the purpose of giving annoyance to him.
Two local Conservatives of repute were nominated
against the three Liberal candidates; but the provision
that was to give him a Conservative colleague was easily
defeated, the Liberals securing nearly three-fourths of
the recorded votes. Birmingham is distinguished by the
fidelity of its political attachments; for during the whole
of its parliamentary history it has happened only twice
that a member nominated for re-election has been out-
voted at the poll.

Bright's constituency was as yet only slightly affected
by the process, dating from the settlement of the Corn-
law question, that may perhaps be called the torification
of the middle-classes—a process that at this election
produced some surprising results in his own county of
Lancashire. The working-classes in general were disposed to vote for the Liberal candidates. "For thirty
years", said a Birmingham working man to a Conservative canvasser, ' I have been trying to get this vote.
For thirty years you have been trying for me not to get
it. I shall not give it to you the first time." The small
loaf and the big loaf were still the most persuasive of
emblematical arguments. Bright himself had established
a hold on the affections of the artisans of Birmingham
which was never weakened. He did not live among
them; he took no interest in their local concerns; his
visits were not frequent, and not many of his constituents
made personal acquaintance with him. But when he
came, he always gave them the best of his wisdom and
eloquence. No one who heard it will ever forget the great

K

roar of cheers that went up year by year when the white
head of the people's tribune appeared on the platform of
the Town Hall.   His annual speech was to many a
hard-wrought man one of the great events and chief
enjoyments of the year.   Each man was proud of his
share in so distinguished a representation; they listened
to him with the unquestioning reverence of discipleship;
and they were never wearied of the punning motto,
" Honour Bright ".

The November returns decided at once the fate of the
Irish Church and of the Conservative Government.
Disraeli immediately resigned, and Mr. Gladstone became for the first time Prime Minister.   In accordance
with general expectation Bright was invited to join the
Ministry.   He accepted after hesitation and with reluctance.   His work had not been such as to satisfy himself that he was well fitted for official life; he already
suffered from a constitutional indisposition for steady
industry which yielded only to the pressure of a loud
call of duty; after saying exactly what he thought for a
quarter of a century, it is probable that he did not relish
the necessary reticence of office; his habits of life were
domestic, and he was easily wearied by the turmoil of
London life.   He declined the arduous responsibility of
the Indian Secretaryship, and accepted office as President of the Board of Trade only when the urgency of his
chief was reinforced by the strong persuasion of his
private friends.   The reunion of his party, of which he
had almost despaired after the experience of the Cave
and the Tea-room, was made ostentatiously complete
when Bright and Lowe, the duellists of 1866, sat more
or less lovingly together in the same Cabinet.

Bright performed the functions of his office with
punctuality and acceptance, but without distinction.
His value to the Government lay in the confidence which
his presence inspired among the large section of the

party in the country whose political creed was contained in his speeches. Those who expected that his counsels in the deliberations of the Cabinet would tend to disunion were entirely disappointed. The passionate orator of the mass meetings proved himself the most reasonable and conciliatory of disputants in the council-chamber. " It is remarkable," said his colleague, Lord Granville, after his death, " considering his vigour and the enthusiasm of his character, how great was the moderation of the advice he gave his colleagues. I never knew a member of the Cabinet who acted more as a peacemaker among his colleagues."

The session of 1869 was occupied in discussing the details of the Irish Church Bill. Those details varied considerably from those which had been twice—in 1852 and again in 1868—sketched by Bright himself. The liberal terms offered, for the sake of a speedy settlement, for the commutation of vested interests, with other payments which Bright had overlooked, made the cost of compensation to the evicted church far larger than he had anticipated. But except that the Maynooth Grant and the *regium donum* were commuted, there were no grants to the other churches. Bright, however, was content with disestablishment on any terms; and the conduct of the Bill was left, as it may fairly be assumed that its preparation was left, to the Prime Minister, whose skill in grasping and expounding a complex scheme was unequalled.

The main question having confessedly been already referred to and decided by the country, the debate on the second reading was not so much deliberative as an occasion for the display of epideictic oratory. Bright contributed a speech which was regarded at the time as one of his most successful efforts. It is carefully elaborated, and abounds in all the skill of a resourceful rhetorician; but modern readers will probably agree that

Bright's eloquence is more impressive when he is defending an unpopular cause against an adverse audience,
than when he was, as now, defending a foregone conclusion, and embellishing a case that had long ago—by
Macaulay, for example, in 1845—been exhaustively
stated.  In a speech made on such an occasion there
must needs be an air as of conscious art, which is altogether absent from the eloquence, spontaneous and as
it were inevitable, of the speeches on the Russian war.

   He showed that dexterity which the House of Commons encourages more than any other school of oratory,
of turning against his antagonists their own phrases and
sentiments.  The Irish Church had been called a light
of the Reformation.  "This light of the Reformation,"
said Bright, "sustained by privilege and fanned by the
hot breath of faction, has not been so much a helpful
light as a scorching fire which has burned up almost
everything good and noble in the country.  Industry and
charity and peace and loyalty have perished in the
flames."  One of the supporters of the establishment
had remarked that ministers of voluntary churches were
rather a low class.  "I think", retorted Bright, "that
many prophets of old were graziers.  The apostles were
fishermen, and theirs was a religion to which not many
mighty, not many noble, were called."  But the passage
of his speech that has most permanent interest was his
reply to the stricture, elicited by an often-quoted admission of Mr. Gladstone's, that the new Irish policy was
due to the Fenian outrages.  If this were so, said
Bright, it was only another proof that it was difficult to
make great reforms unless under circumstances that
absolutely forced them upon the attention of Parliament.
"You know very well that the Catholic Association led
to Catholic Emancipation; that the dethronement of the
Bourbons brought about the Reform Bill of 1832; that
the desperate condition of affairs in the West Indies

freed the slaves in the English colonies; that the famine in Ireland was an irresistible argument to bring about the repeal of the Corn Law; that the mutiny in India drove the House immediately and without consideration to abolish the East India Company; and, sir, if I were to come down to a later time, I might, speaking of what took place in 1867, ask the right hon. gentleman and his colleagues what were the cries that induced them to be enthusiastic in support of a measure of household suffrage."

Bright took very little part in the discussions of the Committee. But on the question of the provision of glebe lands for the disestablished clergy, an amendment being moved that seemed to agree better than the provisions of the Bill with the plan he had proposed, he was obliged to explain the disappearance of his own scheme. That scheme had been of the nature of a compromise between the devotion of the Church property to secular purposes adopted by Mr. Gladstone, and the plan, still favoured by Russell, of endowing the Presbyterian Church in Ulster, and the Roman Church in Leinster, Munster, and Connaught. Bright said that the terms of the Resolutions of the preceding session had precluded the Cabinet from considering his scheme when the Bill was drafting; and that he had not submitted it to the House when the Resolutions were under discussion because he had already found that "the basis he had proposed was not acceptable to the House", that it "was regarded by many as unreasonable and unjust", and was "distasteful to many people in the Church and in general to Nonconformists". It may be said that the scheme was a compromise designed to make the feat of disestablishment easier at a time when it appeared to be difficult, and therefore not wanted when the difficulty disappeared. But the speeches already quoted seem to prove, if due respect be paid to Bright's acknowledged candour, that, had he not failed to win support, he would have preferred his own plan to that of Mr. Gladstone. Matthew Arnold (whose father is cited by Russell as an early advocate of concurrent endowment) wrote at this time that "the Nonconformists were actuated by antipathy to endowments and not by antipathy to the injustice and irrationality of the present appropriation of Church property in Ireland", and that "the moving power by which the Liberal party were now operating the overthrow of the Irish establishment was this antipathy and not the sense of reason and justice". He ought to have excepted Bright from this taunt. But the history of the Education Bill of the next year proves that Arnold exaggerated the weight of Nonconformist counsels in the deliberations of the Ministry.

There was a general expectation that Bright would sooner or later break through the decorous reserve, and say something inconsistent with the moderation, which were at that period of our history supposed to be incumbent on Cabinet Ministers. The expected opportunity came in the month of June, when he was provoked, by the indiscretion of those who predicted that the House of Lords would try to reverse the verdict of the electorate and the Commons, into writing a letter threatening constitutional changes to the disadvantage of the Peers if they should obstruct the Bill. They would, he said, stimulate discussion on important questions which, but for their infatuation, might have slumbered for many years. By throwing themselves athwart the course of the nation, they might meet with accidents not pleasant for them to think of. The Liberal leaders in both Houses were challenged to repudiate the letter; but Lord Granville and Mr. Gladstone found no difficulty in steering a middle course between embracing and disavowing the sentiments of their colleague.

Many years later, in somewhat similar circumstances,

Bright repeated this menace. "The veto of the House of Lords", he wrote in 1884, after the rejection of the County Franchise Bill, "is a constant insult to the House of Commons; and if the freedom of our people is not a pretence and a sham, some limit must be placed upon a power which is chiefly manifested in or by its hostility to the true interests of the nation. A Parliament controlled by hereditary Peers is no better, perhaps it is worse, than a Parliament influenced by and controlled by a despotic monarch."

If we consider the strong antipathy to privilege and to aristocracy which was inbred in Bright's nature by his religious creed of equality, and fostered by that long struggle against the land-owners which gave a lasting bias to all his political career, these momentary outbreaks of indignation are really less remarkable than his habitual reticence in regard to the privileges of the hereditary chamber. He was for years the one man who could, had he chosen, have put himself at the head of a crusade against the authority of the Lords. Like other democratic Liberals, he often used language which seemed to lead him to the very verge of such an enterprise. That he did not go further than an occasional and a conditional menace is another proof of the sincerity of his frequent professions of aversion from violent constitutional change, just as the tolerance of the English masses for that institution is the most impressive example of the conservatism that distinguishes English from continental democracy. Bright had no zeal for artistic perfection in politics; he attacked unsparingly anything, however venerable, that appeared to him evil in practice, but of mere anomalies he was curiously tolerant, so long as he found them practically tolerable. On this occasion he was rude to the Peers, not because they were Peers, but because he supposed them to be meditating unconstitutional behaviour.

In spite of this provocation a majority of the Lords
accepted the verdict of the country, the influence of the
Court being used to avert a crisis.  A dispute between
the two Houses over certain details was, after some
days of anxiety, adjusted.  The Peers, said Bright, in
his review of the session, had taught some other people
a lesson by showing that they had learned it themselves.
The act of conciliation was passed.  It did not conciliate
the Irish people, who had still grievances enough to
satisfy their appetite for complaint.  On the other hand,
it did not destroy the Protestant religion.

Early in 1870 Bright's health again broke down.  The
symptoms of his second illness resembled those of the
first, and it was of about equal duration.  He was
present at the Cabinet meetings at which the Irish Land
Bill of that year was prepared, and, for reasons already
noted, certain clauses of it have always been known by
his name; but he was unable to take any part in the
discussion of the measure in Parliament.

Twenty-five years had passed since the Devon Commission had reported in favour of giving legal sanction
and extension to the equitable custom of Ulster, by
which tenants, on quitting their holdings, were entitled
to compensation for improvements made at their expense.  The Parliament of the middle-classes per-
sistently neglected this recommendation.  The first
Parliament in the election of which the working men
of England took part carried it into effect.  This fact
may fairly be pleaded in justification of the opinion which
Bright had maintained against Lowe.  The Bill also
provided for compensation for disturbance when tenants
were evicted for any cause other than default of rent.
But we are here chiefly concerned with the Bright
clauses.  It must not be assumed that in a Cabinet in
which Bright alone represented the extreme left of the
party he had it all his own way in the drafting of this

part of the Bill; and it is not certain that he is to be blamed for defects that have since been corrected in the maturity of experience by fresh legislation.

A beginning of the new land-purchase system had already been made in those clauses of the Irish Church Bill which empowered the Church Commissioners to advance on mortgage at four per cent three-fourths of the purchase-money to a tenant of Church lands desiring to buy his farm. These clauses are sometimes associated with the name of Bright. The Bright clauses of the Land Act of 1870 provided that any tenant agreeing with his landlord for the purchase of his farm could borrow from the Imperial Government two-thirds of the price, repaying the interest and principal in thirty-five annual payments of £5 for every £100 advanced.

The Bright clauses are sometimes said to have failed in practice. In fact they initiated a successful experiment. The transactions that took place under them, though small in comparison with those under the Ashbourne Act of fifteen years later, amounted to nearly two millions under the Church Act, and more than half a million under the Land Act. A beginning at any rate was made towards realizing Bright's hope of making the land the savings-bank of the thrifty Irish husbandman.

The experience of the working of the clauses was so satisfactory, especially in respect of the trifling proportion of bad debts, as to encourage Parliament to continue the work by further advances of public money on easier terms. The Land Act of 1881 increased the proportion of the purchase-money lent to three-fourths, the rate of repayment remaining the same. The Acts of 1885 and 1891 authorized the advance of the whole of the price, and reduced the annuity to four per cent, with an extension of the term to forty-nine years. All these Acts are to be traced to Bright's original discernment of this method of dealing with the agrarian difficulty, and to the use he elected to make of the vast influence he had gained over the new voters.

The causes of Irish discontent were too deeply rooted to be eradicated by such legislation, and those who have laboured for the welfare of Ireland have long ceased to look to Ireland for gratitude. But Bright's name may yet be honoured in Ireland if ever the fulness of time should bring the accomplishment of the prediction with which he closed his great speech in 1849: "God has blessed Ireland, and does still bless her in position, in soil, in climate. He has not withdrawn his promises, nor are they unfulfilled. There is still the sunshine and the shower, still the seed-time and the harvest, and the affluent bosom of the earth yet offers sustenance for man. But man must do his part. We must do our part; we must retrace our steps; we must shun the blunders, and, I would even say, the crimes, of our past legislation. We must free the land; and then we shall discover, and not till then, that industry, hopeful and remunerative, industry, free and inviolate, is the only sure foundation on which can be reared the enduring edifice of union and peace."

## Chapter VII.

### Education; the Conservative Reaction; and the Eastern Question.

The session of 1870 is memorable not only for the first Irish Land Bill, but for Forster's Bill establishing for the first time a national system of elementary education. Bright was still well enough to do business when the first draft of this measure was submitted to the Cabinet, but his attendance had ceased before it came under discussion. For a great part of the session he was unable even to read in the papers of what was going on in Parliament. His illness therefore befell just at a time to prevent him from doing a service to his party for which no other man was competent—the service of mediating between his colleagues and the Nonconformists, who were provoked to revolt by the educational policy of the Government.

The education question as raised and discussed in 1870 is the only political controversy of his time upon which we cannot collect with certainty a complete account of Bright's views from his speeches and public letters. All his leading supporters in Birmingham were warmly engaged in the opposition offered by the National Education League to some of the provisions of Forster's Bill. Bright's own sympathies were divided, in a ratio that cannot easily be determined, between the League and his colleagues. When he addressed his constituents for the first time after his recovery, he said what he could honestly say on the side of the controversy which they had espoused, and in regard to the rest held his peace.

It has already been related that in his early parliamentary life, as a zealot both of religious equality and of *laisser-faire*, Bright adopted without reserve the views of the Nonconformists who advocated the voluntary principle in education. These views must be carefully distinguished from those of the supporters of what is perversely called the voluntary school system of to-day. The so-called "voluntarists" of 1843, an extinct species, held that all schools should be maintained as well as managed by voluntary effort. Between the time when Bright strenuously resisted all national assistance whatever to elementary education and the discovery by the friends of religious equality of a more excellent way of satisfying their scruples, nearly a quarter of a century elapsed. During that period the education of some millions of unlucky children was sacrificed as a burnt-offering to the religious difficulty, that man-devouring sphinx.

The steps by which Bright gradually changed his views on this question cannot be traced in his public utterances. But in 1866, towards the end of the agitation for reform, he declared in general terms for a national system of elementary education. He then described with admiration the common school system anciently established in New England and already prevalent in all the other Northern States. He used the superiority of American over English education as an argument for democracy, and even seemed to add the meagreness of the national provision for education to his catalogue of the delinquencies of the governing classes. He declared that he would stake everything he had upon the prediction that, if the agitation resulted in a substantial and real representation of the whole people, there would not pass over three sessions of Parliament before there would be the fullest provision for the thorough instruction of every working man's child in the kingdom.

In order to secure this result without further offence to the principle of religious equality the National Education League was established. Its head-quarters were at Birmingham; its president and chief spokesman in Parliament was Bright's colleague, Mr. George Dixon, and its other officers were mostly constituents of his; and the working-classes of the town displayed immense interest in the question. The agitation was conducted with great vigour, and before 1870 the League was invested with authority to speak, not indeed for all, but for a majority, of the Nonconformists. Its policy was in brief, Free, Compulsory, and Unsectarian Education, and after much debate the word unsectarian was interpreted to exclude all religious teaching from schools supported by the State. It was not indeed proposed to withdraw from the voluntary or denominational schools the subsidy they already received from the Treasury; but it was anticipated with confidence that they would painlessly disappear after the establishment of such a system of municipal schools as the League desired.

The solution of the religious difficulty which the League proposed has never yet commended itself to more than a respectable minority of the community. It was rejected by nearly all Churchmen, and by many, perhaps most, of the Scotch Presbyterians and of the Wesleyans. It was proposed that the State should entirely relieve the Churches of the care of secular education, but should leave to the Churches the whole charge of religious education. There was to be a thoroughly national system of secular instruction, and a purely voluntary system of religious instruction. It was held that the qualifications which command success in religious instruction were notably different from those of a good teacher of reading, writing, and arithmetic, and that the same differences between secular and spiritual instruction in respect of time, place, person, and manner, which are commonly recognized by those of riper years who seek edification for themselves, should also be accepted in providing education for children.

Whatever may be justly said against the rejected proposal, it will not be denied that it was simple, complete, and logical, and that it provided at least a real and a final solution of the religious difficulty. It is also apparent that it was, of its own nature and not merely by the obstinacy of its adherents, rigid and unyielding, for the completeness and finality by which it was chiefly recommended vanish at the first touch of compromise. The League principle was not formulated by Bright, nor did he ever declare his entire acceptance of it. But it proceeded from the understanding of men who had learned politics at his feet, and, in its simplicity, audacity, and thoroughness, it bears the manifest impress of his mind. As a work of art it is to be catalogued as of the school, if not from the hand, of Bright.

In his absence it was rejected, in despite of entreaty and menace, by Forster and Mr. Gladstone, who threw education back into that turmoil of the sects from which they had an opportunity, not easily to be recaptured by any other statesmen, of giving it deliverance. "When a contest comes for a School Board", said Bright in 1873, "the question of real education seems hardly ever thought of, but there are squabbles between Church and Chapel and secularists, and I do not know how many other things. And when the School Board meets, there is priest and parson and minister, and they are partisans, and there is no free breeze of public opinion passing over the proceedings, but rather an unwholesome atmosphere of what I may call sectarian exclusiveness from which nothing good may come."

Bright had described the plan of education which he favoured during the election of 1868. He proposed a school committee elected by the ratepayers in every Poor-law Union, rejecting the alternatives of parish or county committees. The committee was to determine whether there was a deficiency of schools in its district, and where new schools were wanted; they were to have powers to borrow money to build schools, and "to levy from all the property in the district a sufficient amount of rate to repay in time the debt, and at the same time to support the schools from year to year". As for the existing voluntary schools he said, "I would leave them at present just as they are. They would work on, doing their meritorious work, and I hope" (alas for the vanity of hope) "without any jealousy of the new schools which would be created." He expected that the new schools "would be in all points so good that gradually all disinclination to this system on the part of the friends of the present schools would vanish", and he added that he "looked to the time when all the existing schools would be given up to the new and general system, until

at last—and it would not be long before that would
happen—the whole common school education of the
country would be placed under a general broad system
of district and municipal management". He did not,
however, indicate his opinion whether the common
schools should be open entirely without fee, and whether
attendance should be compulsory. Compulsion was in
general distasteful to him, as he showed for example by
his dislike of compulsory vaccination. When it came,
he did not actively resist it, but he described himself as
" not a fanatical supporter of any strict or rigid compulsion ".

Of the religious difficulty Bright took a view which
has, unhappily for education, proved far too sanguine.
" It is a difficulty which is every day lessening. It has
never been great in the minds of the great body of the
people. It is a difficulty which has mainly been created
by the ministers of religion, not with any wrong intention, but because their eyes were directed so much to
one question, and to one great object of human endeavour,
that they seemed to feel it necessary to tie it up with
everything else." Bright, it must be remembered, belonged to a religious community which does without a
professional ministry. He looked to the Sunday-schools
to " supplement the general education of the people in
ordinary instruction by giving them that religious instruction which may be of value to them ". Two years
later, just before his illness, he repeated this opinion.
He thought " one day in seven a reasonable time for
religious instruction ", and that the religious organization was " sufficient for teaching religion in the sense
that is meant by those who say that education is of no
value unless it be taught alongside and mixed up with
distinct religious teaching ". In the day-schools he
thought that it would suffice to teach "what every right-
minded teacher would undertake—to teach every child

love of truth, the love of virtue, the love of God and the fear of offending him ".

Such was the basis on which Bright would have tried to induce his colleagues to frame the Education Bill, had he not been removed from their counsels by illness. Of Forster's Act he expressed his opinion after his return in 1873. "The Education Bill was supposed to be needed because the system that up to 1870 had existed was held to be insufficient and bad; and the fault of the Bill is to my mind that it extended and confirmed the system which it ought to have superseded. It was a Bill to encourage denominational education and, where that was impossible, to establish Board Schools. It ought to have been a Bill, in my opinion, to establish Board Schools, and to offer inducements to those who were connected with denominational schools to bring them under the control of the School Boards."[1] This was also the opinion of the Birmingham Liberals; but, even with Bright's assistance, they failed to convince the leaders of their party. It must be remembered that Forster had asserted that the school-rate would not exceed three-pence, except in a few very poor districts, where it might touch fourpence; and that this statement, offered without a word of proof, was accepted without a single question by the House of Commons. The rapid rise of the rate to three, four, or five times this amount drove the Birmingham plan out of the region of practical politics. Having secured compulsion, the League party concentrated their efforts, with ultimate success, upon the abolition of school fees.

In order to complete and dismiss this question, it must be added that in 1876 Bright supported Mr. Dixon's Bill for extending the School-board system.

---

[1] Rogers (*Public Addresses of John Bright*, p. 202) reads "under the control of the Privy Council". I cannot believe that this is what Bright meant; anyhow it is not what he said.

He was not, he said, wedded to School Boards if they were not the best plan; but he called on the Government to produce a better plan if they would not accept School Boards. He declared himself satisfied with the success of the Boards; and, after describing a visit to a Board School in the East-End, he said, with some forgetfulness of the part he had taken in 1847, "When I left that school I confess I did not know whether most to rejoice or to weep. I could rejoice at seeing what I had seen of what is now being done: I could have wept at the thought that for so many generations the children of that class in this country and in this city have been almost absolutely and entirely neglected." He opposed the clauses in the Conservative Bill of the same session which seemed to be prejudicial to the School Boards. But in 1880, after further experience of School Boards, he said that he was sorry that Forster had not adhered to his original proposal of entrusting the education of municipal boroughs to the Town Councils instead of to specially elected bodies.

Bright made one or two appearances in the House of Commons in 1872. In September of the following year, when, after the failure of the attempt made by the Government to establish a new University in Ireland, Mr. Gladstone reconstructed his Cabinet, he rejoined it as Chancellor of the Duchy of Lancaster. But he did not speak in Parliament during the session of 1873, and the speech already quoted, delivered to his constituents in October of that year, marks his return to the activity of public life. His illness had condemned him to four years' silence in Parliament.

Some of the most important victories of his political principles were completed during his absence. The third of his three heads of Reform was accepted by the passing of the Ballot Act. He had peculiar reason to rejoice in the submission to arbitration of the American claims in respect of the depredations of the *Alabama*. "When the pen of history", he said, "narrates what has been done in regard to this question, it will say that that treaty and that arbitration, conducted by Lord Granville and Mr. Gladstone, added a nobler page to the history of England than if they had filled it with the records of bloody battles." Another question in which he had all his life taken the most lively interest, and on which he had made his first speeches even before he joined the Anti-Corn-Law League, had been settled in 1868 by the abolition of compulsory Church Rates.

By this Act the third of the three great purposes which he had pursued with hope and energy that prevailed over the doubt and weariness of disappointment was at last accomplished; and he was disposed to the opinion that the work of his life was finished. This feeling, with the permanent lassitude left by the physical and mental sufferings of his two long illnesses, caused him from this time forward to hint frequently at retirement from public life. But, though his work could never again be as important as it had been to his party and to the country, his political friends were always unwilling to allow him to relinquish the position he had attained. He had laid down the axe of the pioneer; he remained the Nestor of his party, advising its more active leaders, and sometimes composing its strife.

In the Birmingham speech he suggested five more reforms to which the Liberals should devote their energy. These were: the assimilation of the county to the borough franchise, a further redistribution of seats, the repeal of the Game Laws, a Free Breakfast-table, and what was now called Free Land.

He had popularized the term, a Free Breakfast-table, in 1868, in a speech at Edinburgh, after receiving the freedom of the burgh. "I once advised the Financial Reform Association of Liverpool, who are against all indirect taxation, to hoist a flag with the motto 'a Free Breakfast-table'—that, as the bread was no longer taxed, some effort should be made to untax the tea and the coffee and the sugar." But it soon appeared that the new voters preferred rather to spend what could be spared of the national income on education and other objects beneficial to themselves than to save their own contributions. The cry of economy has not been so attractive to the working as to the middle classes.

The term Free Land, unfortunately suggestive of schemes, abhorrent to Bright, which had not yet crossed the Atlantic, owed its acceptance in part to the attractive jingle it made with Free Church, Free Schools, Free Trade. Bright intended by it the removal of all obstacles created by law in the way of the distribution of land among many owners. Although he had held that such reforms of the Land Laws were not so urgently needed in England as in Ireland, because in England the manufacturing industries supplied the gradations of rank and position which it was the chief purpose of his Irish policy to create in Ireland, he had from the first made it clear that he desired those reforms in England also. "What the agricultural class of this country requires is that the land should be made absolutely free; that there should be steps by which the best, the cleverest, the most industrious, the most frugal of the agricultural labourers could gradually make their way to a higher and better social life. They can never do that with land laws such as we have—land laws which tend everywhere to great estates and great farms altogether beyond the reach of the expectation or dreams of the agricultural labourers." "There are natural forces at work", he said in 1876, "which cause or promote the accumulation of land, and natural forces which as certainly cause and promote the dispersion of land. What we are arguing for is that these forces should be allowed to work natu-

rally and freely, and that the law should not in any way
interfere with them, but that land should change just
as easily, and go into the possession of other persons
by that change, as any other kind of property which
men possess. The result of such a change in the law
would be that land as a whole would find itself always
in the possession of that class of the population which
will do the best for the land and for the people who
dwell upon it." The *latifundia*, which he disliked as .
being both the symbol and the mechanism of aristocratic
supremacy, still exist; they would probably, being maintained rather by traditionary habit than by law, survive
any legislation stopping short of such interference with
the liberty of ownership as he at least would not tolerate; but by other methods something has been done
to open a more hopeful career to agricultural industry
and thrift.

Bright's proposals were offered on the presumption
that the next Parliament also would occupy itself with
measures devised by a Liberal Government. That expectation was to be disappointed. In January, 1874,
Mr. Gladstone surprised the country by a dissolution.
Bright and his two colleagues were returned for Birmingham without opposition. But elsewhere the Liberals
lost many seats; the Conservative reaction proved to
be a reality; and Mr. Disraeli found himself not only
Prime Minister, but for the first time in command of a
majority of the House of Commons.

Disraeli had touched with a needle one cause of the
waning of the popularity of the Liberal Government in
his description of their measures as "harassing legislation". Bright retorted that if the Conservatives had
been in the wilderness they would have condemned the
Ten Commandments as harassing legislation. It was
hard for a man who had said that most of our evils are
caused by the interference of the State to confess that

the Government of which he was a member had inter-
fered overmuch.

Bright himself selected for special remark three of
the causes that had contributed to this memorable defeat.   The first was the disunion caused by the *mauvais
coucheurs* of the party, whom he described as "men
possessed not of an idea, but by an idea".   The second
cause was the permanent and solid power of the Land
and the Church; and the third the wrath of the publicans, whose interest had been harassed by Bruce's
early-closing Act, and was threatened by the Temperance party with further interference.   In the early years
of democracy the influence of the publicans was a force
not to be despised.   The old-fashioned publican was in
the position of the chairman of a workmen's club.   He
was often the oldest inhabitant of the street, a man of
substance as compared with his neighbours, and frequently generous in disposition; he was commonly the
best informed of the group that met in his parlour in
the evening, and, if not the only reader, the only man
who had had time to study the politics of the day in the
daily paper.   He was, in short, the interpreter of politics
to a small coterie of voters, and when the election came
he could often take his company with him to the poll.
His political power has since been weakened by the
Education Act, the halfpenny evening paper, and the
tied-house system.   But in 1875 Bright was justified in
respecting him as a formidable antagonist.

No one, however, could at that time discern that the
change in the balance of parties was due to a quality
of the new democracy that has since proved itself to be
of the most serious importance.   Every general election
since the Reform of 1867 has resulted in a transference
of power from one party to the other, if we except the
doubtful case of 1885, when a new army of voters was
called out.   No political wisdom, no legislative success,

no eloquence of advocacy, no art of organization, has prevailed against the imperious force of the swing of the political pendulum.   It is now manifest that the victory of the Conservatives in 1874 was the first example of the operation of a force that works, as it were, with the inexorable precision of a law of nature.

Two causes of this discomposing phenomenon may be suggested.   Under modern democratic conditions each party is so sensitive of the general trend of public opinion that it can always save itself by timely concession from falling into a hopeless minority.   In the freedom of private conversation we can always discover divergences of opinion such as would, unless something checked, split the electorate into many groups.   The check is supplied by the instinct of party, so strong in the English race.   That instinct encourages the surrender of sectional purposes against which the balance of public opinion has decided.   The result is that, in whatever direction the country is carried by the hidden laws that guide the broad current of national opinion, the division between the two parties will, at any moment, approximately bisect the electorate.   When the balance of parties is even, what is called the verdict of the country is the verdict of a body of voters, respectable neither in number, nor in intelligence, nor in public spirit—the grumblers, who are always in opposition.

The second cause may be found in the large expectation which the populace is encouraged to entertain of what Government can do, ought to do, and will do for them.   This expectation, necessarily disappointed by each successive ministry, turns the tongue of the even balance in favour of the Opposition.   The promises that win success for a party at one election ensure its defeat at the next.

These reasons are independent of the theory of reaction,—a very disputable part of the philosophy of history,—the theory that, to take the example most frequently cited, accounts for the indecency of the Restoration by the prudery of the Puritans; as though Dryden would have been less obscene if Milton had permitted himself an occasional indelicacy! So far from offering examples of alternating reaction from one extreme to its opposite, the history of England since 1868 exhibits the policy of each party—Disraeli's imperialism for example—exercising a positive and attractive rather than a negative and repellent influence upon that of its rival, and upon the general tendency of national opinion.

Hitherto the movement of opinion in the Liberal party had been uniformly in Bright's direction. From this time forward it is possible to discern changes which, so far as they went, tended to draw the party away from his ideals. The ear of the democracy was being caught by a new school of Radicals, who did not reject, but who were not content with, the Manchester doctrine. Their outlook was wider, their democratic sympathies broader, their principles less rigid, than those of the school in which Bright was reared. It might be misleading to apply to this group of politicians in any absolute sense the terms Imperialist, Socialist, Opportunist; but, used relatively, these names may serve to indicate the most striking differences between the radicalism of the eighth decade and that of Cobden and Hume.

Bright had seen with exultation the adoption of his principle of non-intervention in European quarrels, and the decaying worship of the hated fetish of the Balance of Power. But the relinquishment of the risky and fidgety behaviour of the Palmerstonian period had left the foreign policy of the party, in the opinion of its younger members, nerveless and indistinct. Bright had not only rejoiced in the policy, for which he gave chief

credit to Molesworth, that acquiesced without demur in
the demand of the growing colonies for self-government,
but he seemed to regard the tie that bound the settlements to England as one that might be broken without
regret; every extension of the area and responsibility
of the Empire made him uneasy; and he lived to treat
with disdain the idea of Imperial Federation. One of
the leaders of the new Radicals was the first man to
popularize the term Greater Britain, which contains in
itself the germ of the modern imperialist idea.

Bright again, as we have so often had occasion to
remark, was disinclined to any legislative interference
with freedom of action and liberty of contract. The
new Radicals were disposed to emulate the Conservatives in social legislation; nor did they share Bright's
distrust of trades-unionism. Bright remembered Joseph
Hume, the terror of Supply, with affectionate regret;
the new Radicals were liberal in their demands on the
public purse. They were interested in expanding the
progressive policy of the party; he retorted that the
party had already "too much policy". He did not like
the word programme, which about this time was introduced into the political vocabulary.

These differences, however, were not yet to be detected
by the ordinary observer. There was at no time any
quarrel or even debate between Bright and the younger
men who represented the newer conception of progress.
His tenacity of opinion forbids us to impute to him
without direct evidence any change of view. In the
weariness and the prudence of old age he became more
and more disposed to prefer silence to speech and
acquiescence to disputation. Whatever fear he may
have had of the socialistic tendencies of younger Liberals,
and whatever disappointment at the failure of his hope
that the new power would be used for retrenchment, were
eclipsed by one great apprehension that beset him in

his old age.   He became subject to depression, due no
doubt in part to physical causes, and disposed to take
a gloomy view of public affairs.   The fear that then
haunted him was that the working-classes, enfranchised
by his efforts, might, as time went on and their independence of thought and action grew, renounce the
doctrine of Free Trade.

This fear was never publicly expressed; for no event
befell that could justify the discussion of such a possibility.   But often when men were assembled to hear
him, he passed by the burning questions of the moment,
and told again the story of what free trade and the
free-traders had done for the country.   Hostile critics
discovered self-complacency in these speeches.   But
they were delivered for the practical purpose of keeping
steadily before the mind of the younger generation of
voters the lessons of the history which the speaker himself had helped to make.   He saw that the working-
classes were setting at nought in their unions what
appeared to him to be the orthodox and irrefragable
teachings of political economy.   Where, then, was the
security that they would not be persuaded by blind
guides to despise the doctrine that forbade protection?
If that doctrine was mathematically demonstrable, not
less so was the doctrine they already disdained.   " I
believe", he said in 1875, " that all combinations which
are intended to affect the rate of wages are acting upon
a principle of protection, which in their case is just as
evil as it was in the case of landed proprietors and the
various manufacturers who at different times have had
protective duties in their favour.   There appears to be
a general opinion among many of them, that, if people
could do less and produce less, by some necromancy
every one would have rather more.   It appears to me
from what I know of the gospel of industry, that it is
as likely by combination to make men immortal as it is

by combination to fight against the laws upon which profits and wages are based."

Not many men dependent for their seats on the votes of artisans would have ventured to say so much. Fifteen years earlier, when there was a strong indignation against the trades-unions and the practice of striking, Bright had declared that, though nine strikes out of ten had better be avoided, the unions were justified in holding strikes as a reserved force to be used in the last emergency. He was no flatterer of the populace. He defended the trades-unions when they commanded no voting power; after he had won them their votes, he gave them unwelcome advice.

When before the session of 1875 Mr. Gladstone resigned the leadership of the Liberal party, Bright's position in its ranks was indicated by his call to the chair of the meeting at which the new leader was chosen. Despite the divergence caused by the innovations of the new Radicals, Lord Hartington was chosen with a unanimity that was in part due to confidence in Bright's mediation. But events were imminent that recalled Mr. Gladstone from his brief retirement, and that aroused Bright to the last outburst of his old energy. Though he was becoming more and more inclined to leave the political battle to other combatants, and though he was incapable of repeating the labours of the Free-trade campaign and the popular agitation for Reform, he could not sit quiet when the Eastern Question was reopened, and when the ghost of the Crimean policy began to walk.

Early in 1875 the revolt of Herzegovina and Bosnia against Turkish misrule excited hopes and fears of the disruption of the Ottoman Empire, unless Britain or Europe should once more intervene to save its integrity. In October of the same year the Porte made what was equivalent to a declaration of bankruptcy. Later in the same year its rejection of the Andrassy Note, a diplomatic instrument by which the Powers essayed to impose reforms on the Sultan, marked the first signal failure of the European concert as the machinery for protecting the Christian subjects of the Porte. In the following May Bulgaria revolted, and the Powers again intervened. But now the European concert was broken, and broken by Britain: for the Berlin Note, demanding favourable terms for the insurgents, and effective guarantees for the reforms, which was prepared by Germany, Russia, and Austria, and accepted by France and Italy, was rejected by Disraeli's Government.

To the Opposition the Government appeared by this action to be sacrificing to their jealousy of Russia a rare opportunity of doing something really effective for humanity and civilization in European Turkey, and their wrath rose to a white heat when the news came to hand of the unparalleled cruelty that had attended the suppression of the Bulgarian revolt. No oratory less copious or less ardent than Mr. Gladstone's could serve to give voice to the popular indignation. He left his books, and led with tremendous effect the cry of outraged humanity. At this point the great majority of Britons appeared to join in the demand that Britain, notwithstanding any engagements of treaty, should at once and for ever dissociate herself from complicity with Turkish misrule. Disraeli however declared firmly that he would never consent to any step that might imperil the Empire of Britain.

In the autumn Servia and Montenegro made war upon the Turk, with the connivance of Russia. They were soon crying quarter; and the intervention of Europe again became necessary. At the end of the year there was a conference of the Powers at Constantinople, Lord Salisbury representing Britain. The European Concert appeared to be restored, but the Turk refused to sacrifice the fruits of victory at the dictation of the Powers. The situation now resembled that which followed the rejection of the Vienna Note in 1854. But the British distrust of Russia had now to contend with the more powerful sentiment of disgust at Turkish misrule. If the crisis was similar, the issue was different. Bright attributed the obstinacy of the Turk to his expectation that, as in 1854, Britain would still support him against Russia though he should neglect her advice. Lord Salisbury's voice, he said, was overpowered by the "rowdy war party" in England, who "were speaking in another voice and stimulating and encouraging the Turk to resist". "There is always a war party", he said later. "It is found in the press constantly. Unfortunately for the public interest, there is hardly anything that tends so much to enhance the profits of the proprietors of newspapers as a stirring and exciting conflict."

In April, 1877, Russia declared war on Turkey. It took the Russians all the rest of the year to bring the Turks to their knees. On December 10 their victory was assured by the unconditional surrender of the Turkish forces beleaguered at Plevna. By this time British opinion, which had been so strongly hostile to the Turks at the time of the Bulgarian atrocities, appeared to be evenly divided between the belligerents. The war fever of 1854 reappeared, and rose higher as the Russian army approached Constantinople. Parliament met early in 1878, and the Government took a vote of credit for six millions, as a warning to Russia not to pursue the rights of conquest so far as to threaten British interests. A notable addition was made at this time to our political mythology. That part of the population which is least distinguished by intelligence and sobriety, in calling upon the Ministry to fight rather than allow Constantinople to become a Russian port, invoked the aid of Jingo, the tutelar divinity of those ambitions which were afterwards oddly associated with the modest primrose.

Bright addressed many public meetings during these events. His views on the question, simplified as they were by his life-long disdain of the traditions of the Foreign Office, admit of a brief summary.

So far from resenting he welcomed the intervention of Russia. After the Crimean war Russia had been compelled to renounce the protectorate of the Christian subjects of Turkey; but the European Powers which had undertaken the duty had proved incompetent to perform it. "The Russian protectorate was a reality; the protection of the conjoint Powers is only a sham. There has been no protection." He admitted that it was impossible to tear up without negotiation the treaty of 1856; but he urged the Government to "negotiate on new terms, with better principles and a better policy". "Let us dissolve partnership", he exclaimed, "with a Power which curses every land that is subject to it." When Russia declared war, Bright justified that action. The verdict of Europe had been given against the Turk; Russia had only undertaken to enforce the verdict; and "if the verdict of the Conference was a righteous verdict, it seemed only in accordance with reason and with logic that someone should enforce it".

He refused to believe either that any British interest was endangered by the action of Russia, or even that Russia had any designs hostile to Britain. "No nation has been in disposition more friendly to this nation than Russia." "There is no nation on the Continent that is less able to do harm to England." The only interest England had in the Levant was "the constant free maintenance of the passage through the Suez Canal", and that freedom would not be more endangered by the presence of a Russian fleet in the Mediterranean than by the presence there of the fleets of other Powers. Even if Russia held Constantinople, why should Constantinople imperil our route to India any more than Toulon and Spezzia? We could always rely on the help of Europe to keep the Canal open. It was written in the book of fate, he said, that the Bosporus would ultimately, and not remotely, be open to all the nations of the world; and why should not the Bosporus be as open as the Canal?

As for the Central Asian aggressions by which Russia was believed to be preparing for an attack on India, Bright was content to say that "the interest of this country with regard to Russia in connection with India is an unbroken amity". The Government seemed to hold the doctrine of 1854, but the opinion of half the country had swung round. "Now a man may have an opinion in favour of peace, and the dogs of war will scarcely bark at him."

On March 3, 1878, the Treaty of San Stefano was signed by Russia and Turkey, and it was found that Russia did not intend to occupy Constantinople. Nevertheless the British Government felt it their duty to intervene with the other Powers for a revision of the terms of peace, which indeed they loudly condemned. Bright taunted them with "going to a conference with shotted cannon and loaded revolvers", and with professing to defend "what they called European law", although "Europe repudiates our European law". He charged them with "constant deception practised on the House of Commons and the country by professing a wish for peace whilst engaged in acts distinctly provocative of war"; and with "interposing obstacles in the way of any arrangement for the settlement of the Eastern Question on any basis favourable to the freedom of the oppressed Christian population of the Turkish provinces".

Before the Conference at Berlin was held the Ministry was weakened by the secession of Lord Carnarvon and

Lord Derby. Lord Derby was on friendly terms with Bright, and it had long been suspected that Bright exercised a strong influence over his mind. Beaconsfield and Lord Salisbury went to Berlin, and brought back "peace with honour". The Prime Minister of Britain had approved himself, in the opinion of European diplomatists, one of the great statesmen of Europe; and Britain had recovered the prestige that had seemed to die with Palmerston. It was not to be expected that Bright would join in congratulating the ministers on their feat. He had never believed in any danger from Russia; Britain, he thought, was afflicted only with a "chronic fear based on ignorance of the facts"; and therefore he had no thanks to give to those who had averted a peril created by a diseased imagination. Moreover, although many provinces were happily delivered from the Turkish yoke by the arms of Russia and the Berlin negotiations, part of Bulgaria was disappointed of its independence. Bright and the Liberals, whom he had at last persuaded to regard the dismemberment of the Turkish Empire as an object of hope rather than fear, believed that the power of Britain had been used "to hand back to the Turkish Government a population which Russia, left to herself, had delivered". If there had been no war, there had been "the menace of needless war". Also the six millions were spent. The Government, said Bright in 1879, had been "imbecile at home, and turbulent and wicked abroad". At the election of 1880 he reiterated his contention that war had been averted not by the prudence and skill of ministers but by the pacific determination of the people.

The sober verdict of history will never agree exactly with the hot recrimination of partisans. But the difference between the conduct of this country in 1854 and 1878 is a phenomenon that historians will have to explain; and no explanation will be complete that omits

the gradual influence of Bright's persistent appeals from
ambition and jealousy to reason and moderation.

---

## Chapter VIII.

### Last Years.

When Bright attacked Disraeli's foreign policy as
turbulent and wicked, he was thinking not only of the
risk the Government had run of war with Russia, but of
their expedition to Afghanistan in pursuit of a scientific
frontier, of the fighting in South Africa that followed
the attempt to annex the Transvaal, and of the responsibility they had undertaken in conjunction with France
for the good government of Egypt. All these transactions were grievous to Bright. He had so little sympathy with the national sentiment that is flattered by
such enterprises that he was hardly able to understand
it, and was in the habit of imputing motives which the
statesmen attacked could have disavowed with entire
sincerity. Yet he was equally sincere in making the
imputations. He was not betrayed into them by the
spirit of party, for he would hold the same language
when his own political friends committed the same
offence. The latest example occurred when in 1885 all
parties called for an expedition against Theebaw, the
bloodthirsty tyrant of Burmah. Bright, who had justified for humanity's sake the American civil war and the
Russian war against Turkey, accused the newspapers
that were exciting British sentiment by reports of
Theebaw's transgressions of "acting in the interests of
the civilians and the officers, all hungry for more territory, for more patronage, for more salaries, for more
pensions, for more honours and promotions when the
war was over". The view that he uniformly adopted

of such adventures having been sufficiently illustrated, it is unnecessary to quote his opinions on the details of Beaconsfield's imperial policy. Between 1870 and 1880, even after his recovery, he spoke very rarely in Parliament; and his condemnation was expressed briefly and in general terms.

At the general election of April, 1880, the Liberals regained a majority. Bright retained his seat without difficulty, one of his opponents being Burnaby, the famous soldier and traveller. The election was immediately followed by the resignation of Beaconsfield; and Bright accepted office under Mr. Gladstone as Chancellor of the Duchy of Lancaster. The policy of the Conservative Government in India was reversed; but in South Africa it was maintained until after the defeat of our forces by the Boers of the Transvaal at Majuba Hill, nor did the new Government retire from the responsibility contracted by their predecessors in Egypt.

Bright spoke with more frequency in this than in the two previous Parliaments. But, though his reputation always ensured a respectful hearing, and though he never spoke without some traces of the old fire and force, it was evident that the weariness of forty years' contention had fallen upon him. Except his defence of the Irish policy of the Government, to which events not then foreseen have given a special significance, there is not much to record in this, the penultimate period of his career.

He took some part in the discussions raised by the claim of Mr. Bradlaugh, member for Northampton, first to make a simple affirmation of allegiance, in the form permitted to Quakers, in place of the customary oath, and afterwards, when it was proved that he was not included in the general permission, to take the oath in spite of his recorded objection. Bradlaugh was widely known as a public assailant of Christianity, and many

members were incensed by his attempt to use the forms
of the House as an opportunity for the ostentation of
his opinions on religion.   But if his object was to adver-
tise himself and his views, the course which the House,
rejecting the guidance of the Government, adopted, was
exactly such as to serve such a purpose.   The dignity
of the Commons was staked, as in the case of Wilkes,
upon a struggle not only with Bradlaugh, but with
the constitutional rights of his constituents.   They
allowed themselves to make an unconstitutional use
of the oath itself, which had certainly been intended
not as a test of religious orthodoxy, but merely as a
guarantee of loyalty.   Bright refused to be a judge of
any man's religious opinions.   "I have myself passed
through many doubts, and have learned not to condemn
without sympathy, or not to condemn at all, those who
are unable to adopt the same views that I entertain."
Still more characteristic was the boldness with which he
struck at the root of the contention.   "Do you suppose
that the Founder of Christianity requires an oath in this
House to defend the religion which He founded?   Do
you suppose that the Supreme Ruler of worlds can be
interested in the fact of a man coming to this House
and taking His name in vain, or in a man being permitted
to make an affirmation reverently and honestly in which
His name is not included?"

He supported a Bill brought in by Sir W. Harcourt,
the Home Secretary, to protect tenant-farmers against
the depredations of ground game.   He was still in favour
of the entire abolition of the Game Laws, and while
supporting the Bill as one introduced with "the honest
object of relieving farmers", he said plainly that it did
not meet his views on the question.   His old antipathy
to the landed aristocracy reappeared in this discussion,
and Sir W. Harcourt was rather insolently warned from
the Opposition bench that if he wanted to carry his Bill

he would do well to "muzzle his right hon. colleague". This incident may be regarded as the last scene of the historic feud of cotton-spinner and squire. The Bill was passed, and the Game Law question has since rested.

In the first session of this Parliament another controversy in which he was interested was decided. The Burials Bill, which gave to Nonconformists the right, under certain restrictions, of burying their dead with their own rites in graveyards attached to parish churches, was passed by large majorities. This proposal had at one time encountered strong opposition from the Church. The subject was one peculiarly adapted to Bright's eloquence, for no other orator of his time could touch with such felicity the springs of pathos and sentiment. "I would say to Churchmen," he had said in 1875, "if you were to deal with the Nonconformists of this country with more consideration and with more condescension, with more of what I call Christian kindness and liberality, in matters of this sort, you would find that the strength of the Church would not be lessened but increased, that the hostility with which in many parts of the country she is regarded would diminish, and that there would be a general subsidence of some of the animosity which must, I fear, to some extent prevail where there is a favoured and established church." There is evidence that Bright's appeals exercised a considerable effect on the minds of leading churchmen. Many of them were now disposed to make the inevitable concession graciously. Bright could not resist the temptation to rally the Opposition on the change in their demeanour. "I have always noticed that hon. gentlemen opposite, when they feel that their cause is nearly at an end, that a great question over which they have been fighting is given up, pluck up their courage and go to perdition in a very happy frame of mind."

In the third year of the ministry Bright withdrew from

the Treasury Bench.    The establishment of British control in Egypt, which is now recognized as having proved
the most beneficent of Disraeli's perilous enterprises,
had been accepted by Mr. Gladstone's Ministry.    But it
became necessary that Britain should either recede from
this engagement or maintain her authority by force.
Arabi, the War Minister of the Khedive, a man strong
in the affection of the army, put himself at the head of a
military revolt, the objects of which were suspected to
be the dethronement of the Khedive, the expulsion of the
Europeans, and the establishment of a military despotism.
He overawed the Khedive, and became possessed of the
fortress of Alexandria.    The French refused to join in
enforcing the authority which they shared with Britain,
but the British Government proceeded to extremities.
On July 11, 1882, Alexandria was severely bombarded
by the British fleet.    Four days later Bright's resignation was announced.    It gave no cause for surprise,
and he was content to give a brief and indefinite explanation of his reasons.    " For forty years ", he said, " I
have endeavoured to teach my countrymen an opinion
and doctrine which I hold, that the moral law is intended
not only for individual life, but for the life and practice
of states in their dealings with one another.    I think
that in the present case there has been a manifest viola-
tion both of the international law and of the moral law."

Bright was subject to some criticism both for staying
in the Cabinet while measures were taken which involved,
in the event of resistance, either stultification or an appeal
to arms, and again for not following his resignation and
his assertion of the moral law by a further attack on the
policy he condemned.    But his conduct is readily explained by the supposition that he was guided throughout by a sentiment of strong personal attachment to
Mr. Gladstone.    He would not desert his leader in spite
of his disapproval so long as a peaceful issue was

possible. Having satisfied his conscience by resignation, he would not embarrass his friend by criticisms
that could serve no practical purpose. It is evident
that according to his principle of non-intervention the
British had no business to go to Egypt at all. But
when they were once there, Bright was not bound by
any general principle of action to which he had ever
committed himself to call for withdrawal. He had never
suggested that we should retire from India. When the
Government of which he was a member was confronted
by the alternative of either engaging in warfare or submitting, for the sake of peace, to a disturber of peace,
he was in a dilemma of which the pacific principles that
he cherished do not appear to offer any solution. He at
least did not disclose the solution. He held his peace;
and we are left in ignorance of the method of dealing
with the Egyptian difficulty which he may have suggested
to his colleagues. During the rest of his life he often
recurred in his popular addresses, with an added touch
of melancholy, to the old topics of the waste of the blood
and treasure of nations on unworthy ambitions. But he
treated the question still in general terms. In the year
following his resignation he delivered an address as
Lord Rector of the University of Glasgow, an office for
which his competitor had been Mr. Ruskin. Here again
he poured out a flood of inspiring eloquence upon the
wickedness of a warlike and turbulent foreign policy.
The democracy had disappointed his hopes; and he
may be said to have spent his old age "ingeminating
'Peace, peace'."

His release from the restrictions of office enabled
him to break silence on the question of disestablishment. He had taken many earlier opportunities of declaring his sympathy with the purposes of the Liberation
Society. In 1875 he had devoted a very vivacious speech
at Birmingham to the Public Worship Bill. This Bill,

designed for the repression of ritualistic extravagances,
had been introduced in the House of Lords by the Arch-
bishop of Canterbury, and effusively welcomed by politicians of both parties in the Commons.    It had been
passed with approximate unanimity.    "I never knew
the House of Commons unanimous and enthusiastic
about a thing," said Bright, "except when it did not
know what it was doing and where it was going."   The
clergy of the Church of England " are set over us by
the State as instructors of morals and religion, and yet
their own friends declare that their conduct is so lawless
that it is necessary to have special legislation to keep
them in order ".    He conducted his audience to the conclusion that "the Church, whether we consider it as a
political institution or a religious institution, is greatly
out of harmony with the time ".    But he added, " I am
not asking you or any party or section of a party to
plunge into a violent agitation for the overthrow of the
Established Church of England.   I think it would be
a great calamity indeed that a change like that should
come through violent hatred and angry discussion—that
it should be accomplished by a tempest which would be
nothing but the turmoil of a great revolution."   In 1883,
however, he gave countenance to the crusade against
the establishment by taking the chair at a meeting of
the Liberation Society in Spurgeon's Tabernacle.   He
said that he had been forced early in life by his study of
the persecution to which his own sect had been subject
after the Restoration to ask himself the question: " Is
the State the better for its union with the Church, or
the Church the better for its union with the State?"
When it was replied that " the Church tends to make
the State more Christian, that is, more just and gentle,
more merciful and peaceful ", he tested this contention
by the behaviour of the Bishops in the House of Lords;
and finding that they had resisted the abolition of slavery

and the repeal of capital punishment for larceny, and had neglected other opportunities of Christianizing the policy of the State, he concluded that the union had had rather the opposite effect. He did not touch on the question of disendowment, though it is proper to infer from his profession of " perfect accord " with the Liberation Society that to him also disestablishment meant disendowment.

Bright's seventieth birthday was celebrated by public demonstrations of the respect and affection of the workmen in the employ of his firm and of his Rochdale townsmen. Two years later, in June, 1883, the completion of his twenty-fifth year of parliamentary service to the borough of Birmingham was celebrated in a fashion to which it would be hard to find a parallel in the history of parliamentary representation. He was received by his constituents with such honours as are rarely paid except to royal personages. An imposing procession carried him through the town in the midst of vast crowds of cheering citizens. In the presence of a throng of twenty thousand persons he received and acknowledged the gifts of his constituents and addresses from nearly two hundred political associations and clubs. Nothing could surpass the enthusiasm of these festivities; and no more memorable example has ever been exhibited of the spirit of gratitude of which it is sometimes cynically said that our political life is destitute. The secret of this extraordinary popularity is not far to seek. His eloquence no doubt contributed to it. Yet if there were but few orators of his time worthy to be classed with him, English public life produces many popular speakers of the second rank, and the crowning grace of style that raises him, in the estimation of critics, into the order of the few whose speeches are an abiding possession, was not a quality that would captivate the affection of a multitude of plain working men. A transparent sincerity that never condescends to dexterous evasion or plausible excuse is the quality which the people of this country chiefly delight to honour. Of all the public men of the century, Bright had won the highest reputation for saying exactly what he meant and for doing exactly what approved itself to his conscience as righteous.

It was generally recognized that the household suffrage established in the boroughs must be followed by household suffrage in the counties. Bright had supported the motion regularly introduced by Mr. Trevelyan for an equal franchise, and saw with satisfaction the Liberal Government addressing itself to the necessary completion of the scheme of Reform. It was not to be expected that this measure should be heralded by such popular agitation as had preceded the Reforms of 1832 and 1866. The villagers who were desirous, or who were assumed to be desirous, of admission to citizenship, a scattered population and slow of movement, could not be gathered together in processions or mass meetings; nor was any popular clamour necessary to stimulate the Ministry. Meetings were indeed held; but they were rather the rallies of a party anxious to carry its principles to a conclusion, and also to recruit its strength by a new enlistment, than demonstrations of unenfranchised men knocking at the gates of the constitution. Bright took some share in these proceedings. He attended a Reform Conference at Leeds, at which there was no lack of enthusiasm; but it was an organized enthusiasm, and the creak of the machinery was audible.[1]

In the year 1884 the Government proposed to deal with this question in two Bills, extending the suffrage

---

[1] For a fuller account of the course of events preceding and accompanying the third Reform Act, see the first volume of this series, *The Rise of Democracy*, ch. xiii., by J. H. Rose.

in the first, and making the redistribution of seats necessitated by the enlargement of the rural constituencies in a second Bill, which was to occupy the session of 1885. The Opposition met the Bill with an amendment declining to consider the extension of the franchise unless a measure of redistribution were at the same time submitted. Bright was put in the forefront of the battle, as though to revive the recollection of the days when he was the leader of an impassioned popular movement, and brought to the House the inspiration of the great meetings. He spoke immediately after Lord John Manners, who moved the Conservative amendment. But though he spoke, as always, with conviction, the fire of 1865 was not easily to be rekindled; and he had the unusual experience of seeing the audience that had crowded the House to hear the old orator on the old theme diminish as he spoke.

The Bill passed the Commons; but the Lords, encouraged to resistance by the apparent failure of popular enthusiasm, while recording their assent to the principle of equal franchise, postponed their acceptance of the Bill until the production of the scheme of redistribution. If the Liberals of the boroughs had called for the enfranchisement of the rural labourers with little more than a drilled and factitious earnestness, they were cordially indignant when the decision of their representatives on such a question was overruled by the hereditary chamber. Bright led the attack on the Lords with all his old impetuosity. "It was once said in ages past that the path to the Temple of Honour lay through the Temple of Virtue. The law-making peer goes into the Temple of Honour through the sepulchre of a dead ancestor." He quoted against the peers, who were arrogant because undisturbed by any fear of a coming election, some verses of the 73rd Psalm. "They are not in trouble as other men, neither are they plagued like other men;

therefore pride compasseth them about as a chain; they speak wickedly concerning oppression, they speak loftily." In the same speech he exhorted his constituents to "curb the nobles as their fathers had curbed the kings". Many proposals for facilitating this feat were produced in the excitement of the hour. Bright selected for his approval the suggestion that the veto of the Upper House should be disallowed in the case of a Bill sent up from the Commons a second time after its first rejection by the Lords.

Other Liberal leaders however showed a strong indisposition to raise so grave a question of constitutional reform, and preferred to avail themselves of the door which the Lords had left open for accommodation. Parliament was convened for an autumn session; and the dispute between the two Houses was soon conciliated. The scheme of redistribution proposed by the Government was shown to the Conservative leaders, and declared by them satisfactory. Having carried their point that the extension of the franchise should be accompanied by a measure giving adequate representation to the counties, the Lords accepted the Franchise Bill. The Redistribution Bill passed without difficulty early in the session of 1885. This measure approximated to the Chartist ideal of equal electoral districts as nearly as was possible without entire disregard of ancient boundaries. The few small constituencies that still remained were mostly in Ireland. Bright had been prominent in supporting, against those who asked for a more exact distribution of seats according to the number of electors, the claim of Ireland to retain, notwithstanding the decrease of her proportionate population, the representation apportioned by the Act of Union. His influence also contributed to the final relinquishment of all plans designed to secure the representation of minorities. He had always regarded these devices with peculiar aversion; and their disappearance must count as a victory of popular over philosophical radicalism.

The Parliament elected in 1880 will be remembered in history, not so much for its completion of the work of democratizing the constitution, or for its other efforts in legislation, as for the developments it witnessed of the perplexed Irish problem. It is not necessary here to attempt more than the briefest summary of the series of events that led to the momentous change of the Irish policy of the Liberal party in 1886, and to Bright's rupture with the colleagues with whom he had associated himself for so many years. The course of events was such as to bring into relief a side of Bright's public character and of his political creed which had indeed always been discernible, but had never had occasion to display itself so prominently.

The term Home Rule had long been familiar to the House of Commons when the Parliament of 1880 assembled; and for ten years the case of the Irish Home-rulers had been presented to the House with ability and moderation, but without much effect. As early as the beginning of 1872 Bright had had occasion to contradict a report circulated at an Irish election that he was " an advocate of what is called Home Rule in Ireland ". He wrote: " To have two representative legislative assemblies or parliaments in the United Kingdom would, in my opinion, be an intolerable mischief; and I think no sensible man can wish for two within the limits of the present United Kingdom, who does not wish the United Kingdom to become two or more nations, entirely separated from one another ".

In 1879 Isaac Butt, the first leader of the Home Rule party, had died, and had been succeeded by Mr. Shaw. In the same year the Land League had been formed by the efforts of Mr. Michael Davitt and others, and was conducting, both by the methods of the English leagues, and by other methods which those leagues had sedulously avoided, an agitation for Home Rule and for further reforms in the Irish land-system. When the Parliament met, Mr. Parnell, who had been elected for Meath in 1875, sat as the leader of an advanced section of Home-rulers, apart from those who under Shaw's leadership still offered a qualified support to the Liberal Government. This section of the Irish party had already in the former Parliament initiated the Irish method of enlisting the interest of the House in Irish grievances by obstructing its ordinary business.

The first Irish measure of Mr. Gladstone's Ministry was conciliatory. A Bill was passed by the Commons providing for compensation for disturbance to evicted tenants, even when the eviction was for omission to pay rent, provided that omission was due to the failure of crops. This Bill was rejected by the Lords in August. Its rejection was followed by agrarian crimes in Ireland; and the organized persecution of Captain Boycott furnished agitators with a striking example of a new method, and added a new word to every European language. In the same autumn Parnell and other Irish leaders were prosecuted for seditious conspiracy; but the jury disagreed. In 1881 a Bill authorizing the Lord-lieutenant to imprison without trial persons suspected of treasonable practices or intimidation was passed. It was followed by a Land Bill designed to establish Fair Rent, Fixity of Tenure, and Free Sale; the first of the three F's being secured by the appointment of a Land Court, with power to fix judicial rents. On October 13 Mr. Gladstone's announcement of the arrest of Mr. Parnell was received with great enthusiasm in England, and with unmeasured indignation in Ireland. Parnell retaliated by issuing the famous No-rent manifesto. Towards the close of the year reports of a convention of American Irishmen and Irish politicians, and of speeches there uttered that burned with implacable and unscrupulous enmity to the Crown and people of England, filled Englishmen of all conditions and opinions with strong indignation, and seemed for the moment to separate the Parnellites more widely than ever from the sympathies of all the English parties alike.

In the spring of 1882 the Government decided to release Parnell. This release was sharply criticised by the Opposition, and was displeasing to Forster, the Irish Secretary, who had made himself grievously unpopular in Ireland by his rigour in using the powers given to him by the Coercion Bill. He resigned, and was succeeded by Lord Frederick Cavendish. On May 6, the day of his arrival in Dublin, Cavendish and Burke, one of the permanent officials of the Irish Government, were assassinated by a secret society in Phœnix Park. A new Coercion Act was immediately carried. The Irish juries having habitually failed to convict in cases where the evidence was clear, provision was made to substitute a special commission for the jury. The remedial measure of the year was a Bill providing for the payment of arrears of rent out of the Irish Church fund. In the same session a new weapon was forged to be used against Parnell's obstruction, the House of Commons assuming the power to limit the duration of its debates.

Throughout this troubled period Bright gave a cordial support to the policy of Mr. Gladstone's Government. To the Irish Nationalists his speeches were often highly offensive. He was frequently selected by them as the object of their most animated invective, and the disappointment they professed at finding him among their most vehement antagonists was not necessarily insincere, however unreasonable it may seem to the candid student of his career. He was almost the only English statesman of eminence who had attained a high degree of popularity with the Irish people; and the opposition, always resolute and sometimes acrid, which he offered to the demands of the party led by Parnell, was an obstacle to be broken down, as such obstacles are broken down in politics, by the battery of vituperation. A just examination of all his speeches and letters on the Irish question will discover nothing to support any charge of inconsistency, or to justify the surprise which the Parnellites expressed when he denounced their methods and rejected their proposals as dishonest.

Bright was above all things a lover of order. He had striven with surprising success to restrain within the limits of order a hungry populace calling for bread, and a voteless populace clamouring for citizenship. No man was more strongly disposed to abhor the disorderly, not to say criminal, methods of agitation practised in Ireland—the systematic breaches of contract, the refusal of rent, the boycotting, the hamstringing, the moonlight outrages, the threatening letters, the secret assassinations. He was a democrat; and for democracy's sake he was troubled at heart by an infection of the Irish populace that seemed in danger of bringing democracy itself into contempt. His dislike to intimidation is measured by the earnestness with which he had cried for the Ballot; and the intimidation of the Land League and the priests, whatever may be pleaded in its excuse, was in itself vastly more cruel than any intimidation charged against the English squires. He always strove, even against the weight of evidence, to relieve the Irish populace from the burden of opprobrium by throwing it wholly upon their leaders. If he judged the Irish members too harshly,—and no man judged them more severely, —it was because his judgment was prejudiced by his desire to save the credit of the Irish people.

He had devoted himself to reforms intended to purge

the House of Commons of the excessive influence of a dominant class. He had succeeded; and the House was at last, to his mind, a legislature capable of large and popular achievements. When therefore the Irish members tried to impair by obstruction the legislative activity of the Commons, Bright regarded their action with the indignation of an artificer who should see a machine that had been repaired and improved by his own skill and patience thrown out of gear by the malice of mischievous enemies; and when they adopted a course of action avowedly based on disbelief in the capacity and inclination of the Imperial Parliament to redress the grievances of their constituents, Bright could not admit that distrust without admitting also the failure of his own labours. He could not bear to hear the reproach of neglect of popular interests and contempt of popular appeals, which he himself had urged against the oligarchy, repeated against the perfected organ of the English democracy. Parliament had, indeed, actually adopted measures of justice and conciliation that had been devised by his sagacity or approved by his advocacy; the Church had been disestablished, the Land Law reconstructed, the franchise extended; and the outcry of the Parnellites sounded in his ears like a declaration of the incompetence of himself and his party.

Finally, Bright was an Englishman. His love of England was not the less fervid though he disdained the national vainglory and imperial ambition that feed the same passion in other men. All the prejudices and limitations that can be with any reason attributed to him are of the sort commonly called insular. Hence his indignation admitted no excuse for the vindictiveness of the Chicago Convention. Hence, too, he was not predisposed to assign any weight to the contention that Ireland must be governed by Irish and not by English ideas. The ideas of English Liberalism seemed to him good enough not only for Ireland but for the whole human race. They were as sacred and universal, he often said, as "the laws that were given amidst the thunders of Sinai". Thus his principles, his prejudices, his achievements, his experience, all combined to set him in an attitude of resolute defiance to the leaders of the national movement in Ireland.

Nothing moved Bright's indignation more strongly than the comparison between the behaviour of the Land League and that of the Anti-Corn-Law League. "From 1839 to 1846", he said, "no man ever heard any of the recognized leaders, or lecturers, or speakers of the League say anything that was calculated to bring the people to disobey the law, and to the violence we have seen in Ireland. There was strong language used. I am not a bit ashamed of strong language. But it did not stimulate any man to violence. We directed the people to political efforts and to the ultimate justice of Parliament for the remedy of their grievance. What is it that these gentlemen have done? They have to a large extent demoralized the people whom they professed to befriend."

In a speech made in November, 1880, during the disquietude that followed the rejection of the Compensation for Disturbance Bill, Bright said: "Is there a remedy for this state of things? Force is not a remedy. There are times when it may be necessary, and when its employment may be absolutely unavoidable. But for my part I would rather discuss measures of relief as measures of remedy than measures of force, whose influence is only temporary, and in the long run, I believe, disastrous." A few months later he was supporting a stringent measure of force. But this Bill satisfied his condition, because it was accompanied by a remedial measure —the Irish Land Bill of 1881.

His contributions to the discussion of the Land Bill

were not important. There were five or six hundred thousand tenants, he said, who made public opinion for good or evil against fourteen thousand proprietors, who could by no means stand up against it. "The opinion of property is always in favour of property. The opinion of people who have no property is not any very great safeguard to people who have property. If land is to be made secure in Ireland, it must be by a system which by dividing the property in land will furnish it with a multitude of defences." With such terse and sagacious sayings as this he illustrated the general purpose of the Bill; but in accordance with a custom imposed on him by his consciousness of the limits of his powers, he left to others the defence of the methods proposed.

When he addressed his constituents in January, 1882, he defended the policy of coercion. "What I am in favour of is as much freedom as will give security to freedom. But I am not in favour of that freedom that would destroy it." There were English Liberals to whom the suspension of *habeas corpus* and like measures seemed a more grievous evil than the organized persecution of the Irish societies. "I am driven to the belief", said Bright, "that some of our friends are to some extent ignorant of principles on which alone democracy can be made tolerable in any country. What would these gentlemen do on board ship? In a storm they might protest if the captain took in canvas or closed down the hatches. Or if there happened to be any attempt at mutiny or piracy, they might object to the captain exerting his powers and putting the troublesome men in irons. They might prefer the loss of the ship to the infringement of their democratic ideas of freedom."

Bright eagerly supported the measure by which the House of Commons sought to free itself from the obstruction of the Irish members. "I believe", he had said at the Mansion House in 1881, "that the debates might be shortened; that is, when a man has said what the House evidently considers enough, there should be some mode of reducing him to silence." When the Closure was proposed he addressed himself to the fallacy that the right assumed by a deliberative assembly of limiting its own debates was at variance with freedom of speech. "What I have always understood by freedom of speech was not so much the quantity of the speech as the quality. It is freedom of speech when you can say whatever you think right, and when neither the power of the Crown on the one hand nor the law of libel on the other can interfere with you." The Irish members, he said, were "at liberty to hold their opinions—at liberty to conspire and rebel; but they were not at liberty to make it impossible for the imperial Parliament to transact the business of the nation".

The Conservative Opposition joined the Nationalists in resisting this proposal. Bright's indignation at this coalescence inspired a remark that was submitted to the censure of the House of Commons. Speaking of the Conservatives at his silver celebration at Birmingham he said: "They are found in alliance with an Irish rebel party, the main portion of whose funds for the purpose of agitation comes directly from the avowed enemies of England, and whose oath of allegiance is broken by their association with those enemies. The reform that is coming and must come cannot long be delayed, for it must suppress the power and close the era of the men who now afflict the House of Commons and from night to night insult the majesty of the British people." A week later Sir Stafford Northcote, the leader of the Opposition, moved that this language constituted a breach of the privileges of the House of Commons. Bright withdrew the word alliance, by which he said he had intended to imply no more than that the Conservatives and the Nationalists were acting together. But he refused to withdraw or modify his description of the Irish members. He repeated his charges; and the Liberals, not yet prescient of 1886, applauded him with enthusiasm. Although his withdrawal of the word alliance seemed to remove the immediate cause of offence so far as the Conservatives were concerned, many of them supported the protest of the Nationalists against Bright's imputation of disloyalty by voting in favour of Northcote's resolution.

Two years later this incident was repeated in circumstances that made it still more ominous. In June, 1885, the Liberal Government, weakened in public estimation by the Egyptian disasters, was unexpectedly defeated in a division on the Budget by the Nationalists and Conservatives; and a Conservative Government succeeded. Lord Spencer, who as Lord-lieutenant, with Mr. Trevelyan as Secretary, had administered the law in Ireland with courage and stringency, had been assailed by the Nationalist leaders with an acrimony that far exceeded the rather wide limits permitted by the custom of our party warfare. Accusations were brought against him which are now admitted to be absurd, and which were at the time regarded by his friends as insincere. Some of the younger Conservatives had permitted themselves to join in the less offensive of the attacks on Lord Spencer; and there were other indications which suggested the fear that, if the young Conservatives had their way, a bid would be made by their party for the Parnellite vote. Such was the suspicion of the Liberals; such too the expectation of the followers of Parnell, who ordered the Irish vote in the English constituencies to be given to supporters of the new Government.

Lord Spencer was entertained at a banquet by his political friends. There was much plain speaking, and

Bright's was, according to his habit, the plainest. "Who", he asked, "are Lord Spencer's assailants? They are to be found in some conductors of the Irish press, and in some of those who profess to be representatives of Ireland. These men are disloyal to the Crown, and directly hostile to Great Britain. They have obstructed all legislation which was intended to discover or to prevent or to punish crime. They have insulted and denounced every man in Ireland concerned with the just administration of the law. They have attacked indiscriminately every magistrate by whom any guilty man has been convicted. They have exhibited a boundless sympathy for criminals and murderers. There has been no word of pity for their victims."

When these words were read on the motion of an Irish member to the House of Commons, the whole Liberal party loyally associated themselves with Bright by their applause. Again he refused to apologize. "Every word of my speech was accurate and true. Two hundred of the first men of England accepted it as such." He put the supposition that he had said the contradictory of these remarks, and asked whether the Irish members would not have taken such a speech as insultingly ironical. Northcote refused to support the motion that Bright had committed a breach of privilege; however, he "much regretted" Bright's speech, and sympathetically advised the Irish members that "having repudiated these remarks with indignation they could afford to leave them unnoticed". Lord Hartington retorted by declaring that nine-tenths of the people of England would admit the truth of what Bright had said. For this indiscretion he was in his turn rebuked by Lord Randolph Churchill, the leader of the younger Conservatives, who was designated as Bright's antagonist at the coming election.

Birmingham had been divided by the Redistribution Act into seven parliamentary divisions. Bright was nominated for the Central Division, in which the chief strength of the local Conservative party lay. In Lord Randolph Churchill he met with the strongest opponent the Conservative party could place in the field against him. Churchill had seen more clearly than older Conservatives the changes of policy, of manner, and of organization, that were necessary to adapt the aristocratic party to a democratic environment. His popularity was then at its zenith, and he was the political hero of the younger generation. By his opposition to coercion, and by joining in the Parnellite attacks on Lord Spencer and Bright, he had secured the Irish vote. Although Bright was, for the first time in his career, meeting an opponent whose personal qualifications were formidable, he did not relinquish his dignified custom of taking no share in the personalities of the contest. In his election speeches he dealt chiefly with a recent and temporary revival of protectionist doctrine under the specious name of Fair Trade. The contest was sharp, and the issue at first doubtful. In the end Bright was returned by a large majority.

At this general election the Liberal party throughout the country had made effective use of the suspicion of a possible alliance between the Nationalists and the Conservatives. They based their appeal to the country upon their resistance to the Parnellite claims, and upon the sense of the danger that would ensue if the Liberal majority were insufficient to maintain a Government against a combination of Conservatives and Home Rulers. The effect of this appeal was weakened partly by the disasters in the Soudan, and partly by the fear of disestablishment. They lost many seats in urban constituencies; but when the counties were polled, these defeats were in part counterbalanced by the attractive-

ness of the Liberal promises to the agricultural labourer.
The majority of Liberals over Conservatives was slightly
smaller than the whole strength of the Irish Nationalists.
With such a Parliament no Government could be stable,
unless indeed it should be founded on some hitherto
unheard of coalition.

At first the Liberals scarcely recognized the possibility
that their own leaders might yield to the very temptation
to which they had begged the country not to expose
their Conservative rivals; and a rumour, circulated just
before the New Year, that Mr. Gladstone meditated an
alliance with the Nationalists was received at first with
incredulity and afterwards with consternation.  His assurances, however, were sufficient to secure the temporary
support of the Parnellites, and with their assistance the
Conservative Government was defeated early in the
session of 1886.  Mr. Gladstone formed an administration; but Bright and other leading Liberals withheld
their support until they should be better informed of
the new Irish policy which their leader had conceived.
When the new Government produced a Bill for establishing a separate Legislature in Ireland, and another
Bill under which the State was to purchase at a vast
outlay the estates of Irish landlords, the party was rent
by a formidable secession.  It soon became evident that
what was to be feared was not merely the temporary
withdrawal of malcontents into a Cave of Adullam, but
the formation of a new party in the State, started upon
its orbit with an impulse strong enough to counteract
the gravitation of the parent mass.  There had been for
some years reason to prognosticate a division of the
Liberal host, for the political aims of the new Radicals
were becoming more and more incompatible with those
of the less enterprising section.  But the most remarkable feature of the Unionist secession was that the new
fissure was transverse to the threatened line of cleavage,

the Radical wing of the old party contributing about one-half of the Liberal Unionist strength. Bright used his influence effectively to promote this revolt. He did not address the House in debate, but when the dissatisfied Radicals met to consult whether they should abstain from voting, or by voting against the Bill ensure the downfall of the Government, a letter from Bright announcing his own determination to vote was read, and encouraged his friends to take the bolder course.

On June 8 the division on the second reading of the Home Rule Bill was taken. It was defeated by a majority of thirty, ninety-three Liberals voting against it. Mr. Gladstone appealed to the country. Many of the Liberals who had forsaken the Government lost their seats; but the Conservatives, supported by the Liberal Unionists in the constituencies, won many victories, in spite of the transference of the Irish vote. The verdict was decisive; and the first Home Rule Ministry fell after a distracted existence of less than six months.

Birmingham returned six Liberal Unionists and one Conservative to the new Parliament. Bright himself was returned without opposition. He made one speech to his constituents justifying his desertion of the leader whom he had followed for so many years. This was the only speech he made upon the new issue, except one delivered a year later as chairman of a dinner at which the Liberal Unionist members entertained their leader, Lord Hartington. But in the confusion attending the rupture of the party many perplexed Liberals wrote to him for advice, and published his letters.

These letters, about forty in number, written hastily, but with great vigour and terseness, may be regarded as his last contribution to the guidance of his countrymen. They are distinguished even among Bright's utterances by the vehemence of their invective. He stood at the parting of the ways like a Hebrew prophet

testifying against backsliders. The controversy raised
by Mr. Gladstone's policy included a very large number
of points of dispute. Bright however, whose habit was
always to simplify discussion by concentration upon a
few salient points, confined himself mainly to three
topics. "I have not been moved", he wrote to Bishop
Magee, "by fears as to the breaking up of the Empire,
or as to the effect the proposed measure would have
upon Great Britain."

In the first place, he reiterated his refusal to believe
in the sincerity of the Liberals who had followed Mr.
Gladstone's lead on the Irish question. He was habitually severe, not to say uncharitable, in his moral judgments; and having once, with whatever justification,
formed the opinion that the newly-converted Home-
rulers had enslaved their conscience to that of their
chief, it was inevitable that he should condemn, with a
severity that no other Unionist ventured to assume,
their infidelity to the inward light. He took up the
position of a political Protestant asserting the right of
private judgment. "There are men in the House of
Commons", he said in his speech at Birmingham, "who
have no notion of anything but following. They have
no trouble in considering great questions. There is
their leader, and where he leads they follow. They
remind me very much of those gentlemen who go out
as tourists with Mr. Cook. They enjoy great security,
because they are personally conducted." His indignation did not often permit him to treat the subject in this
vein of good-humoured satire. "Surely", he wrote to
Mr. Gladstone, "when you urged the constituencies to
send you a Liberal majority large enough to make you
independent of Mr. Parnell and his party, the Liberal
party and the country understood you to ask for a
majority to enable you to resist Mr. Parnell, not to
make a complete surrender to him." "If Mr. Glad-

stone's great authority were withdrawn from these Bills,
I doubt if twenty members outside the Irish party in
the House of Commons would support them." "It is
notorious that scores of members of the House of Commons have voted with the Government who in private
have condemned the Irish Bills." "I have not been
able to march with the clubs and associations which
shout for measures which little more than a year ago
they would have condemned. We have not yet had
an infallible leader, and till he appears on the scene, I
must preserve my own liberty of judgment."

In the second place, Bright repeated again and again
in the new circumstances the unfavourable opinion that
he had formed long ago of those Irish politicians to
whom, in his view, Mr. Gladstone was making a capitulation. "I am asked why I cannot trust those leaders.
I do trust them most entirely. I have seen their course
for seven years past, and have heard and read their
speeches, and see in them only hatred to England and
disloyalty to the Crown." "The great English Liberal
party is called on to abandon its past policy and pros-
trate itself before an odious, illegal, and immoral
conspiracy." His patriotic sentiment was grievously
shocked by the suspicion that the Irish members sub-
sisted on "contributions from America, from men whose
avowed object is to separate Ireland from Great Britain,
and permanently to break up the union of the three
kingdoms". He spoke of "the disloyal and rebel
party", of "a conspiracy whose main object was to
plunder the landlords and excite bitter hatred of England", and of "men who had wholly ignored truthful-
ness and wisdom and justice for the last seven years".
The reasons which appear to have led the great English
democrat to adopt so detrimental an opinion of the
leaders of the Celtic democracy in Ireland have already
been noticed. What was new was his astonishment at

the new sympathies of those who had seemed to share that opinion with him. "I believe", he said, "that history has no example of a monarchy or a republic submitting to a capitulation so unnecessary and so humiliating."

The third topic on which Bright laid stress was the injustice which Home Rule would, in his opinion, inflict on the Englishry in Ireland, and especially in Ulster. "You are asked", he said in his speech at Birmingham, "to thrust out from the shelter and the justice of the United Parliament the two millions who would remain with us, who cling to us, who passionately resent the attempt to drive them from the protection of the Parliament of their ancestors." In his letter to Magee he wrote: "Nothing seems to me more shocking than the scheme of handing over the loyal portion of the five millions of the Irish population, being in number, I believe, at least two millions, to the government of men who have disturbed and demoralized Ireland during the last seven years."

In the early days of the disruption many schemes of compromise were suggested. Bright made the suggestion that every Irish Bill should after its first reading be submitted to a committee consisting of 103 Irish members, who should treat it as Bills are treated in committee of the whole House. The second reading was to be omitted, and the decisions of the Irish Committee were to be reviewed by the House only in the stage of report.

In the midst of the gloom that fell on his spirit at the snapping of old ties and the failure of the great engine of progress from which he had hoped so much, Bright slowly and sadly descended to his grave. "The moral sense of the Liberal party", he wrote in December, 1887, "seems to have become depraved, and all that we boasted of in its former character has for the time forsaken it. I suppose the cloud will lift some day, but

just now we are in great darkness.    Our duty is to go
on, honestly acting up to our convictions of what is true.
I am sorry I am not able to do more, but years creep
on, and their warning must not be disregarded."

In 1886 he was admitted to an honorary degree by the
University of Oxford.   His last speech at Birmingham
was delivered on March 29, 1888, on the occasion of a
banquet celebrating the return of his colleague, Mr.
Chamberlain, from a mission of peace to America.   He
spoke chiefly of projects already in the air for Imperial
Federation.   He rejected Federation as a "dream and
an absurdity", relying for the support of this opinion on
"the question of the tariffs, which divide the colonies
among themselves and divide them from us, and on the
question of our foreign policy, which tends to place
the colonies all over the world in a situation of peril
because of the uncertainty of the peace we are able to
maintain".

A few days later a statue of Bright was unveiled at
Birmingham.   His effigy now stands in a place of honour
in each of the three towns with which his name is im-
perishably associated—Rochdale, Manchester, and Birmingham.

When he made the speech just quoted the hand of
death was already upon him.   He had been ill in the
previous winter, and in May his trouble returned.   He
rallied again in the late summer, but in October he took
to his bed, and was never afterwards strong enough to
come downstairs.   In December his death was daily
expected, but the enemy was kept at bay for a few
months longer.   His daughter has recorded some simple
incidents of his last days.   He was weary and silent,
but patient and grateful to those who tended him.   He
called for Addison's versification of the 107th Psalm to
be read over to him till he had learned it by heart.
"His love for animals was amply repaid by the devotion

of his little dog Fly, who was always by his side, never willingly leaving the room from the time he was taken ill in May till the end came. She was a constant source of pleasure to him during those long months, and her head received the last caresses of the dying hand when all other power of expression was gone. The end came at last, quietly and without suffering, after many hours of unconsciousness, early in the morning of March 27, 1889."

He was buried with the studiously simple rites of his community in the graveyard attached to the Friends' Meeting-house at Rochdale. Many men whose names will be forgotten before his have been buried in the enviable sepulchres of our national temples. But to all who loved Bright it seemed most fitting that his grave should be encircled by the tombstones of those homespun worthies of his sect and kindred, from whose quiet lives he had inherited the creed, made famous and potent by his genius, of peace and amity and the equal dignity of manhood.

## Chapter IX.

### Bright's Oratory.

Lord Salisbury, speaking immediately after Bright's death, said of him: "He was the greatest master of English oratory that this generation—I may say several generations—has seen. I have met men who have heard Pitt and Fox, and in whose judgment their eloquence at its best was inferior to the finest efforts of John Bright. At a time when much speaking has depressed, has almost exterminated, eloquence, he maintained that robust, powerful, and vigorous style in which he gave fitting expression to the burning and noble thoughts he desired to utter." This judgment might be supported by the testimony of many other competent critics; it is indeed so generally accepted that it requires illustration rather than defence. Lord Salisbury's epithets do not, however, do justice to the most distinctive and admirable feature of Bright's oratory. If it was robust and vigorous, it was also emotional, sympathetic, sentimental. It was by virtue of a well-tempered combination of what may be called the masculine and the feminine elements of rhetorical persuasion that Bright claims the first place among the British orators of the century. It is impossible to give an adequate critical account of eloquence worthy of such high commendation. In the best oratory, as in poetry, there is a quality, the rarest of all, that eludes critical analysis and can only be referred vaguely to genius. A critic, applying one after the other the accepted critical tests of the art, might defend the judgment that Macaulay was a greater orator than Bright. The sense by which we revolt against such a judgment is the sense by which we perceive the last inimitable grace that lies beyond the reach of study and cleverness.

Although Bright owed his supremacy to an incommunicable gift of nature, it must not be supposed either that he achieved his oratorical triumphs without sedulous endeavour, or that his art reached the full perfection of accomplishment otherwise than by degrees. That his speeches in the days of the Anti-Corn-Law League were full of inspiration and conviction is proved by the rapidity with which his fame spread through the country, and by the popular association of his name with that of Cobden, the undoubted protagonist of the great struggle. But those who heard him during this period of his career describe his speeches as animated, impetuous, and exhilarating, but as consisting of mere passionate declamation, disorderly in arrangement and amorphous in style, and anticipating but rarely the majestic manner of his later orations. Many extracts from his speeches at Covent Garden and Free-trade Hall may be read in Prentice's *History of the League*. It is only here and there that the reader lights on some phrase that in humour or vividness or ingenuity or elevation gives promise of something better than the ordinary fluency of a demagogue content with emphasizing commonplaces. Perhaps the first speech in which Bright displayed his full power was a speech on Ireland delivered in the House of Commons on April 2, 1849. This speech was evidently carefully prepared; it was based upon genuine study of certain aspects of the Irish question. The peroration is not merely powerfully composed, but, unlike many of Bright's perorations, it really completes and summarizes the argument of the whole speech. The speech elicited a very high encomium from Disraeli.

Nor can there be any doubt that he took great pains in the preparation of his speeches. It was not his habit to write them out. He told a correspondent that his written notes contained only the heads of the leading arguments and facts, and that he "left the words to come at call while he was speaking". He added that he almost invariably wrote out the concluding words and sentences. The evidence of those who were in his society before he spoke proves that it was his custom to revolve his speech in his mind for some days. He must have chosen and rejected this or that turn until his forethought, perhaps unconsciously, had extended to the phrasing as well as the substance of his sentences. If he had to make a speech in the evening, his nervousness and preoccupation made him almost unapproachable for the whole of the day. When the speech was off his mind he became again genial and disposed for conversation. He once said, with humorous exaggeration no doubt, "I am always ill for a week before speaking". One of his hosts at Birmingham made the curious observation that he always complained of the cold when he came down to breakfast on the morning of a meeting. This preoccupation cannot have been caused merely or chiefly by his sense of the moral responsibility laid upon one who assumes the office of advising his countrymen on affairs of state; for it is difficult to conceive that Bright ever suffered misgivings as to the soundness of the counsel that he had to offer. It was rather the nervousness of the artistic temperament. He had a cultivated respect for his art, for his audience, and for his reputation. He was afraid, not that he might not say the right thing, but that he might not say it well. The notes that he took with him were merely a few heads and catchwords. Those that he used in his speech of July 1, 1886, have been preserved. They cover nine pages of note-paper; they are neatly written, and, being without erasure or interlineation, must have been copied from a first rough draft. A familiar quotation from Scripture is written in full, as though Bright distrusted his memory.

Mr. S. H. Butcher, discussing the art of the greatest orator of antiquity, finds none of the moderns worthy to take rank with Demosthenes, save only Edmund Burke. "John Bright", he says, "has almost every Demosthenic gift except that of strong and persistent reasoning. He is easily led away into emotional digression; some of his noblest passages are loosely connected with the subject, they are not wrought into the texture of the thought. The two most perfect types in which the eloquence of impassioned reason has hitherto expressed itself are found in Demosthenes and Burke."

The comparison here suggested between Bright and Burke is one from which those may shrink who wish to praise Bright without disparagement. Burke's understanding was far more ample and profound, his knowledge greater, his imagination more vigorous; his eloquence had a stronger wing and a loftier flight; he had at call the full opulence of the English tongue. One might prefer to measure Bright against a less august figure. Burke left a message for posterity; it may be found that Bright served only his own generation. If, however, the comparison is to be made, we may claim some compensating superiority for Bright. He possessed, whether by nature or art, a far greater power of adapting his eloquence to his audience. If the end of oratory is to convince the judgment and to guide the passions of those who hear, rather than to accumulate treasures of wisdom for the student, Bright's eloquence was far more successful. He also possessed the saving grace of humour, in which the great Irishman, like the great Athenian, was almost painfully wanting. This is surely no small matter. To men who take so grave a view of political responsibility as these two statesmen, who strove, as they strove, to teach political morality and a political religion to an untoward generation, the burden of affairs is intolerable if it cannot be lightened by laughter. Bright's humour was not penetrating like that of Carlyle; it only played on the surface of his earnestness; but it helped to save him from the gloom of Burke and the Prophets.

The oratory of Bright is distinguished from that of the great orators of an earlier generation chiefly by the quality of simplicity both of matter and diction. This simplicity reflects the most striking quality of his mind. He was for the most part content to deduce his political conclusions from a few very broad principles. He did not lead his hearers through any long processes of argumentation, because his own mental processes were simplified by his indifference to so many considerations that count with more patient observers. He did not weigh reason against reason and strike the balance, because the conclusions he propounded commended themselves to him, not as resulting from a calculation of comparative expediency, but as following directly from comprehensive premises to which his hearers were assumed to have already assented. He did not weary them by marshalling facts, because his own methods of thought were intuitive rather than inductive. There is a sort of insincerity which is almost inseparable from political rhetoric. Most speakers are constrained to adapt their words to their hearers by choosing for rhetorical purposes reasons more popular but less weighty than those by which they were themselves convinced. For simplicity's sake they present as absolute and universal a conclusion which is really conditional and dependent on circumstances. Hence comes, when conditions change, the scandal of inconsistency. Bright spoke as he thought; he revealed his true reasons and his real motives; and because his reasons were naïve and easy, the very candour with which he disclosed them led him into a method that might have been commended to him by the tact of a rhetorician gauging the receptive power of his audience.

A discussion was once proceeding in his presence on the difference between his speaking and that of Mr. Gladstone. At last he struck in himself. "I think", he said, "that the difference between my speaking and Mr. Gladstone's is something like this. When I speak, I strike across from headland to headland. Mr. Gladstone follows the coast-line; and when he comes to a navigable river he is unable to resist the temptation of tracing it to its source." Those who by more painful processes had reached a different conclusion were irritated to hear Bright pass over as mere irrelevancies arguments that appeared to them pertinent and weighty. It seemed to them that his conclusions were easy because his grasp of the science and of the facts was wilfully incomplete. They had followed the coast-line,

and had discovered on the journey many things, ignored
by Bright, to be counted and measured.   Philosophers
may prefer the completer survey, but to a mass meeting
there can be no doubt that the shorter voyage from cape
to cape is more agreeable; and even the House of Commons is not yet an assemblage of philosophers.

⌊ The simplicity of his diction corresponds to that of
his thought. ⌋ His vocabulary was stinted by comparison,
not indeed with that of the common run of speakers,
but with that of most of the great masters of his art.
The comparative scantiness of Bright's *copia verborum*
may be attributed in part to his neglect of subtleties of
thought and the finer distinctions that require the rarer
sort of words; in part to the instinct of the popular
orator discarding words unfamiliar to his audience; in
part to the frankness that avoids the trick of making
common ideas seem impressive by pretentious phrasing.
No speaker made less use of what Bentley called " common and obvious thoughts dressed and curled in the
beauish way".

Much has been said about Bright's "homespun phrase",
"vigorous Saxon", and the like.   It is true that he did
not elevate his ordinary style so far above the level of
conversation as the classical orators of former generations.   But there is always some elevation; he did not
commit the disrespect of talking to people who had
come to hear him speak.   If his speeches are fairly
examined, no justification whatsoever will be found for
the suggestion that his rejection of words employed by
Burke or Fox or Mr. Gladstone was due to any preference for the Saxon to the classical element of the
language.   He would often use a Latin word even though
an English equivalent was at hand, for the sake of sound
or of rhythm, or from mere indifference of choice.   Such
words as *potent, dominant, turbulent, enormous, multi-
tudinous, disastrous, commensurate, interminable, incal-*

*culable*, are quite characteristic of his style. He would say *constantly, inculcate, trepidation, profligate, decorous, penurious, eradicate, assembly*, when he might, except for sound or dignity, have said, *always, teach, fear, wicked, seemly, stingy, uproot, meeting.*

If his vocabulary was limited, his choice of words within those limits was singularly just and delicate. In his popular addresses,—the conditions of which admitted a more accurate preparation than his speeches in Parliament, where any speaker is partly at the mercy of the course of debate,—there are few sentences in which the boldest critic would venture to suggest the replacement of a single word. He had a most delicate sense of rhythm. In this respect not one of our most admired orators has excelled him. To one who has caught the suavity of Bright's cadences the accent of Macaulay sounds like the stroke of a blacksmith's hammer, the sentences of Burke strike the ear like the tramp of a regiment, and the periods of Fox or Mr. Gladstone like the tumult of a hurrying crowd. To make rules for rhythmical prose is the despair of criticism. Probably there is no rule that will work except that which prohibits rhythms that suggest any familiar form of verse. But if the reader will refer to the peroration quoted on p. 66, and will substitute the word *Ministry* for *Administration*, and read the last phrase thus: "the squandering of the treasure of my country or the shedding of a single drop of her blood"; or if in the famous passage on the future of America, quoted on p. 107, he will try the effect of any of the following substitutions: *confederacy, ocean, liberty, asylum, nation, climate*, for *confederation, main, freedom, refuge, race, clime*; he will realize how much of the beauty of these fine passages is due to the artful disposition of the accents and of the long vowel sounds.

Another phase of Bright's characteristic simplicity

remains to be noticed more particularly.  He differed from those orators who have hitherto taken classical rank in nothing more strikingly than in this—that he was content with a plain and unadorned phrase for the statement of a simple fact.  He did not think it due to himself or to his art to trick out a plain narrative with oriental embellishments.  He gained far more than he lost by this Wordsworthian reversion to natural simplicity.  It is usual to ascribe Burke's failure to keep the ear of the House of Commons to some defect of that body—its stupidity or its prejudice.  But many admirers of Burke will admit, if they are pressed, that it is not easy to read one of his speeches through at a sitting.  We read a few pages with immense admiration; but soon the ear and the mind are surfeited of his grand manner, and we can understand how those magnificent sentences failed of their due effect because they fell on ears wearied by the strain of so much highly-coloured eloquence. Bright is always interesting and never wearisome.  Some of the finest effects of his eloquence were produced by the sudden transition from some simple statement or some plain argument presented in plain terms to a stroke of passion or imagination.  There is ample contemporary testimony of the extraordinary effect produced by his reference to the death of Colonel Boyle.  He is speaking of the loss of life in the Crimean war.  "We all know what we have lost in this House.  Here, sitting near me, very often sat the member for Frome.  I met him a short time before he went out, at Mr. Westerton's, the bookseller's, near Hyde Park Corner.  I asked him whether he was going out.  He answered, he was afraid he was—not afraid in the sense of personal fear; he knew not that—but he said, with a look and a tone I shall never forget, 'It is no light matter for a man who has a wife and five little children'.  The stormy Euxine is his grave; his wife is a widow, his children fatherless."

The subdued tone of the introductory narrative, and the odd triviality, as of a conscientious witness, in the details of the place where the speaker met Boyle, add vastly to the irresistible force of the stroke of pathos.    When the effective sentence comes, it needs only the slightest touches of art—the substitution of *Euxine* for the commoner *Black Sea*, and the addition of a single ornamental epithet—to give it elevation.    The eloquence comes like a flash of lightning, and fixes itself for ever in the memory; but it has obeyed the primary rule of pathetic utterance, that it should be unlaboured and simple. Such an effect is beyond the reach of the gorgeous style. This little touch of pity probably moved men nearer to tears than all the woes of Sheridan's Begums.

The foregoing remarks may be illustrated and other criticisms suggested by the following specimen of Bright's ordinary parliamentary style.    The passage is chosen, not as having any special excellence, but because it treats of topics by which the great Whig orators of the last century frequently displayed their method of arousing compassion and indignation.

"I beg the Committee to consider this matter, notwithstanding that the right hon. gentleman is not disposed to take a gloomy view of the state of India. Look at your responsibilities.    India is ruled by Englishmen; but remember that in that unfortunate country you have destroyed every form of government but your own, that you have cast the thrones of the natives to the ground.    Princely families, once the rulers of India, are now either houseless wanderers in the land they once called their own, or are pensioners on the bounty of the strangers by whom their fortunes have been overthrown. They who were noble and gentle for ages are now merged in the common mass of the people.    All over these vast regions there are countless millions, helpless and defenceless, deprived of their natural leaders and their ancient chiefs, looking with only some small ray of hope to the omnipresent and irresistible power to which they have been subjected. I appeal to you on behalf of that people. I have besought your mercy and your justice for many a year past, and if I speak to you earnestly now, it is because the object for which I plead is dear to my heart. Is it not possible to touch a chord in the hearts of Englishmen, to raise them to a sense of the miseries inflicted on that unhappy country by the crimes and the blunders of our rulers here? If you have steeled your hearts against the natives, if nothing can stir you to sympathy with their miseries, at least have pity upon your own fellow-countrymen. Rely upon it, the state of things which now exists in India must before long become more serious. I hope you will not show to the world that, although your fathers conquered that country, you have not the ability to govern it. You had better disencumber yourselves of the fatal gift of empire than that the present generation should be punished for the sins of the past. I speak in condemnatory language because I believe it to be deserved. I hope that no future historian will have to say that the arms of England in India were irresistible and that an ancient empire fell before their victorious progress, yet that finally India was avenged because the power of her conqueror was broken by the intolerable burdens and evils which she cast upon her victim, and that this wrong was accomplished by a waste of human life and a waste of wealth which England with all her power was unable to bear."

Certainly Bright is not at his best here. Some of the language is not only plain but almost too common. A more fastidious speaker might have tried to avoid such worn-out locutions as *ray of hope, steel your hearts, touch a chord.* In one sentence the style seems to sink suddenly; probably in speaking some art of delivery rescued it from the sense of bathos. The word *con-*

*demnatory* sounds oddly, though it has good authority. Bright seems to have substituted "condemnatory language" for the usual "language of condemnation" because he had just used the word *generation*. His ear was very sensitive to this jingle, which most speakers find it impossible to avoid. He could never have spoken, as Disraeli did in the eulogy already referred to, of "a speech to which I listened with pleasure and gratification, as I must to every demonstration that sustains the reputation of this assembly".

These things are mere trifles, and are only worth noting for the sake of the remark that Bright would have been more careful of his language if he had been speaking in the Birmingham Town Hall. What is really noteworthy in the style of the passage is this— that just because the ground tone is pitched rather low, the vivid and touching phrases require no elaborate workmanship to make them effective. Burke would have laboured the picture of the dispossessed potentates until he had forced us to resist his pathos by reminding ourselves that they were after all rather worthless persons paying the penalty of selfishness and incompetence. He might have introduced some of the oriental scenery of the tragedy; we should have heard of Rannies and Zamindars, of diamonds and palanquins. Bright's appeal to the sentiment of compassion for fallen greatness, and to our sense of the perplexity that follows the uprooting of institutions, is sufficient, and it does not overshoot the mark. The whole passage satisfies the three proverbial aims of rhetoric—*ut doceat, moveat, delectet*. It is good oratory, because the sound is grateful to the ear, because it stimulates the imagination, and because it touches the sensibility. The mind is powerfully impressed with the sense that it is easier to conquer than to govern, to destroy than to reconstruct. The hearer may have learned nothing new of

the resources of the language or of the power of the
orator, but he is left with a quickened perception of the
gravity of imperial responsibility. That is the effect
intended; and it could not have been achieved more
skilfully by the use of more recondite diction or more
sonorous periods.

Mr. Thorold Rogers, in his preface to a selection of
Bright's speeches,—excellently chosen, but edited with
reprehensible carelessness,—commends "the clearness
of his diction, the skill with which he arranges his
arguments, the vigour of his style, the persuasiveness
of his reasoning, and above all the perfect candour and
sincerity with which he expresses his political convictions". Certainly Bright was lucid, persuasive, and
eminently candid. If there is one of these heads of
commendation to which exception may be taken, it is
that which touches the arrangement of his arguments.
Bright does not seem to have paid any attention to the
architectonics of oratory. In reading his speeches we
are rarely conscious of that effect of the gradual
accumulation of the force of reasoning which has often
been attained by the skill of inferior orators. It must
be recorded, not as a fault, but as a fact, that some of
his finest speeches have really no structure at all. No
critic of to-day will wish to revive the importance which
ancient writers on rhetoric attached to this part of the
art. To an audience coming to the hall of meeting or
to the House of Commons with their minds already
occupied by the burning question of the hour the order
in which topics are taken may be immaterial. Each
sentence will carry its full weight of meaning to the
mind without the aid of any artifice of arrangement.
The reader, who is not prepared, as the hearers were
prepared, for the reception of the speech, will sometimes feel that the orator might have helped him by a
more orderly disposition of the argument. In par-

ticular, the transition to the main course of the argument after a digression, perhaps unrehearsed, will sometimes appear to be awkwardly managed.

Bright rarely made any show of being severely logical. But the affectation of logical precision in a popular or even a parliamentary orator is rarely more than a delusive pretence. It must be added that, like other orators, he was not altogether exempt from logical fallacies. If the arguments implied in the extracts quoted on p. 100 and p. 91 of this book be treated in the Socratic manner, the former will be found to owe its plausibility to the ambiguity of the term *property*, and the latter to the ambiguity of the term *conscience*. Such things do not make much difference. The part of a popular orator is to make people see things immediately by common sense; if he cannot do this, he will not make much way by a train of reasoning.

The opinion has already been expressed that Bright's reputation would be secure and lasting if it depended entirely on the speeches on the Russian war. Future compilers of a florilegium of British oratory will probably resort to these speeches for their specimens of his eloquence. The strength of resistance against him brought out the full force of his powers. He had to contend against the belief in the minds of nearly all his hearers that his opinions were not only unwise and quixotic but informed by a defective sense of national honour. Nothing short of the very finest tact could have saved him from ridicule. The admiration which these speeches won at the time was the more valuable because it was given grudgingly and of necessity.

Although he won so many triumphs in the House of Commons, it was as a popular rather than as a parliamentary orator that Bright attained the very first place among his contemporaries. By comparison with other speakers of the first flight, he was in a manner dis-

qualified for the highest success in debate by certain
qualities of his mental habit.   A great debater is a man
who is not afraid to allow his opponents the advantage
of choosing the field of combat.   He will either essay
to prove that the premisses of his antagonists are mistaken, or that their conclusions do not follow their
premisses.   Bright's method was to go on reasoning
from premisses of his own choosing.   His opponents
did not think that he came fairly to close quarters with
them.   In his numerous republished speeches on parliamentary reform the reader will find the reasons for
reform enforced with the highest rhetorical skill.   The
appeal to emotion is irresistible; the indignation is in-
fectious and virile, it is free from feminine shrillness of
complaint; the hot air of controversy is cooled just at
the right moment by a whiff of humour or ridicule.
What the reader will not find there is any adequate
reply to the reasons against democratic reform urged
by Lowe and others.   Again, in the controversy of 1886
Bright, as we have seen, seized on three reasons of
weight against Home Rule.   No other man then living
could enforce those topics with more authority; and
when the controversy has reached its final issue and its
history is written, the narrator will not fail to allot to
Bright a large share of praise or blame for the defeat
in 1886 of the new policy.   But it must be conceded
that in his speeches and letters he ignored the reasons
which the majority of his party accepted as sufficient to
justify their change of purpose.   To recur to his own
metaphor, he left to others the task of following Mr.
Gladstone up the navigable rivers.

Bright, therefore, does not take quite the highest
place among the athletes of debate.   But all his mental
powers combined to equip him for the work of a popular
orator.   Those who assemble at public meetings love
the note of certainty; and Bright was always confident,

unhesitating, resolute. They are disposed to accept on authority an opinion laid before them distinctly by a man of whose sincerity they are already convinced; and Bright's sincerity was guaranteed by every possible test. They are eager for generalities, and the form of reasoning that affects them most favourably is that which refers the special case to some general maxim. The Radicals wisely supplied them with a little treasury of such maxims—a bunch of keys to fit many locks. Of such maxims those which are, or which affect to be, rules of morality rather than of prudence are the most valuable to an orator; for ethical maxims are accepted as absolute, while it is known that there are two sides to a question of expediency. In taking his stand on morality, Bright was simply obeying his own conscience; but he was also occupying the position most advantageous for the control of public opinion. The popular orator will do well to say, if he can, It is wicked not to do this, rather than, It is expedient to do it. He will refer the errors imputed to his opponents to their moral delinquency rather than to mere infirmity of judgment; and this he may safely do, provided that he has first satisfied his audience that he is himself in earnest. The appeal to reason is ineffective unless it is followed by an appeal to emotion; and of the emotions indignation is that which is most readily excited. A public meeting never enjoys itself more thoroughly than when it is crying Shame!

It is unnecessary to add to the examples already given that show how exactly Bright's manner fulfilled all these conditions of success. The reader of his speeches, if he is a man anxious to think as well as possible of everyone, may have a feeling of revolt when one group of ministers, some of whom have now been honoured by statues and Lives in two volumes, is described as "incompetent and guilty", another as "tur-

bulent and wicked", or when a statesman of good repute
is accused of "haughty unwisdom". But the populace
rejoices to be told that it does well to be angry. Nothing, it may be said, is easier than scolding. Every
man has at hand a sufficient supply of offensive epithets.
But Bright did not scold; he had the art of speaking as
one having authority to condemn, and he said these
things in such a way that they sounded like the judgments of Rhadamanthus.

This prophetic sternness of denunciation was relieved
by the faculties of humour and wit. Without the gift
of humour no speaker could have sustained so constant
a habit of earnestness, or have made so many bold
incursions into the region of pathos, without sometimes
incurring ridicule. Bright was grave and sentimental,
yet his audience never laughed at him. His mental
refinement saved him from the easy flippancy that
besets many popular speakers. His wit was displayed
in the invention of those happy and effective comparisons, of which the best-remembered is the proverbial Cave of Adullam. In one of the earliest of these
sallies he likened Russell's Government, whose financial
measures seemed to him exactly adapted to make them
unpopular with the electorate, to "the religious order
of La Trappe, who are said to have employed themselves diligently in digging their own graves". The
last, contained in the same speech with the parable
of the Cook's tourists, was his description of the result
of a proposal that the Irish members should speak and
vote on Irish questions only as "a sort of intermittent
Irish fever in the House of Commons". He compared
Disraeli to Voltaire, "who wrote history far better without facts than with them". He revenged himself on
the eminent writer who had attacked him and Cobden
under the protection of anonymous journalism by comparing him to the American of whom it was said that

"he was a just and righteous man, and he walked up-
rightly before the world; but when he was not before
the world his walk was slantindicular". The reluctance
of the Conservatives to mend grievances reminded him
of a Lancashire miser, who would not have his clothes
repaired "because he found that a hole lasted longer
than a patch". He suggested as a motto for the Whigs,
"A place for every one, and every one in his place".
When a high-church baronet, who sat for Oxford University, opposed the admission of a Jew into the House
of Commons, Bright gave an unexpectedly humorous
turn to a really pertinent argument. "Take, for instance, what may be called the morality of politics.
You will find that the hon. baronet draws nearly all his
opinions from the very same source as Baron Rothschild.
We have discussed in this House the question of capital
punishment. I find the hon. baronet quoting against
me, with his accustomed bland dignity, the ninth chapter
of the book of Genesis. I have a strong suspicion that
he takes his notions of the priesthood from the times of
the book of Exodus. When the question of marriage
with a deceased wife's sister was under discussion the
hon. baronet referred the House with perfect confidence
to the book of Leviticus."

Bright had a strong and beautiful voice, clear rather
than loud, rich and sympathetic in tone, and so admirably controlled that he could produce a fine effect by a
very slight increase in the volume of sound or force of
utterance in passages of denunciation, or by a very
slight fall of pitch for humour or irony. In his old age
some weakness of the throat often made his voice husky;
but when it was at its best he could make himself heard
without painful effort by an audience of twenty thousand
people. He relied for colour and emphasis almost
entirely on choice of words and modulation of voice,
making little use of gesture and action. He would call

attention to a strong point by leaning forward and rais-
ing his right arm. He had also a trick of putting his
finger between collar and neck under the ear and moving
it round to the chin when he was about to say something
playful. The flashing eye and curling lip sometimes
attributed to him when scornful are figments of imagina-
tive reporters; and indeed such grimaces belong rather
to the mock oratory of the stage. His bodily attitude
in speaking was dignified; and his manner was as far
removed as possible from the shouting and gesticulating
style of the ideal demagogue of fiction and the satirists
—a style which, it must be added, is the least likely to
make a favourable impression upon such audiences as
Bright was accustomed to address.

His quotations, which were generally felicitous, were
taken chiefly from the Bible and from the English and
American poets. Some of them were used repeatedly.
His occasional use of the words of Scripture with a
humorous intention may be traced to his fondness for
American literature, which is itself to be associated with
his admiration for American institutions. No political
orator has ever used citations from the Scriptures with
more fortunate results. They harmonized admirably
with that "undercurrent of religious emotion" by which
his speeches were distinguished. No literary quotations
can be so effective in addresses to a popular audience
as those taken from the Bible. The essential value of a
quotation is that to those versed in literature it suggests
by association ideas not directly expressed. To the
majority of any popular audience a passage from Milton
or Pope means what it says and nothing more. But
when Bright, for instance, quotes from the Psalms,
"The needy shall not alway be forgotten: the expectation of the poor shall not perish for ever", he achieves an
effect not otherwise to be attained. The thoughts of
the most ignorant are carried back to antiquity, and the

needs and hopes of the moment are linked with the im-
memorial needs and undying hopes of humanity. So
again, when he replied in debate, to an orator who had
spoken sadly of "the dark cloud that hangs over Ireland" by citing the words, "Unto the upright there
ariseth light in the darkness", he gave dignity to his
appeal by claiming, as it were, the alliance of the eternal
forces of justice, and seemed to invest the trite exhortation to do justly and hope for the best with the lustre of
a universal faith.

He, therefore, not only owed to his study of the Bible
the elevated and half-religious tone of thought that per-
meated his utterances, but used it directly in some of
the most impressive strokes of his eloquence. Many
critics have suggested that his style also was indebted
for some of its fine qualities to his familiarity with the
English of the Bible. The present writer, having given
a different account of Bright's simplicity of style, and
having discarded the suggestion that Bright shared that
preference for Saxon words which is one of the charac-
teristics of Tyndale's version that in part survived the
pedantry of King James's revisers, finds himself, after
due consideration, unable to concur in this view. Probably no man's style ever owed less to conscious or
unconscious imitation. The books with which, after
the Bible, Bright was most familiar were Byron and
Milton. Milton, it is said, has contributed more to the
equipment of English orators than to that of English
poets; but Bright does not seem to have been under any
special obligation to him for words and phrases. Nor
is there any evidence in his speeches that he had paid
any great attention to the earlier English orators.

Though plain, direct, and economical of embellish-
ment, his style is never without distinction. Even at its
plainest it is rarely bald. It will not perhaps be thought
fanciful to compare the difference between the manner of

Bright on the one hand, and that of orators like Burke and Fox, Pitt and Canning, on the other, to the difference between Demosthenes and Cicero. The influence of the Roman in forming what may be called the classical manner of English oratory is not to be gainsaid. Bright renounced many of the qualities of that manner—its studied sonority, its balance of clauses and epithets, its antithetic emphasis, its well-knit structure of sentences. Without considering whether it is longer or shorter than the sentence that preceded it, and with no care to give it equipoise upon its own centre of gravity, he brings a sentence to a conclusion because he has said what he meant to say in it, or carries it on with a new subordinate construction because he has something to add. This again was a reversion to nature in defiance of the traditions of his art. His manner, if we may coin a word in imitation of preraphaelite, was preciceronian. Unconsciously, it was also a reversion to the manner of Demosthenes.

A word must be added on what may be called the educational value of these speeches. Mr. Challemel-Lacour, speaking in particular of the speeches on Reform, declares that, in spite of the aggressive tone of some of the speeches, and though he recognizes here and there the impassioned accent of the Tribune, the quality that strikes him most forcibly is their moderation. "When I read those orations delivered at the great popular meetings at Birmingham, Manchester, Glasgow, and London, before easily inflammable mobs, whose applause is so strong a temptation to the orator, I am amazed by their didactic character and by the sobriety of their manner. Are these really the speeches of an agitator or of a professor of politics? It seems incredible that such disquisitions, with their apparatus of statistics and details and searching analysis, were addressed, not to an assembly of professed politicians,

but to immense audiences almost entirely composed of
men who were not even voters." It suited the exigences
of controversy to represent Bright as inflammatory, passionate, a sower of disaffection. But let his speeches
be compared with the incoherent diatribes of the eloquent
Chartists, or the perverse contentiousness of Cobbett,
or with the demagogic eloquence of Ireland or America
to-day. We are dealing now with the manner rather
than the substance of his harangues to the masses—
with the fashion of popular exhortation which he adopted
and established as an example. The number of his
countrymen who listened to him in the course of his
career was larger probably than any other orator could
count. What did they learn? They heard the English
language used with all the lucidity and force of Cobbett,
but also with a graciousness and dignity that cannot
have failed of a refining influence on the minds of unlet-
tered men. They heard a man who in every word he
uttered showed that he treated politics as a subject
worthy of the fullest tension of his intellectual powers.
They heard appeals to morality in which the most sensitive ear could not detect a suspicion of hypocrisy.
They were moved to laughter; but by jests that differed
as widely as possible from the buffoonery of the smoking-
carriage or the commercial-room. Their indignation
was aroused, but not their envy; they were armed with
resolution, not stimulated to sedition. They learned
self-respect, earnestness, loyalty, patriotism.

We can expect no unanimity in approval of the substance of his teaching. He attacked institutions that
still command the affection of many of his fellow-
countrymen; he tried to undermine sentiments that still
hold their place in the prevalent conception of patriotism.
But even those who see in his doctrine the exaltation of
the narrowness and prejudice of a commercial middle-
class, will, if they turn from the substance to the manner

of his speeches, agree that it is by such oratory as this that the victorious populace can best be educated to the duties of citizenship.

## Chapter X.

### Characteristics.

Bright was a man of middle height and stoutly built. In his youth he was lean and spare, but his figure soon thickened to the comfortable proportions that suggest a prosperous and not too active life. A head and face of the leonine cast, mild blue eyes, clear-cut and handsome features, the forehead both broad and high, the mouth large and firm, an abundance of white hair and a fringe of white whisker, the lip and chin shaven, an expression indicating firmness, dignity, benevolence, and a thoughtful habit of mind, but giving little promise of eagerness and vivacity—such was the outward aspect of the man who for so many years stood first in the affections of English democrats.

He was entirely devoted to politics, and published his opinions on any other subject only under some sort of compulsion, with diffidence and embarrassment, and for the most part ineffectively. His mind was eupeptic, contented, conservative; even in politics he was not greedy of novelty; and in the mental disquietude that in other domains of intellectual activity calls itself modern thought, or claims to represent this or that phase of the Revolution, he remained, so far as any public utterance reveals his state of mind, happily uninterested. It is not very often that we can collect any opinion outside politics and political ethics from his speeches. An exception may be cited for the sake of supplying a necessary note to one of his best-known speeches. In 1854, accusing ministers of neglect of their duties, he remarked that Palmerston had "undertaken a labour left unaccomplished by Voltaire, and when he addressed the Hampshire peasantry, had in one short sentence overturned the New Testament and destroyed the foundation of the Christian religion". What Palmerston had said was something to the effect that children are born good, and become bad only by bad training. This amiable doctrine—which is to be found in Diderot if not in Voltaire, and may therefore claim the dignity of an idea of the Revolution—would, if announced to-day, encounter severer criticism from the scientific than from the theological side.

Few men from an obscure origin can ever have attained so great an eminence of fame with so small an expenditure of industry. From the time when he accepted Cobden's invitation until the Corn Law was repealed, he did not spare himself. The record of his League speeches implies a large amount of labour. It must, however, be remembered that the admirable organization of the League employed a vast number of zealous volunteers, who worked together under an excellent system of division of labour. One set of men took charge of the finances; another worked at the production of handbills and pamphlets for popular distribution; another arranged statistics, and collected facts and illustrations for the use of the speakers and lecturers. Bright and the others to whom the propagation of the faith on the platform was allotted, were supplied with matter for their speeches from Newall's Buildings, and were in the position of advocates speaking from a well-prepared brief.

At more than one crisis in his later life the old activity was resumed for a time. But the indications are too numerous and too precise to be misread, that he was, not morally, but physically and constitutionally, disposed to indolence, and was only saved by a dominant sense of duty from living an idle life. Hard mental labour was actually perilous to him; in both his long illnesses it was necessary to protect him with the utmost care from any mental exertion. Except when roused to energy by some crisis, he accepted invitations to speak with reluctance; and it is apparent that he was an exception to the rule that a man finds enjoyment in doing what he can do extremely well. If the whole of the work he got through during the forty-six years of his parliamentary life be summed up, it does not amount to much more than the average of unofficial members; and he was exempted from the *petits soins* which most constituencies exact from their representatives. Many men have given as much time to public work who have also satisfied the claims of an arduous occupation.

Like most men of this habit of life he was fond of miscellaneous reading. His services to the League were recognized by a handsome present of books; and he gradually accumulated a large library. He had acquired in youth a great love for English poetry. He was once, when passing an idle afternoon in a drawing-room, asked by the ladies to read to them the last new volume of poems. The book did not please him. He laid it down, and repeated by heart with spirit and enjoyment a surprisingly large quantity of Byron. It has been remarked that his love of Byron is evidence of early independence, for it is improbable that in the early years of the century such a taste should have been encouraged by Quaker parents. Milton he read constantly; he preferred *Paradise Regained*, and made a point of reading it once a year. Notwithstanding these laudable tastes and his genuine love of books, his faculty of literary criticism was not highly developed. It was matter of surprise that an orator whose own productions were marked by so fine a sense of language that they seem secure of an

honourable place in the history of English prose, should
have given such recommendations of books as seemed
to show that he was scarcely sensible of the difference
between good writing and bad.  It must, however, be
recorded to his credit, that he was one of the first Englishmen to recognize the merits of the incomparable
*Biglow Papers.* While the reading of books was a
favourite recreation, he always regarded the newspapers
of the day as having the first claim on his time.  Contemporary politics were, in fact, the one subject of which
he made a serious study; and with all his reading his
mental equipment remained inferior to that of most
Englishmen who have been eminent in politics.  After
reading, his favourite recreation indoors was billiards.

He had a taste for travel, and saw a good deal of
Europe and something of the East.  He declined invitations to visit the United States, pleading that he was
a bad sailor.  If there was any admixture of generous
illusion in his estimate of the American polity, he did
not incur the risk of losing it by personal observation.

He loved the fresh air and wild open scenery, and
had a keen relish for the diversion of salmon-fishing,
especially in Scotch waters.  When reproached with the
cruelty of his favourite amusement, he would answer
the objector according to his folly.  Fox-hunting, he
remarked, might be called cruel, because you routed
out the fox and hunted him willy-nilly; but the salmon-
fisher merely laid his fly before the fish, who had always
the option of not taking it.  His attachment to Llan-
dudno was well known, and helped to make the fortune
of the place; it was associated with the memory of a
little boy who died there, and whose grave in the little
churchyard on the cliff he visited annually.

But his chief happiness, as befitted a man who stands
as the representative of the best type of the English
middle-class, was found in family affection.  He had a

large family of sons and daughters, and, except for the
early bereavement that condemned him to a six years'
widowhood,[1] his domestic life was fortunate.  One of
his boldest appeals to pathetic sentiment illustrates this
side of his character.  During the American war the
feeling in favour of the South was so strong that Roebuck ventured to move the House in favour of the
recognition of the Southern Confederacy.  There were
Englishmen to whom the Southern cotton-planters appeared to represent the virtues of a landed aristocracy
and the loyalists the abominations of commerce; to them
the South was the home of gentlemen and chivalry, the
North of bagmen and vulgarity.  Bright resisted Roebuck's astonishing proposal, and treated his palliation
of negro slavery with fierce indignation.  " I want to
know whether you feel as I feel upon this question.
When I can get down to my home from this House, I
find half a dozen little children playing upon my hearth.
How many members are there who can say with me
that the most innocent, the most pure, the most holy
joy which in their past years they have felt, or in their
future years they have hoped for, has arisen from contact and association with our little children !  If that be
so, if, when the hand of death takes one of these flowers
from our dwelling, our heart is overwhelmed with sorrow, and our household is covered with gloom, what
would it be if our children were brought up to this
infernal system—a hundred and fifty thousand of them
every year brought into the world in the slave states,
among these ' gentlemen ', among this ' chivalry ', among
these men that we can make our friends !"

Although he was probably never so happy as in the
seclusion of his own circle in the pleasant home that he
had built for himself at Rochdale, he was not disinclined

---

[1] In 1847 he married Margaret Elizabeth Leatham, the daughter of a
Wakefield banker.  She died in 1878.

to society.  Those who met him on social occasions are
agreed in their testimony to the singular charm of his
conversation.  It had many of the fine qualities of his
eloquence, and impressed those who heard it with the
same sense that they were listening to a man of remarkable mental endowments.  The "undercurrent of religious emotion" could be discerned in his talk as well as
in his speeches.  "In his graver conversation", remarks
one who often heard him talk, "he always spoke as if
living continually in the presence of the Deity."  But
he was well disposed also for conversation of the lighter
sort.  He abounded in entertaining reminiscences of the
shrewd homely wit of Lancashire characters.  He was
an admirable narrator of humorous stories.  His son,
who succeeded him in the representation of Central
Birmingham, once incurred the reprobation of Mr. Peck-
sniff and Mr. Podsnap by repeating in public a story
incautiously selected from his father's table-talk.

He accepted as though expecting it the deference
that was commonly paid to him in any large company.
Though habitually courteous, he was not effusive or
disposed to indiscriminate affability.  But he readily
recognized the claim of other members of the Society
of Friends to treat him with the brotherly familiarity
encouraged by the customs of the society.

He asserted his opinions in private conversation in the
same decisive and uncompromising manner that char-
acterized his public utterances.  This assertiveness,
whether on the platform or at the table, implied self-
confidence but not self-conceit.  He was by no means
intolerant of contradiction.  When he first visited Birmingham in 1858 some of the younger Liberals of the
town met him at dinner.  The question of Gibraltar
turned up in conversation, and Bright expressed with
his usual emphasis his opinion that Gibraltar ought to
be restored to Spain.  The young men, though listening

to Bright with becoming reverence, had courage enough to controvert this opinion. So far from taking offence, Bright afterwards told his host that he was much pleased by what he had heard. He had not expected, he said, to find men of such intelligence in Birmingham. The experience of the League had led him to rank his new constituency much lower than Manchester in the scale of political intelligence and energy. Manchester seems always to have occupied the first place in his affection. His Birmingham constituents observed that to the last he always spoke of "your city", never of "our city".

His habitual use of terms of moral censure in speaking of differences of policy or opinion laid him open to the charge of deficient charity. But the hardest things he said about his opponents will be found, if fairly examined, to be entirely free from the element of personal rancour. His conversation showed no want of reasonable allowance in his judgments of men. The respect with which he and Disraeli, both hard hitters, and differing so widely, treated one another, in spite of a few passages of hostility, often excited remark. It has been suggested that they were drawn together by their common antipathy to Palmerston. Lord George Bentinck's remark that "if Bright had not been a Quaker he would have been a prize-fighter" has often been quoted. A jest that had so much vogue cannot have been pointless. Yet it need not be supposed that Bright's invective seemed improperly severe to a generation that had seen Disraeli make himself at last acceptable by his famous assaults upon Peel. The point was that some people's sense of humour was touched by the incongruity of Bright's vigour with the current conception of Quakerly meekness. He neither cherished personal animosity, nor excited it except in minds of the smaller sort.

Bright was a moderate smoker, and is said to have been fastidious in his choice of cigars, exhibiting embarrassment when any man of whose good taste he was not assured proffered a cigar-case. He practised teetotalism habitually, though not rigidly. It was his custom when proposing a toast at a public dinner to announce his own intention of drinking it in water. In early life he was active in the Temperance movement; but he ceased to attend Temperance meetings because he could not tolerate the uncharitable language which at that time, as he tells us, the orators of the Temperance cause permitted themselves to use. He did not support the attempts at legislation made by the friends of Temperance, except that he was willing to empower localities that desired it to close public-houses on Sunday. In 1864 he spoke against the measure that was then called the Permissive Bill, and that has since reappeared under other insincere names; and he never receded from the opinion that he expressed in that debate. He was always suspicious of legislative interference with freedom of action; and he took many opportunities of reiterating his view that "Parliament was not justified in inflicting unnecessary difficulties and unnecessary irritations upon the trade of the licensed victualler". He looked to education rather than legislation for the remedy of intemperance; this, he used to say, must be the sheet-anchor of the reformer.

He had, however, a modest proposal of licensing reform of his own. He suggested that a clause of the Municipal Corporations Bill of 1835 should be revived. By this clause, which passed the Commons but was taken out by the Lords, the power of licensing was to be transferred from the magistrates to the Council in every municipal borough. If the experiment proved successful, a similar reform might be devised for rural districts. The Councils were to be forbidden to increase the number of houses, except in proportion to the growth of population. They were to be empowered to reduce the

234

234l be a grand volume that
234

## John Bright.

number of licensed houses by not more than one-half. The taxes paid on licensed property were to be transferred from the Treasury to the corporations, who were to have the power of levying further taxes on such property in consideration of the monopoly. Out of this fund compensation was to be paid to dislicensed publicans. The essence of his counsel on this difficult question was given in these words: "The temperance opinion in this country, if you can combine, is very powerful. But it is only powerful, and will only be successful, when brought to bear in favour of practicable and moderate measures." This was said in 1883.

It remains to estimate the historical and permanent importance of Bright's work. Speaking to his constituents in October, 1873, Bright said: "The history of the last forty years of this country, judged fairly, —I speak of its legislation,—is mainly a history of the conquests of freedom. It will be a grand volume that tells the story; and your name and mine, if I mistake not, will be found in some of its pages." No one will be disposed to disallow so modest a claim as this.

There are seven leading political ideas of which Bright was a conspicuous advocate, and with which he attempted, with more or less success, to indoctrinate the British electorate. These were: Free Trade, Free Land, Democracy, Religious Equality, Retrenchment, Peace or non-interference abroad, *Laisser-faire* or non-interference at home.

After the account that has already been given of Bright's opinions and purposes, it is not necessary to attempt any further definition of these terms. Of these principles four made enormous advancement in popular favour and in their influence on actual legislation during his lifetime. No other politician ever had the satisfaction, in respect of so many subjects of deliberation, of seeing a small minority under his guidance grow into a majority of the popular House. There is hardly a single prominent publicist of his time who did not at some time come to give his support to a measure which he had formerly opposed and which Bright had consistently supported. So striking a record can scarcely fail to attract the attention of any careful historian of our era. The question remains, how far we are to attribute this good fortune to Bright's faculty for guiding public opinion, and how far to his sagacity in forecasting its direction; and in what proportion the credit is to be distributed between Bright, his coadjutors, and the impersonal forces of political development.

Bright's share in the victory of Free Trade seems more likely to be over-estimated than unduly disparaged. The public memory naturally retains four eminent names —Cobden and Bright, the agitators; Villiers, the parliamentary leader; and Peel, the man who actually repealed the law at the cost of political martyrdom,— whilst the pioneers of the movement, and the army of essayists, pamphleteers, and organizers, are forgotten. Work which, like Bright's, was performed in the open and in the midst of applause, is secure of recognition. The practical triumph of the Free-traders was the conversion of Peel; and it seems improbable, if we consider how much less effect popular oratory and popular response were likely to have upon the mind of a statesman then than now, that Bright's share in this feat was considerable. Bright outlived Cobden by many years, and he displayed vastly greater aptitude for politics in general than others of his companions; we may mislead ourselves if we judge the Bright of 1845 by the Bright of 1854 or 1865. The French critic whose admirable essay on Bright has already been quoted, remarks: " For a long time he was regarded as one who merely followed the inspiration of Cobden. He did not allow his self-esteem to take offence at this. Rejoicing to fight side by side with such a man, he did not dream of claiming originality for his ideas, or of making any display of independence.   So long as Cobden lived John Bright was content, in spite of the indubitable superiority of his talents, to take the second place among the representatives of the Manchester School."   These remarks do no more than justice to the absence of jealousy between the Dioscuri of Free Trade; but they do much less than justice to the commanding ability of Cobden. If we look at Free Trade only, Cobden's name deserves to be mentioned, as Peel mentioned it, alone.

On the other hand, it must not be forgotten that subsequent history compels us to form a higher estimate than seemed necessary fifty years ago of the power of the men who carried the policy of Free Trade in the United Kingdom.   If it is fair to urge the failure of Free-trade principles to win acceptance in America and the Colonies as a reason for disparaging the confidence with which Bright and Cobden asserted their doctrine, it is fair also to use it as a measure of the resisting forces over which they won their famous victory.   The modesty that ascribed their success to the inherent strength of the cause rather than to the prowess of its champions, must yield to the consideration that the cause has elsewhere been a losing cause.   It is now apparent that this success was one of the most remarkable of its kind in all history; and even though we assign to Bright only a secondary share of the credit of the achievement, the honour to be distributed is large enough to bear subdivision.

Bright's devotion to the principles of the Free Churches, which was not less ardent than his faith in Free Trade, was rewarded by the abolition of church-rates, the admission of Jews to Parliament, the removal of religious tests in the Universities, in part by Mr. Gladstone and completely by Lord Salisbury's Commission, and by the passing of the Burials Bill. The disestablishment of the Irish Church ought perhaps not to be counted among the triumphs of the principle of Religious Equality.

In appraising Bright's contribution to the work of winning for Dissenters equality of treatment by the State, we ought to count, not only the persuasive value of his speeches in themselves, but also the fact that he was the first son of the free churches who attained a high position in political life. He was the first Protestant Nonconformist since the Restoration to become a minister of the Crown. He was, indeed, the first, since Defoe and Penn, to attain eminence of any sort likely to command the respect of politicians. The Dissenters had long been the humble followers of the Liberal party. They had been content to accept the patronage of such men as Fox and the Russells. The condescension of one of the great parties was hardly less contemptuous than the enmity of the other. They had been neither loved by the Whigs nor feared by the Tories. This contempt, the unfortunate effects of which are not yet exhausted, was due chiefly, no doubt, to the narrowness of the aristocratic *régime*, but partly also to the failure of the free churches to produce men of commanding ability. In Bright for the first time they found a champion of their own whose advocacy was made effective not only by the inherent force of his case, but by the authority of his acknowledged position in the first rank of orators and politicians.

It is more difficult to ask assent to any estimate of Bright's success in winning approval for a peaceful or "un-English" course of foreign policy. It is indisputable that his opinion that the war with Russia was on the further side of the lines that limit political prudence and political morality, gained ground immensely after the event. That may have been so in part because, when the fever had subsided, when the war was ended

and the remnant of the ill-used soldiery were home again,
and when, in Bright's phrase, "all was over except the
tax-gatherer and the sorrows of those who had lost
their friends in the war", it was scarcely possible to
deny that the results of the war were not commensurate
with the sacrifices it had cost. It is conceivable that if
the issue had been more flattering to national pride, if
another Trafalgar had been fought in the Baltic, and if
Sevastopol had become a name of pride like Blenheim or
Waterloo, those who condemned Bright at first would
have condemned him still. The fact remains that there
has been a strong current of opinion in Bright's direction, and that, if he was not the author of the change,
there is no other man to dispute the credit with him.
Tennyson, whose satire generally missed fire, had put at
this time into the mouth of the cross-grained hero of
*Maud* the well-known description of Bright as

"The broad-brimmed hawker of holy things,
　Whose car is stuffed with his cotton, and rings
　Even in dreams to the chink of his pence".

It would be fair to retort that Bright took less trouble
about the profits of his cotton-spinning than his assailant
is credited with taking to get the best market price for
his verses. But this gibe really represented at the time
the average estimate of educated Englishmen; and yet
Bright, without any apology, and whilst reiterating the
despised opinion in and out of season, lived it down
very completely.

We have already quoted from Mr. Morley instances,
sufficiently striking when every allowance has been
made, of foreign crises in which England did not interfere, although interference was prescribed by the Palmerstonian tradition. On the other hand, it has to be
admitted that the year after Mr. Morley published this
remark Bright was driven from office by the warlike

behaviour of his colleagues; and that since his death we have seen a Liberal Opposition calling for interference, and trying to revive the conception, condemned by Bright, of England's vocation to be " the knight-errant of the human race". It is also to be admitted that even now it is hardly conceivable that any party would invite a statesman holding the fulness of Bright's views to become Foreign Secretary, and that still the majority of Englishmen would regard such an appointment as an invitation to the wolves. But all this is no more than to say that Bright represented an extreme of opinion that is not, or that is not yet, accepted as practicable. It remains true that he led, at first almost unaided, a revolt against the opposite extreme; and that, if he did not carry conviction as far as he desired, he did promote a change in the national spirit comparable to the revolution of sentiment by which it is recognized that a man may preserve his personal honour without fighting duels.

It may, however, be anticipated that those who write the history of the reign of Victoria with knowledge of the fuller and remoter issues of our controversies and our legislation, will pay attention to Bright's career chiefly as the leader of the Reform movement of the sixties. It is true that the results of the Leap in the Dark have hitherto been much less momentous than they were foreshadowed to be by the hopes and fears of the crisis. The hero of *Water Babies*, on arriving after much tribulation at the Other End of Nowhere, " found it much more like This End of Somewhere than he had been in the habit of expecting ". This is a true parable of political as of other enthusiasm. Nevertheless, those who will have the advantage of comparing the politics of the twentieth and the eighteenth centuries may find reason to treat both 1832 and 1867 as memorable epochs. The more closely the history of the period is studied, the more disposed will the student become to treat as impor-

tant the propulsion and the direction that Bright gave
to democratic opinion. We do not yet know whether
the Reform of 1867 was a great event; but, if it was a
great event, Bright is a great character in history. It
is of course certain that the wage-earners would have
been enfranchised sooner or later though Bright had
died with Cobden, or though he had spent his life in his
cotton-mill at Rochdale, mute and inglorious. But very
few names would be left in our histories if we included
only persons who did something that would not have
been done without them.

Let us try to estimate again the service that Bright
rendered. He found a great mass of discontent, often
inarticulate, produced in part by the necessary inequali-
ties of a civilized community, but in part also by the
artificial privileges against which he waged a lifelong
warfare, by unsympathetic government, and by the dis-
sociation of what he called the governing classes from
the populace. Since the collapse of the Chartist agitation—of the perils of which Bright was fully aware—
the aristocratic Liberals were content to ignore a malady
which had certainly not disappeared because one particular manifestation of it had failed through unwise
guidance. To Carlyle at this time Bright appeared
one of the foolishest creatures he had ever heard of—
''clamouring about America and universal suffrage, as if
there was any sensible man anywhere in the world who
put the smallest confidence in that sort of thing nowa-
days!'' Certainly Bright's performances did not resemble
those of Mirabeau, Governor Eyre, and the rest of the
heroes. On the other hand, he was doing something to
prevent one of those crises at which the Carlylean hero
makes his distinguished appearance—generally too late
to do much good without doing also a great deal of
harm. Bright did not create this discontent; he guided
it towards a definite purpose, which was not a revolu-

tionary purpose. He dug a channel for waters that were already flowing, and that might have become a torrent. He exhibited a constitutional remedy for complaints that were likely to tempt the sufferers to accept the panaceas of empirics. The accession of Bright to the leadership of English democracy put a stop to a good deal of crying for the moon, and marked the end of a period of riots and rick-burnings, of Peterloo massacres and indictments for sedition.

He was, in short, the chief educator of the wage-earning classes at a time when they were acquiring, and when they had newly acquired, a power perilous to the nation, if it should be used without sobriety. They have turned to other masters, and have already unlearned some of the lessons that he tried to teach them. He would have regarded their aberrations with no great discomposure if he were satisfied that they had not lost their hold of the central article of his political faith. "May I ask you", he said, "to believe, as I do most devoutly believe, that the moral law was not written for men alone in their individual character, but that it was written as well for nations, and for nations great as this of which we are citizens. If we reject and deride that moral law, there is a penalty which will inevitably follow." This sentiment has been the commonplace of innumerable orators; to Bright it was a real inspiration.

# Index.

PRINTED BY BLACKIE AND SON LIMITED, GLASGOW.